THE SECRET
OF
KEYSTONE CITY

by

William Hallstead

The contents of this book regarding the accuracy of events, people and places depicted; permissions to use all previously published materials; all are the sole responsibility of the author, who assumes all liabiliaty for the contents of this book.

Also by the author

Raging Skies
Hard Days in Paradise
River of Madness
Pursuit of the Weapon from Hell

Writing as "William Beechcroft"
Position of Ultimate Trust
Image of Evil
The Rebuilt Man
Chain of Vengeance
Secret Kills
Pursuit of Fear

1

Gary Samuels took a final drag of lukewarm coffee, set the thermos back on the floor of his Ford pick-up and stepped out. Really isolated out here in all this bought-out Northeastern Pennsylvania farmland. And chilly for an early morning in March.

He raised the collar of his jacket and surveyed the lakeside cottages. Three of them, all the same. Wood siding with its white paint chalky. One step up to their back doors. A window on each side of the doorway. Kitchen, probably, and a back bedroom. Untended lawns out front, then a narrow strip of imported sand so decades-ago realtors could offer rural "beachfronts" on Lake Linden way out here in the Appalachian foothills.

Now the focus was a hell of a lot bigger. Sixteen square miles of this open land were destined – doomed, in Gary's view – to become the new city of Keystone. All existing buildings had to go, including these three little "beach cottages." Susquehanna Salvage had won the bid, so here he was.

A well-muscled six-footer with a not-pretty-facial scar from his Vietnam misery, Gary liked his work. The hours could be tough, the weather often rugged. But he could take out his still-lingering 'Nam bitterness in the crunch and crash of splintering walls and tumbling bricks. These three little cottages wouldn't be all that therapeutic, but this morning he didn't feel much more than the creeping chill.

He walked to the Caterpillar D-8, poised a few yards behind the cottage on the left. After his interior inspection late yesterday, he had left the dozer aimed straight at it. He climbed onto the left side chain treads and felt the familiar twinge. He'd been crouching on a tank when that sniper got him in the cheek. He shook it off and wedged into the enclosed cab.

With a snort and cough, the D-8 started up. He raised the big steel front scoop as high as it would go. Not ideal for major building razing, but okay for jabbing these one-story cottages until they collapsed.

Gary opened the throttle and geared up. The D-8 lurched forward. He tried to ease off on the power. But the engine's roar persisted. The Cat lumbered toward the cottage.

He banged on the throttle. No change. Steering jammed. The gears froze. In a wave of sweat, he turned the key. But the engine roared on.

My God! *Time to bail ou* –

The scraper blade rammed through the kitchen window. The wood siding crumpled. The D-8 roared across the linoleum, shattered the oncoming wallboard partition. The peaked roof collapsed over him. The door of the cramped little cab wouldn't budge. Gary felt a surge of panic worse than he'd ever felt in 'Nam.

With a fractured section of roof trapping its helpless driver, the out-of-control Cat burst through the front of the cottage and rumbled across the narrow lawn. Gary threw himself sideways, thrust both feet against the cab's far side.

He heard a splash. *Sweet Jesus! We're in the lake!* The chilly water closed over his head.

2

Just as I settled into my office chair for a day of...sitting in my office chair, the phone jangled.

"Detective Elrod Montgomery?"

Jeez, how I hate *El*rod. "Yep, this is *Rod* Montgomery."

"Maxwell Sturdevant."

That, in the tone of a guy who expected his name to impress. I'd never heard of him.

"The president of Sturdevant Developers," he said into my silence. "Surely you've heard of Maximalls. They're nationwide."

"That I have. There's a Maximall a couple miles from here. What can I do for you, Mr. Sturdevant?"

"I've been referred to you by the Philadelphia Police."

"Referred?"

"I'll explain—in person. At ten this morning. Give me directions to your office."

"Hold on a sec, Mr. Sturdevant. What's this all about?"

"It's about hiring your services, Montgomery. You've been recommended by Sergeant Lucas."

That explained the unlikely recommendation from the Roundhouse, Philadelphia Police downtown HQ. Pete Lucas was one of only a few Philly cops who knew—but would never reveal — the true circumstances of my retirement in my mid-forties.

"Ten o'clock will be okay, Mr. Sturdevant."

I gave him directions to my house in Orchard Glade. In the city's southwest suburbs, the Glade, as we residents call it, is a cluster of outdated post-World War II building boom split-levels. Not a fruit tree in sight in this former apple orchard. When Leahla and I moved in five years ago, the bottom level was her sewing room. Then she switched her fickle affections to Sidney son-of-a-bitch Simpson six houses up the street and moved up there two years ago.

As our marriage collapsed, so did my career with Philly's finest. I coped, more or less, by converting the bottom room into an office. With help from a few fellow officers who knew the real story of my police disgrace, I converted myself into a licensed private investigator.

***

Precisely at ten, my gimmicky doorbell chimed. I climbed the seven steps to the main floor and opened the front door on two black suits.

"I am Maxwell Sturdevant," the taller one announced. Clean shaven, piercing blue eyes, neatly trimmed black hair with gray sideburns. In his mid-fifties, I guessed. A shade over six feet, several inches over my five-ten.

"And," he added, with a nod at the other guy, "this is my younger brother Clifford."

"Call me Cliff. Gladda meetcha." He thrust out his right hand. The other hand held a black briefcase. A good six inches shorter that Maxwell, Cliff sported buzz cut mustard-colored hair and a fringe of blond beard.

Black suits and black briefcase. Dark green Lexus in my driveway. If Maxwell hadn't told me who they were, I'd have wondered what federal reg I'd broken.

I stood aside. "Let's go down to my office."

Trying to have some kind of psychological advantage, I offered them the two chairs in front of my desk and plunked down behind it.

"Coffee?"

Maxwell turned that down. Cliff said, "Sure."

I stood up and poured a mug from the Silex behind me. Handed it to Cliff, and there went my psychological edge. Sat back down. Folded my hands on the blotter.

"What can I do for you?" Got a little mojo back with that, I thought.

"Are you currently engaged in a case?" Maxwell's eyes stayed on mine.

"At the moment, I'm between cases." There went my mojo modicum.

"So, you could be available full time."

"That depends, Mr. Sturdevant, on what you have in mind."

Maxwell gazed at me, speculating, I thought.

Cliff stirred in his chair. "Oh, for God's sake, Max. Get on with it."

Maxwell shot his younger brother an icy glance, pulled the briefcase off Cliff's lap, zipped it open, pulled out a map, and spread it on my desk.

"Northeastern Pennsylvania, Montgomery. This area north of Hardington, outlined in red, is the twelve-square-mile site of the city of Keystone."

"Looks like empty acres to me."

"It is empty acres. It was mostly farmland with a lake— Lake Linden— along its western edge. Now the entire tract is owned by Sturdevant Developers."

"Yeah," Cliff said. "And it took six shell companies—"

"Montgomery doesn't need such details," Maxwell broke in.

"The hell I don't, Cliff. To decide if I'm going to work with you and Max, I need all the details I can get. So, what are 'shell companies'?"

Maxwell sighed. "If we had gone in there as Sturdevant Developers, the price per acre would have doubled, tripled, quadrupled with each succeeding acquisition. To circumvent that, we set up six dummy companies to buy several parcels each, over a two-year span."

"At 'reasonable prices.'"

"At affordable prices, Mr. Montgomery. Now we are ready to develop the property. But we have a problem."

"More than one," Cliff grumped. "Newspaper editorials. The damned court cases..."

"I'm speaking of the latest occurrences, Cliff."

"Occurrences?"

"Yes, Mr. Montgomery."

"'Rod' will do."

"A series of incidents...Rod. Our chief planner was injured in an automobile accident by a hit-and-run driver who has yet to be found."

"One auto accident hardly seems—"

"Three auto accidents. And a fire in our contractor's on-site motor pool. Cost us two Dodge Rams and a Ford Explorer."

"But the worst—"

"I'm getting to that, Cliff. Two days ago, a Cat D-8 operated by one of our subcontractors ran into Lake Linden. Just this morning I got the call I—"

"Sabotage!" Cliff burst out.

"Yes. The controls were jammed. The driver couldn't get out of the cab. He drowned."

Max gave me a beleaguered look. "Those are specific incidents. We also have an ongoing situation. I have reason to believe somebody in my own company is supplying information to unknown interests who intend to bankrupt the Keystone project."

"Which is why we're here," Cliff said.

"Right, Cliff. We need to place someone in the company, someone to determine who the hell is disloyal enough to abet whoever is at the root of all these occurrences. Someone who has investigative experience and is not from the Hardington area. That's why we drove down here to consult the Philadelphia Police. We were referred to Sergeant Lucas, and he has sent us to you. You may be our man."

"May be?"

"I'm concerned with what Sergeant Lucas called the 'Schuykill Scandal.' He said we shouldn't be deterred — if it came up at all. But before we go any further, Rod, I'd better know what it was, and what was your part in it."

3

"The 'Schuylkill Scandal,' as the newspapers called it, concerned a not-exactly-huge case of bribery."

Maxwell and Cliff hung on my every word.

"Stripped to basics, a certain Philadelphia Police Department lieutenant asked a detective on a case if he would pick up a necklace, a gift for the lieutenant's wife. I was that detective. I took the package from Schuylkill Creative Gemstones back to the precinct and gave it to the lieutenant. I had no idea there were ten one-hundred-dollar bills under the silk lining of the necklace case. And that a damned cell phone camera shot had been taken of me at the pick-up."

"By who?" Cliff asked. "The PD?"

"By a flunky for the never-identified briber. Obviously, somebody with a serious resentment of the lieutenant."

"You had no idea you were picking up and delivering a thousand-dollar bribe?"

I looked straight into Max's cold blues. "Hell, no."

"So, it was a set-up."

"Yeah. To nail the lieutenant. I was just the delivery boy. When the cell photo was mailed to Internal Affairs, serious hell broke loose. They jumped all over me to give them the name of the person I delivered the package to. But I just couldn't get myself to turn in the guy who'd saved my life."

"Why the hell not? He took the damned bribe."

"Back off, Cliff," Max rumbled. "Let the man tell the story."

And kill off my chance of working for Sturdevant Developers. But I plunged on. "Way back when the lieutenant-to-be and I were detectives together, he purposely took a bullet—right in the gut, a bullet intended for me. I nailed the shooter, but I made sure my partner got the glory. I was glad he got the promotion."

I took a long pull of coffee. Max and Cliff didn't say a word.

"The mess boiled down to satisfying the damned newspapers'—and the department's—clamor for a name to blame. That was me. Publicly fired. Privately retired early, with benefits intact and quietly cleared for a P.I. license. So here we are."

Max's eyes stayed on mine for what seemed like a full minute. Then he said, "You find any equanimity in all that?"

"I still feel uneasy about early retirement as payment for avoiding months in legal mumbo jumbo and court appearances over a bribe case I had only an incidental part in. But I feel justified in repaying a debt to the man who took the bullet meant for me."

I'd never discussed that miserable experience in such detail with anyone outside the department. I still wasn't sure how I should feel about the whole ugly mess.

"You sleep well?" Max persisted.

"Not every night."

Long silence. Then he said, "Open-end agreement until our situation is resolved. Your daily rate plus expenses. I recommend the Anthracite Hotel in Hardington. You'll be on our staff as… as…

"A PR specialist," Cliff suggested.

"Hold on a minute. On-staff won't cut it. An Internet check of name and SS number by your personnel department—"

"Human resources department." Cliff's tone was a tad disparaging.

"Using an assumed name might work. I could be a consultant on some aspect of the project. Maybe its impact on the area's — "

"I got it!" Cliff announced. "History. We've talked about writing a history of the project. So we give you an office and a laptop."

"Good idea, Cliff." Max sounded surprised that his younger brother actually came up with something plausible.

"Rod?" Max prompted.

"Not bad. Let's have the phony first name begin with Rod. That could avoid my blank look in an off moment when somebody called me something else. So how about... Rodney, uh...Rodney..."

"Stevenson," Cliff suggested. "That sounds like a writer."

"That *is* a writer," Max said.

"Not bad, though." I thought a moment. "How about Stevens? Rodney Stevens."

"Rodney Stevens," Max said as he reached across my desk, "you are under contract to write the history of Keystone."

"Let's amend that. I'm under contract as a phony history writer to find out who the hell is sabotaging the Keystone project."

"Well said. Start tomorrow?"

"I'll need a day to close up here. Stop my mail. Buy a notebook. Gas up my Jeep."

"Wednesday, then. Report to my office."

"Which is where?"

"Maximall Hardington, on the city's north side. You can't miss it."

Maximall Hardington? This fast spinning big wheel had his office in a *shopping mall?*

On a rainy Tuesday, I locked 435 Red Apple Road, fired up my aging Dodge, and wound through the southwest Philly suburbs to Philadelphia International Airport. Left the Dodge in long-term parking and rented a Jeep Patriot. If anyone up in Hardington had the perception to track down my license plate, they'd be stymied, I hoped, by the rental plate.

From the airport, I backtracked to I-476. I skirted Allentown around noon; then the highway took me into the Pocono Mountains. Actually, onto the Poconos. You twist *through* most mountain ranges; you climb *over* the rolling Poconos.

In mid-afternoon, I coasted down the exit ramp into the valley that cradled the sprawl of Hardington. I'd visited here with my parents, when the once-booming coal city was still working its way out of its anthracite past. Now as I glided down the south valley's slope, I could see progress. New housing developments up both sides of the valley. Couple of sparkling new buildings downtown. A city still in recovery from the decreasing demand for the coal that had built it.

As I passed central city's grassy block with the brownstone county courthouse in its center, I caught a flash of reflected afternoon sunlight. Partway up the valley's north slope. Looked like a shopping mall up there. Some developer had bet his money on future growth. Of course! I was looking at Sturdevant Developers' Maximall Hardington.

A few minutes of upslope macadam took me to the mall's sprawling parking area. I pulled up close to the classy glassy mall entrance, stepped out and locked my SUV. From up here, I had a great view of the whole valley. And surely Max had realized the whole valley had a grand view of his two-story Maximall.

I walked through the automatic sliding doorway and found an info kiosk to my left. Manned by a woman—a lovely young woman with a swirl of glistening auburn hair.

"Rod...ney Stevens to see Maxwell Sturdevant." First real use of my phony name.

"Second level, sir. The elevator is right over there."

A big project with a little office crammed into a busy mall's crowded retailery.

Hard to believe.

Well, maybe the second level was less traffic-laden. I touched button 2. The elevator was so smooth I was startled when the door slid open onto a wide balcony that ringed the whole second floor. With offices. Sturdevant Developers wasn't crammed into an available retail space. It circled the whole second floor with a grand view of the entire retail extravaganza below.

Another lovely lassie approached, this one with smooth mahogany hair, hazel eyes, and a look of cool confidence. As tall as I am, in her gray skirt, gray jacket and white blouse, she exuded efficiency.

"This way, Mr. Stevens." She knew my name...well, my cover name. Oh, sure— from the girl at the info kiosk.

"I'm Priscilla Killian," she said, "Mr. Maxwell Sturdevant's executive assistant."

Her title, I sensed, perhaps included more than the euphemism for "secretary."

We walked only a few feet then turned into a quite spiffy reception area above the mall's main entrance. She tapped at its far door then swung it open on a big office agleam in chrome and tan leather. Behind a desk the size of New Hampshire, Max stood and thrust out his hand. At least, I thought that was what he did. Hard to see him against the afternoon glare from the huge picture window behind him.

We shook. He nodded at a suede upholstered chair in front of the desk. I sat.

"That will be all, Ms. Killian."

She strode out, shutting the door behind her. Max dropped into a black leather swivel. Tapped the huge mahogany desk top with his left-hand fingertips. Sighed. Caught my eye.

"Damned glad you're here...Rod. We've got a new problem."

4

Max Sturdevant folded his arms. A gesture of defiance? "The problem, Rod, is that the Keystone Project has been shut down."

"Shut down! By the city?"

"It's not in the city."

"By the county, then?"

"No, not by the county. By the Feds."

"By Washington? What the hell—"

Max held up a silencing hand. "Cliff will fill you in." He pressed a button on his phone cradle. Ten seconds later, Priscilla Killian stood in the office doorway.

"Show Mr. Stevens to his office, Priscilla."

That beat "show Mr. Stevens to the door." So the federal clampdown wasn't considered fatal. Yet.

Priscilla, somehow projecting warmth despite her gray ensemble—could be that silky-smooth mahogany hair—led me along the balcony to a small cubby. Modest oak desk, naked except for a phone; bare-bones swivel, a plain side chair. Small and empty bookcase. Everything utilitarian plain...except for the view through the single window. If I'd been assigned a space on the other side of the building, I'd be looking straight into the ascending hillside. But on this side, the spectacular view took in almost the entire city of Hardington.

"Thank you, Priscilla."

"Door open or closed?"

"Open. I've got nothing to hide." Uh huh.

I dropped my notebook on the desk. As she walked out, younger brother Cliff strode in, blue shirtsleeves rolled up, pink tie askew. "Gladda see ya again, 'Mr. Stevens.' Helluva day so far." He plunked into the side chair.

I sank into my rock-hard swivel. "Max says the whole project has been shut down by —"

"By OSHA, NTSB, EPA. The lakeside is swarming with federal investigators probing the obvious. Hell, if a plane had been flying over when the D-8 went under, the FAA would be out there, too."

"What's Sturdevant Developers doing about it?"

"We had a meeting this morning. Max, me, and our department heads. The problem is 'under study.' In other words, at this point we don't know what the hell to do. The only thing I can do at the moment is to help you get started."

"Hell, with that, Cliff. You know where are all those bureaucrats are?"

"Lakeside, at the D-8. Susquehanna Contractors pulled it out of the drink, got the driver's body out, then were ordered by OSHA not to move the Cat any further."

I stood and picked up my notebook. "I'm going out there."

"What good will that do?"

"I won't know until I get there."

"Waste of time." Then he brightened. "Better, though, than sitting here 'studying the situation.' I'll go with you, if that's okay."

"You're one of my bosses, Cliff. Let's go see what all those Feds are up to."

***

At the parking area exit, I turned left. We climbed out of the valley and through the cut in the ridgeline to emerge into rolling farmland. A quarter mile farther, the two-lane macadam branched left and right.

"Take the left," Cliff said. "That's the way to Lake Linden."

We rolled through a couple miles between scrubby acreage on the left and a forest on the right.

"Good pheasant hunting here. We haven't closed it down yet. Good in-season PR." Cliff squinted ahead. "There they are."

I pulled in near a gaggle of guys, some in coats and ties, others in black T-shirts marked NTSB in big white letters. Plus, several cops in gray uniforms and peaked campaign hats. I parked near three vans and a police cruiser.

"State police," Cliff said. "The county sheriff handles prisoners, but he's got no investigative department. That's why those state cops are in on this."

He made a move to get out. I put a hand on his shoulder. "Hold on a bit, Cliff. I've got an idea."

I stepped out and walked toward the milling minions. The D-8 had been hauled out at an angle to park between the wreckage of the cottage on the left and the first of the two weather-faded but intact cottages to the right. Deep ruts all the way to the road marked the struggle to haul the D-8 and its drowned driver out of the drink.

A tall Fed official in power-suit blue detached himself from the confabulating cluster. His head was stylishly shaved, but a trim orange mustache told me he hadn't given up hair altogether.

"Wendell Phillips," he announced in the tone of a prosecutor. "OSHA. This project is closed."

"Closed to redevelopment, I assume. I'm not here as a developer. I'm fact finding with the developer's permission. So I'm not even trespassing." I stuck out my hand. "Rod Stevens, historian."

He gave me a curt handshake. "What the hell is a historian doing out here?"

"Sturdevant thinks a book on his Keystone project will have wide appeal. I think so, too. Especially if I spark it up with intriguing anecdotes." I'd browsed through a book on writing when I bought my three-ring notebook. Bought the writing book, too.

"Anecdotes?"

"Interesting incidents. Not just a...uh...chronology. Events and people." I flipped open my notebook, pulled out a ballpoint pen. "Like this, for instance."

Phillips scowled. "'This' what?"

"Ten..." I peered past him. "No, eleven people. From three federal agencies and the state police."

"Mandated procedure," he snapped.

I scrawled in the notebook. "Got it. I know why OSHA's here. Why the National Transportation Safety Board guys?"

His scowl softened a bit. "Slight misunderstanding there. It was misreported to the NTSB as a bus accident."

I gave him a sympathetic smile and scrawled away.

"Stop your damned note taking!"

"Too good to pass up, Phillips. And why the EPA?"

"Look, we all got phone calls. Caterpillar D-8 killed a guy. Bus accident. Big pollution in Lake Linden."

"And nobody checked before sending out investigators?"

"I did. The call to me was accurate. The rest of them—"

"Same voice on all three calls?"

"A man's."

"I love it, Phillips. The local papers, too. Maybe even the AP."

"*Get the hell out of here, Stevens!* We don't need this kind of interference."

"Oh, that's good, too!" I kept the ballpoint moving.

"GO! This is a federal—"

"Great! Great!" I closed the notebook. "Thanks a lot, Phillips. Wendell, isn't it? See you in print eventually. Maybe sooner if the local papers find this of…Well, thanks." I walked back to my Jeep.

Cliff gave me a puzzled frown. "So what was all that?"

"Just a nosy historian doing his job." I turned the key, and we drove on up the road.

"Loops around couple miles north. Not much up there 'cept for Susquehanna Contractors' motor pool. That's where the D-8 came from."

We passed a series of dirt driveways, all leading to crumbled foundations where, I assumed, farm structures once stood.

"How many of those, Cliff?"

"Thirty-one. Should be thirty-two, 'cept for old man Sikorski. Ivan. Got the only place still standing. He refuses to budge. We been working on him for months."

"All these families you dis— All of them turned over their property without a protest?"

"Oh, sure there were protests, but we bought them out at more-than-fair prices. Some were happy to sell. None of them put up a struggle beyond some price bargaining."

"Except for Mr. Ivan Sikorski."

"Yeah, him."

We rolled around a long eastward curve, passed Susquehanna Contractors' fenced-in motor pool sheds and parking lot crowded with dozers, scrapers, and cranes. A few miles farther, where the road curved south, Cliff leaned forward.

"There it is. Sikorski's place."

A substantial-looking and well-kept three-story frame job with a columned front porch dominated a rise at the end of a paved drive. A big, dark-blue Hummer was parked in the turn-around out front, but no one was in sight.

"No out-buildings. Not a farm."

"Nope. It's Sikorski's 'old homestead,' and no matter what we offer, he's hanging onto it."

"What's your next move?"

"You know what 'eminent domain' is?"

"Government seizure of private property for the public good."

"That's it. And that's next."

We rolled southward, back toward the city. I felt a qualm. All those farms... But what was done was done. I wasn't hired as a moralist. I was here to find out who was trying to kill the project.

5

From the street, the Anthracite Hotel looked to me like the undistinguished stone box architecture of the 1930s. I parked under it, took the elevator to the main floor and — surprise! Still the aura of the '30s, but beautifully restored. The dark wall paneling, intricate parquet floor and imposing reception counter gleamed in the light of three huge brass-and-crystal chandeliers. In comparison, the casually placed chairs and two sofas looked fairly up-to-date: comfortably plush seating. Only a few were occupied.

The "room key" card looked like intrusive science fiction. The sullen college-aged reception clerk banged his counter bell. An elderly guy shuffled through a doorway beside the counter, still chomping on whatever he'd been eating when the bell rang. He nodded at me, picked up my bag, and off we marched to the surprisingly modern, steel-doored elevator bank.

My third-floor room was larger than I'd expected. A single queen-size bed. Twin windows looking out on Laurel Avenue's early evening traffic. And lots of color, all of it green. Dark green carpet, light green walls and closet door, forest-green blankets on the beds, grass-green chest of drawers; even a sea-green blotter on the oak writing desk.

"You from outta town?" the bellcodger asked.

"Philadelphia."

"Thought so."

"Why?"

"Way you talk."

"I haven't said anything to you until now."

"Give you a turn, did I?" He grinned. "Took a peek at your luggage tag in the elevator."

Hardington humor. I tipped him and refrained from giving him a kick in the butt as he sauntered out the door. I unpacked, stashed the bag in the closet—God, inside the closet was green, too.

Then I recalled I'd read somewhere that green is the color most likely to inspire "effort." Could be. When I walked in here, I'd intended to flake out on one of the beds. Sparring with Feds can do that to you. But now I found myself at the small desk. I unfurled the paper roll Priscilla had given me. She'd handed it over with a wee smile that seemed to say, "Look at *this*, dumb Philly man." Or, maybe a more hopeful interpretation: "We could have things in common we don't even know about yet?" I flattened out the roll and peered at a plat map of the future city of Keystone.

Three villages surrounded a park-like central area of shops, office buildings, a school. The core of an apparently well-planned small city. On its west side, bordering Lake Linden, lay the future residential Village of Heron Glade. Where the motor pool now sprawled along the loop road's northern sweep, the Village of Deer Walk was to rise. The third residential area, currently centered by the obstinate Mr. Sikorski's old homestead, was destined to be the Village of Stag Run.

All this was a touch too artsy for me. At least the village names were an improvement over the likes of some current Pennsylvania town names—like Blue Ball, Virginsville, and

Intercourse. But who was I to judge? I live in Orchard Glade, built on a hillside without a fruit tree for miles.

I rolled up the plat, stepped from bedroom green into hallway tan and elevatored down to dinner.

The dining room was also semi-preserved 1930s-style. Dark paneling, lush cherry-red carpeting. Apparently designed for grand parties, tonight it served a scatter of business bodies. Like me. I opened the plastic-bound menu. Surely clothbound in plushier days gone-by.

Whaddya know! At the top of the page-3 sandwich list: Philadelphia cheesesteak. Good reinforcement for what I planned tomorrow. A visit to the only outspoken opposition to Keystone I was aware of. Mr. Ivan Sikorski.

***

At nine-thirty the next morning, I found my way to Cliff's office, a carpeted set-up not as spacious as Max's, but large enough to be destined a bookstore or dress shop at conversion time. The younger brother's view out his picture window? The ascending mountainside.

"Coffee?" He had a half-full carafe on his desk. Poured a Styrofoam cup for me. No cream or sugar in sight. I sank into the side chair nearest the desk and sipped the coffee. Black and bitter.

"Good news for a change, Rod." He gave me what I felt was a conspiratorial smile. "I don't know how you did it, or even if you did do it. The Feds are pulling out this morning. Back to their land of alphabetical authority, presumably to compile multi-hundred-page reports. If you're here to gloat, I'm a willing gloatee."

"Either they were about finished when I got there, or the mention of big press coverage wasn't part of their agenda. Good riddance. Now tell me about the car accidents you mentioned down at my place."

"Three of them. All at night, all hit-and-run. Nobody got a license number. First, Marty Elman, our chief planner. He rammed a car that stopped dead in front of him for no apparent reason on an almost empty county road. The air bag saved him from ramming the steering wheel. But the car slewed sideways and his head slammed into the left door. That put him in the hospital overnight. Next one was a sideswipe in Hardington. Our chief surveyor. Pushed him in the path of oncoming traffic, and he barely missed a head-on with an oncoming Mac truck. No injury on that one."

Cliff took a coffee pause then kept fingering the empty cup. "The third one could have been fatal. Couple weeks ago. Al Crofton—he's the Susquehanna Contractors' foreman— he was driving home late. Just as he passed here on his way into Hardington, somebody pulled out of the mall's parking entrance and whacked him on the right rear."

"The kind of a hit the cops use to knock a runner out of control?"

"Well, yeah. Now that you mention it. Coulda been real bad 'cause just past the parking entrance, there's a drop-off on either side. But Al managed to straighten out and keep going on down to the city."

"Any witnesses? Anybody else coming in or going out of the parking lot?"

"Not at midnight. Mall closes at ten. Parking lot lighting is cut down to a couple safety lights near the mall building's two entrances."

"Why was Crofton going home so late?"

"Sometimes he stays out there at the motor pool after quitting time. Catching up on paperwork. When he finally got to his car that night, the battery was dead. Seems he'd left his headlights on all day after driving to work during a rain squall. He swears he turned them off. By the time he got back in action, thanks to the motor pool's recharger, it was almost midnight."

I'd never heard a more obvious set-up. Cliff looked at my expression and nodded. "Uh huh. I think so, too. It was a big vehicle, barreling out of the night with no lights."

"Like, maybe, a Hummer?"

"Come to think of it..."

I pushed out of my chair. "I'm going to visit Mr. Sikorski."

"I'll go with you."

"Not this time, Cliff. I'll play independent writer. I doubt your showing up with me would soften his heart."

"But, dammit...No, you're right. Fill me in when you get back."

Flexibility. I was beginning to like this guy.

***

This time at the loop road's fork, I swung right. Ten minutes later, Sikorski's mansion reared into view. Big, dark-blue Hummer still parked out front. I pulled in behind it.

I stepped out of my SUV. He stepped out of his front door. Big guy, a good six-feet-plus, and well over 200 pounds. Black turtle neck, rumpled blue jeans, brick-red scowl on his square, high-cheekboned face. His head was aggressively shaved bare and glistened in the late morning sunlight.

Hands on hips, naked head jutting forward, he rapped, "You with Keystone, you can git!" He flung out an arm southward. "Back wherever you come from. Now!"

"I'm—"

"I don't care whatchu are. *Git!*"

"—a writer, Mr. Sikorski. Here to get your side of the situation."

"My side? Hell, I can do that in three words: *I'm staying put!*"

I walked to the bottom of the porch's five marble steps. "I'm sure there's more to it, sir."

"More, hell!"

"Like how long have you been here? Did you buy or build? Stuff like that."

The hands slipped off the hips. His arms began to cross his chest in an obstinate fold, then dropped to his sides. "Nobody's ever cared about that. They just want me out of here, this place gone, and their damned Cape Cod-split-level-ranchers sprawled all over my acres like spilt sugar cubes."

"Tearing down what's good to make way for not-so-good?"

His glare lost some of its brittleness. "You say you're a writer?"

I nodded and flourished my notebook.

He surprised me. "Too late for coffee, Mr...?"

"Stevens. And it's never too late for coffee."

"Get your butt up here. If you're lying to me, I'll throw you right back down. But if you really care about what they're trying to do to me...Well, you're the first one."

He held open the massive oak door with its pair of stained glass windows. I stepped into — My God!

6

When I stepped into Ivan Sikorski's living room, I felt I'd walked into an age much grander than the one we live in now. The first stunner was the huge oriental carpet, surely worth thousands. Then the furniture — Victorian, I guessed — all of it highly polished with brass work gleaming. On one of the cherry-paneled walls, a stern-looking gent in a high stiff collar glared at me from his heavy gold-leafed frame.

"My father, Stefan Sikorski. I've kept this place exactly as he left it when he died. Forty years ago. My mother had passed two years before. I had no brothers or sisters. And I never married. All that's left of my family is me." He waved an arm. "And this house."

"It's sure some house."

"What does your company care?"

"I'm not part of Sturdevant Developers, Mr. Sikorski. I'm —"

"Come on," he snapped.

I trailed him down a dark hallway, through a large dining room with an oak table and chairs for six.

He must have noticed my raised eyebrows. "My father had a lot of friends here. Nearly forty farm families. Places knocked flat now and carted away to some dump. What's left are house foundations. And the empty hills and most of the trees, which is fine by me."

We walked into a spacious kitchen with a central table and four chairs. Big electric stove and... Was that big wood-faced thing an *icebox?* I remembered seeing one on my grandmother's back porch. She used it for storage after refrigerators took over.

Sikorski swung open the big door and pulled out a bottle of milk. The thing was an up-to-date refrigerator in disguise as an icebox of a century ago when frozen chunks to keep it chilled were delivered by an iceman in a horse-drawn wagon.

Sikorski's coffee, though, was by modern Mr. Coffee. He pulled two heavy china mugs from a cabinet. We sat at the table. He poured for both of us, a seemingly friendly touch in ominously cold silence. I took it black and bitter. He tipped a dollop of milk into his, stirred. Then he sat back with his eyes on mine.

"They keep the power line out to this place. County made 'em do it." He clunked his mug down on the table's white oilcloth. Last time I'd seen oilcloth was in my grandmother's kitchen.

"You lived here all your life?" I asked him.

"I left when I was eighteen. Out of high school and out to see the world."

"No college?"

"Hell, no. I banged up and down the East Coast taking whatever jobs I could find. I didn't know what I was looking for, so I never found it out there. When my mother died, I came back, worked as a driver for a hauling company down in Hardington. Then my father died and here I am. Found out what I'd been looking for was right here all the time."

He took a coffee sip. Put down the mug a bit easier this time. "So you can see why I'm fighting to hold this place."

"But you could move almost all these things to wherever you—"

"Damn it! It's a lot more than 'things'! Lemme tell you something. My grandparents came here from the old country in the late 1800s. Settled in Hardington when anthracite was beginning to boom. When my father was nine, he worked as a breaker boy. Know what that was?"

"Sat over the breaker chutes to pick out anything that wasn't coal."

"Yeah. When he was old enough—that was twelve—he was down in the mines, down there breathing the coal dust that would kill him. But not before he made foreman, then mine boss, then part owner of the damned mine. Hell of an accomplishment in those days. The mine owners came from England and Scotland. The bosses were Irish, and anybody with a name ending in a, e, i, o, or u did the digging."

"So how—"

"How did this old place come about? When my father retired, he sold his share of the mine. That let us escape, as he put it, to the country. To here. This was a farm. Big frame house, big barn, chicken coop, pig sty. We tore down everything but the house. Big, but just a plain farmhouse. He spent the rest of his life making it what you see today. And you're the only one of the Sturdevant crowd—"

"I told you, I'm not—"

"Yeah, yeah. None of 'em cares about anything but building a goddam 'new city.' So they'll pollute this whole countryside with their damned little cracker boxes."

"The Village of Stag Run seems to me to be a cut above—"

"Stag Run? Well here's one stag ain't running!" He banged his fist on the table. "Whatever it takes, goddammit!"

Whatever it takes? That I put in my mental file.

"You might want to reconsider, Mr. Sikorski."

"Jesus, you too? I thought you told me you're—"

"Writing a history of the project. You'll be part of it." I was surprised at how authentic that sounded, at least to me.

"In your book as the guy who gummed up the works, I suppose."

"Credit where credit is due, Mr. Sikorski."

I could see he liked that. "No," I said. "You'll be in it as someone struggling to preserve his heritage. A losing struggle, I'm afraid. Have you heard of eminent domain?"

"That's when the government throws you off your own property 'for the public good,' right? I see that as a chance to tie 'em up in court." His fist banged the table again, and his face flared red. "If Keystone can't be stopped one way, court's another!"

He gave me a hard look. "You say you're writing a history of all this?" He nodded at my notebook. "I don't see you making any damn notes."

"I'll jot down the highlights in the car. I've got a good memory."

Time to get out of here. I thanked him for the coffee, wished him well and headed for the door. As I crossed the living room, I noticed the only modern touch in that grand holdover from the past. A jolting touch. On two intricately carved pegs over the doorway hung an assault rifle.

He saw my upward glance. "M-14. Memento of my army days. 'Nam. The war nobody wants to talk about. Including me." He yanked the door open. "Good luck with the book." The door closed behind me with a bang.

Yeah, the "book."

Now alone on the porch, I strolled off to my right, shading my eyes with a hand, admiring the view — or so I hoped it would appear to Ivan, were he peering through the living room's lacy curtains. Actually, I was scanning the front of his Hummer for battle scars. Specifically, evidence of that midnight ram job near the Maximall's parking lot entrance.

But I saw only pristine polished midnight-blue and chrome. Could have had it repaired. Or was I grasping at my only straw?

***

Back in my temporary office at Maximall Hardington, I pondered for maybe five minutes. Then Cliff walked in, his mustard-colored brush cut and fringe beard bristling.

"Anything?"

"Concerning Sikorski's determination to shelter in place? Not an inch of give. And now that I've seen what he's protecting, I know why. You ever been in that house?"

"I don't go into any of the houses we level. I don't want to feel… Well, let's say it helps to stay impersonal."

A glimpse of unexpected sensibility in this bastion of hard-driving developers.

"It's more than the guy's old homestead. The whole place is museum quality."

Cliff sighed. "Good thing you were out there fact-finding and not negotiating. See what I mean about going into houses you know are condemned?"

He plopped into the desk-side chair. "Well, sounds like the most relevant fact you got is that we are headed toward eminent domain."

"I mentioned that to Sikorski. Instead of dismay, I saw eagerness. He's looking forward to a long, drawn-out court fight."

"His money against ours. And we've got more."

"Every time I hear something like that, I'm reminded of the Jewish definition of a lawsuit."

"Such as?"

"A litigant yanking on each end of a cow while the lawyers get the milk. By the way, one of these prospective litigants has a gun. An M-14 semi-automatic rifle. Which, he told me, is a souvenir of his Vietnam service. If so, it could be the fully automatic version."

Cliff shook his head in exasperation. "I don't know any humane way to…hell, I'll let Max worry about that. My big concern for the moment is the ground breaking."

"Ground breaking?"

"Nobody told you?"

"I've been in and out. Maybe nobody could catch me."

"You're being diplomatic. Anyway, it's scheduled for Saturday morning. Groundbreaking for Keystone's first building. Town Center, until we come up with a more glamorous name. Plan is to move our offices up there and free up this level of the Maximall for additional shops."

"Sounds efficient, but six pols with gold shovels to celebrate the birth of an office building doesn't—"

"We're way past the pols-and-shovels routine. Ten a.m. Saturday. Be out there. That's when the balloon goes up. Literally."

7

Friday, the day before the groundbreaking, I perched in my temporary office on Maximall Hardington's top floor and spun my wheels. Well, not exactly. It just felt that way. If Max were to ask me for a formal report on what I was doing at the moment, I would tell him "I'm acclimating to the overall situation and familiarizing myself with various staff members."

The first to pop in was a guy who looked to be in his mid-thirties but exuded enthusiasm like a college kid. Blue turtleneck, khaki slacks. Tall, slim, thick black hair combed straight back, which always strikes me as aggressive.

"Hi! I'm Mitch Newman, head of PR. Heard you're holed up in here to write a history of our Keystone project." He stuck out a hand. Grip of eagle talons. "Want to make sure you get out to the groundbreaking tomorrow. It's gonna be worth writing about."

"Wouldn't miss it, Mitch."

"They tell me you're from—mind if I sit down?" He plunked into my butt-numbing desk-side chair. "—from Philly."

I felt an uneasy twinge. I was being talked about.

I nodded. "Yeah."

"A writer. That's what I really want to be. What've you written?"

Oh, fine. But I was ready for this inevitable question. "Mostly annual reports, those thick volumes of data-speak that nobody reads."

"Oh man, that sounds double dreary."

"Pays well."

"I've tried a few pieces for inflight magazines. Two rejections and two never answered at all. You got any helpful hints?"

"One. Keep trying."

He gave me a speculative look. "Yeah." Pushed out of the chair and glanced at my open notebook. "Guess you'd like to get back to what you're working on. See ya." And he walked out. The fewer casual conversations I had with probing Sturdevant employees, the better.

Lunchtime. I closed the three-ringer, took the elevator down to the shopping level and worked through the Friday frenzy to Ye Olde London Pub. Cool and cozy, but a pub without a bar. Had to be a jolt to any Brit tourist who might wander in here. I spotted a booth with a dandy view of the valley, slid in, reached for a menu then had the prickly feeling I was being watched.

From a booth across the room, Priscilla Killian waggled her fingers at me. She pointed at herself then at me. I nodded.

Tall and trim in a navy-blue slack suit, she grabbed her purse, strode over, and slipped in across from me.

"Everybody's hesitant about getting chummy with the boss's right hand." She consulted the clothbound menu then said, without looking up, "I heard you paid a visit to our friend Mr. Sikorski."

"The immovable Gibraltar of Stag Run. Got a whole chapter for my book out of that."

A chubby blond girl in a blue-and-white-striped uniform appeared, pad and pencil at the ready. "Cheerio," she said in a passable British accent. "I am your food arranger. The Friday special is kidney pie."

My American stomach turned over. Maybe Priscilla's too. "I'll have the avocado salad plate," she said. "And iced tea."

"BLT for me, and iced coffee." That got the hint of a frown from our food arranger as she flounced away.

"What do you think of our leading hotel?" Priscilla asked.

"A nice try at preservation-of-the-past." And to my relief, we chatted amiably about the Anthracite Hotel. Our lunches arrived. And distracted, I made a slip.

"The hotel could be worth a mention in my book."

"Oh, speaking of your book, that whole idea intrigues me. In fact—don't be angry now—I Googled you."

Uh-oh. On the job four days, and Sherlock Killian is checking on me? What can I say? As little as possible. So, I said, "And?"

"And I found two authors named Rod-odd Stevens. Roderick Stevens in California. Rodgers Stevens in New Mexico. But no Rodney Stevens anywhere. Isn't that interesting?" She nibbled a cherry tomato, her eyes unblinking on mine.

I had sudden inspiration to launch into a fable about how a famous writer must occasionally use a false name to avoid… Realized that fleeting idea could backfire in my face, so I let it fleet.

And said, "Not surprising I'm not Googleable." I unfurled my "writing annual reports" dodge. While I jabbered on about how dreary an occupation that was, she pulled what looked like a black cigarette out of her purse. Didn't light it, but when she took a puff, it glowed blue.

"An e-cigarette," she said. "I'm blowing water vapor, not smoke."

I'm the one blowing smoke, I thought, as I malarkyed on about the dullness of narrating profit-and-loss statements.

Her interest withered fast, and she said, "I'm sure you'll find something more compelling out on the site tomorrow morning."

"The groundbreaking. Cliff said something about a balloon, and your PR chief dropped by to make sure I'll show up."

"Mitch's inspiration. Another highlight for your book. How many other—"

"How long have you been with Sturdevant?" I broke in. Had to get her off the damned book probe.

"Since the Keystone project began two years ago. Well, almost at the beginning. I came on board a month or so after it was announced."

"You from around here?"

"No, from New Jersey. Cherry Hill. Saw an ad in the newspaper classifieds. It sounded more exciting than what I was doing."

"Which was?"

"Administrative assistant for the president of a trash hauling company. I gave up clamor for glamor."

"You think Keystone is glamorous?"

"In comparison to what I was doing. I'd read about the new cities of Reston and Columbia, and how successful they've been. Keystone can be right up there with them. So now I'm a Pennsylvanian."

I glanced at her naked ring finger. "Never been married?"

She nodded. "Years ago, but it didn't work out. You?"

"Briefly, but she walked out."

"Life's bitter experiences," she murmured and looked down at the table. I gathered that was the end of marital discussions.

She looked to be in her mid-thirties. Not young but still plenty viable.

Our kewpie doll food arranger arrived with the check. I grabbed it. "My treat, Priscilla."

"After breakfast together," she said with mock shyness, "you can call me Pris. But never Prissy. See you tomorrow at the Y."

"The Y?"

"Where the access road forks into the loop road. That's where the City Center will be built.

***

At sun-drenched 9:30 a.m., a dozen cars, including two county sheriff blue-and-whites were already parked along the north sides of the "Y" intersection. A couple hundred yards out in the newly-mown grass with a leafy forest looming behind them, Max Sturdevant and a group of guys in coats and ties settled into folding chairs flanking a small speakers' stand. They faced a three-tiered bleacher closer to the road. Near its board seats on a metal framework, a small crowd milled around an open-sided refreshment tent. I joined them. Got myself a cup of black-and-bitter from a huge steel urn. I nodded at the two county cops sipping coffee nearby, then took a seat on the near end of the bleacher. That gave me a good view of the real point of interest out here in the blinding morning sun.

The red-and-yellow striped balloon was easily fifteen feet in diameter. Tethered to the ground between the speakers' stand and the bleacher seats, it bobbed gently in the morning's light breeze. A three-man handling crew in tan jumpsuits rolled a half dozen bright green pressure tanks clear.

The coat-and-tie dignitaries settled in chairs flanking the speaker dais. The crowd deserted the refreshment tent and clambered onto our bleacher boards. I opened my notebook across my knees and jotted a few notes, half legit and half play-acting for any Sturdevant employees who might wonder just what I was doing here.

Max stepped up to the portable speaker's stand, tapped the mic. The crowd stilled.

"Good morning and welcome to this historic occasion in the birth of what will be one of the Keystone State's most vibrant communities: the City of Keystone."

That got him a smatter of get-on-with-it applause.

"The imaginative project about to arise from these picturesque hills and dales, these very grounds..." And on and on until I could feel restless shuffling through the board I was sitting on.

Finally, after fifteen minutes of "pioneering development" boilerplate: "And now, the dramatic symbolic moment to mark the ascendancy of the first structure in our nation's most exciting new city-to-be: the sixty-foot rise to mark the apex of the six-story City Center."

He pointed at the balloon crew then gave them a hearty thumbs-up.

They cut the mooring lines. Trailed by its unreeling tether line, the big balloon began to rise. I had to admit this was impressive. A trifle corny, but impressive.

As the big red-and-yellow balloon floated past what I guessed to be the twenty-foot level, the morning breeze drifted it southward, almost directly above us.

Craning high, I heard an odd sound. From the parking area behind me. A muffled gunshot?

Something fiery bright streaked overhead.

My God, a flare.

Had somebody fired a flare at the crowd?

No, *at the balloon.*

8

ifty feet above our bleacher seats, the flare punched into the balloon. The plastic fabric glowed briefly; then the flare died. A ring of flaming fabric around its entrance point widened the breach. Then it, too, sputtered out.

If the guy expected an explosion, he'd heard or read too much about the Hindenburg. Now even party balloons use non-flammable helium so the damage to our "ground breaking" balloon was the ragged hole near its top.

As helium gushed out, the balloon began to sink. Panicky feet rattled and banged the bleacher boards. I launched off my seat but my feet snagged in the collapsing folds. I managed to pull clear just as the balloon gasped its last and flopped over the people still struggling on this end of the stand.

"Help! Help!"

"Get me outta here."

Panicky munchkin-voice shouts. A couple whiffs of helium do that to the vocal cords. Too many whiffs can kill you.

As I turned back to lend a hand, I spotted a guy running toward a gray SUV in the parking area. Looked like a flare gun in his right hand. The two sheriff deputies raced for the stand. I swung toward the fleeing flare shooter. I wasn't about to yell "Stop! Or I'll shoot!" in a helium falsetto. And I'd left my .38 back in the hotel. He dived into the gray SUV. The engine roared. Wheels spun. He bounced onto the loop road.

One of the deputies swerved my way. I yanked open the door of my Jeep and scrambled aboard.

The fleeing SUV, a Nissan, headed for the Y intersection. I charged onto the loop road just in time to see him swerve into the road back to the valley.

Wow! A car chase! My highlights as a P.I. had mostly been dreary suburban stakeouts spying on errant spouses — interrupted once for a trip to Florida, where I was briefly kidnapped — but no car chases till now.

I swung hard right and rushed downhill to see him bounce into the air over a road hump a hundred yards ahead. I leaped airborne over the hump and gained a few yards on the fleeing balloon killer. Behind me, I heard the yowl of a siren. One of the deputies at the ground-breaking must have been sharper-of-brain and fleeter-of-foot than I'd expected. I was a pursued pursuer.

We bounded past the Maximall access road and into the fairly empty streets of Hardington's northern suburbs. Swerved around several Saturday morning drivers, then roared into downtown.

Talk about dodging and weaving! A traffic light half a block ahead showed green as the balloon buster sailed through. Yellow, as I screeched after him. The deputy's car behind me ran the red.

This was getting damned dangerous. But I stuck to my accelerator-stomping, brake-ramming, wheel-twisting dance because I figured the guy causing all this was a link to whoever wanted the Keystone City project closed down.

We snaked through mid-town traffic. When I pulled around a slow-moving bus, the street ahead was clear. No gray SUV in sight. A Houdini disappearing act... until I noticed the alley between two apartment buildings on my right. Yep, there he was, barreling down the alley. I barreled right after him.

Then his brake lights flared.

He stood the Nissan on its nose. Barely ten feet short of plowing into the huge trash hauler that had just pulled into the far end of the alley.

I slammed on my brakes. Close behind me, the deputy's car screeched rubber. He jumped out and headed for me. I popped out and headed toward the Nissan. Its driver flew out, left his door gaping, and scuttled around the truck. By the time I squeezed by with the blue-and-white close behind, the guy had disappeared in the sidewalk shuffle.

"Okay," the deputy rumbled behind me, "back to your car."

"I hope you were after him, not me."

"I'm after both of you, but for the moment, you'll do."

He was a big guy, muscles bulging beneath his tan uniform shirt, wrestling quality. But I thought I detected a "what's going on?" expression in his wide-set eyes.

"Your license," he ordered.

As I handed it over, a quote from my high school English class hopscotched through my concern. "The best laid schemes o' mice and men Gang aft a-gley." My hastily laid "Rodney Stevens" scheme could be ganging a-gley right in this cop's chunky fingers.

"Elrod Montgomery from Philly," he read. "What the hell are you doing chasing that idiot in your rented vehicle?"

Now I knew he had a computer aboard, and managed to check my Jeep's license tag. I took a deep breath; better than "er-ah-well-uh." His car-borne Google could strip me naked.

I was forced to take a chance on this gruff-looking county cop. Glanced at his name plate. "I'm a private investigator, Sergeant Stoddard." I pulled out my P.I. license. "Hired undercover by Max Sturdevant, head of the Keystone project—"

"I know Max. You'd better be leveling with me."

"And I'm sure you know about the three car incidents, the sabotaged D-8 that killed its driver. And we both witnessed the death of the balloon."

"Dumb idea to start with."

"The balloon or the attack on the balloon?"

"Both."

"Yeah, well...Sarge, I hope you'll keep all this under your hat as long as possible." What else could I hope for? "I am making some progress." I nodded at the open-doored SUV. "And we have the guy's car. And something of a description: brown turtleneck sweater, tan pants. Maybe five-six or -seven."

"Right." Stoddard peered at the Nissan's license plate. "Lemme check that out." He trotted to his blue-and-white. A couple minutes later, he motioned me back there.

"Belongs to a Mrs. Stella McHugh way up in Binghamton, out of state. Stolen weeks ago. Dead end, Montgomery. Unless state cop forensics turn up anything. County uses them."

"Call me Rod. Rodney Stevens. That's my cover. I'm working the case as a writer hired to write a history of the Keystone project. You keep that quiet as long as you can, and I'll pass on anything substantial directly to you. Deal?" I held my breath.

"Unless you're —"

"Whatever you're thinking, I'm not. What I'm thinking is that somebody wants that project to fall apart. I'm here to find out who and why. If I do — *when* I do — you'll be the next one to know."

"Damnedest bribe I've ever been offered. I'll take it. But if you're snowin' me, you'll be one sorry private dick."

"Fair enough. Let's get out of here."

He backed out, peering behind him as he talked into his shoulder-mounted two-way, presumably for a pick-up of the stolen Nissan. I hoped his getting credit for its recovery would help keep his mouth shut concerning Keystone.

As I drove back up the hill to my barebones office in Maximall Hardington, I wondered if I had a confidential contact with the county police or a bemused leaker who was about to blow my flimsy "historian" cover into uselessness.

9

After my heart-clutching car chase and the encounter with County Sheriff Sergeant Stoddard, I drove carefully back to Maximall Hardington. To my surprise, in my barebones office, I found Priscilla.

"A refuge," she said, "from the not-much-fun fallout in Max's office. He and Cliff are trying to calm down the press mob jammed in there with them. They crowded me right out of my administrative assistant cubby."

"Hell of a morning." Again, I was impressed by the appeal of this business-intense woman. No-nonsense gray skirt and jacket. Not a hair out of place in her mahogany sheen. Hazel eyes on full alert. Yet I thought I detected a hint of...

"How about lunch?" I suggested.

For the second time, we shared a table at Ye Olde London Pub down in the mall's sales level. Waldorf salad for her, grilled cheese for me.

"I didn't see you at the groundbreaking, Pris."

"I was catching up on paperwork. Max gave me a pass."

"Too bad. It turned out to be quite a spectacle."

"So, I heard. You think that goof with the flare was expecting an explosion?"

I took a drag of iced coffee. "Maybe. His obvious intention was to make the ceremony look like yet another stumble by an inept developer. Enough stumbles could kill public and private support and doom the Keystone project."

In the midst of that speculation, I realized an oversight on my part.

"You know who I haven't talked to yet? The guy in charge of Susquehanna Contractors' on-site motor pool."

"Jacob 'Workaholic' Waller. He's probably there now."

"On Saturday?"

"On every day. He has a paperwork fetish. Scared to death it'll get impossibly ahead of him. When we get back upstairs, I'll give him a call. Make sure he's receiving visitors."

***

"A *historian?*" Waller snorted on the phone's speaker back in Pris's now deserted little office. She rolled her eyes. "What the hell does he want with—Well, okay," Waller rasped. "Send him out here."

"Wouldn't want to keep him waiting," I told her. "Enjoyed lunch, now back to historical research."

Out in the mall's parking area, I fired up my rented Jeep, swung left at the exit, climbed the hill to the loop road intersection. In the afternoon shadows of the forest behind them, a three-man crew cleaned up remnants of the chaotic groundbreaking ceremony. I swung to the right. In a few minutes, I passed Ivan Sikorski's defiantly still-standing homestead. With his Hummer parked nose-in near the front porch, he was presumably in residence. Serenity, while calamity pends.

A couple miles farther, I pulled up in front of the motor pool's three long, tar-papered sheds, temporary construction equipment shelters to be gone when Keystone City blossomed into reality. A sign on one end of the center shed told me this was the office. I parked beside a dark brown Kia Soul, the model with the chopped-off back end. Had to be Workaholic Waller's.

I stepped into a bleak workspace, its two-by-four framing exposed. No windows. A single exceedingly bright light bulb hung over a pair of two-drawer filing cabinets with a flush door laid flat on their tops. Behind this paper-choked makeshift desk, a narrow-shouldered guy with gray hair falling over his forehead perched on a folding chair. The place was thick with cigar smoke. One butt was mashed on a tin can lid in front of him. Another butt hung in the corner of his mouth. I wondered if he put in long hours here because a wife wouldn't let him smoke at home.

"Stevens?" His voice was as flat as his door desktop.

"That's me." I shook his casually offered hand.

"Jake Waller. What're you doing out here on a Saturday afternoon?"

"Same question to you, Jake."

"Paperwork. Never catch up. Max's steno said you're a — what was it? Oh, a historian. What the hell is a historian doing on this project?"

I'd pegged him around fifty, but his voice had a much younger bite. "Max's idea. He wants a detailed history of the project. Might be thinking of national publication. Or maybe he just wants a record for posterity. I'm only concerned with getting the facts straight and down on paper."

"Such as, where I'm concerned?"

"Guess you could call it a 'sequence of misfortunes' your motor pool has been involved in."

"You sound like a cop."

I almost said I once was a cop. Caught it just in time. I gave him what I hoped was an ingratiating grin. "Only trying to get the facts, man. And the D-8 that killed a guy did come from here."

"Don't remind me."

"And I heard a fire here destroyed several vehicles."

"Don't remind me of that, either."

"And there was that attempt to knock you off the road the night you were held up here by a dead battery. Plus, a couple accidents by Keystone staffers."

"Wait a minute! You can't tie Susquehanna Contractors into everything that's gone wrong. Next you'll be trying to pin that messed-up groundbreaking this morning—"

"Were you there?"

"Hell no. Buncha photo-op nonsense."

"It sure did impress the media, Jake."

"So, I heard." He pointed at a small radio half-buried in his desk clutter. "Also, heard some yonko tried to chase the guy who wrecked the stupid event."

"Said 'yonko' sits in front of you, Jake."

"Huh. Did you catch up with the guy?"

"On the far side of Hardington, he drove into a clogged alley, jumped out and disappeared. His SUV turned out to be stolen up in Binghamton. All I got was a partial description. Medium-size guy, tan pants, brown turtleneck sweater. He—"

"Hold on, Stevens. Brown turtleneck sweater? That sounds like Vinny Parson. Jesus!"

"Who is Vinny Parson Jesus?"

"Just Parson. He showed up a while back. Said the auto business he worked for back in—hell, I forget where. Anyway, it went out of business, and did I have a spot for a part-timer? We were being pushed hard to clear the site, so I took him on."

"So, your company has his SS number on file."

"Well...no. I took him on like you hire a lawn worker. No paper, except the weekly cash I paid him out of our general fund."

Dead end. Again. "You know where he was living?" Maybe a landlord could give me more than I was getting from Jake Waller.

"No need to know that," Waller said. "He showed up, worked, I paid him cash. Period."

Well, not quite. "Did he live up to his alleged automotive background?"

"He was damned good at it." Waller gave me a speculative squint. "Does all this have to go into that Keystone history you say you're working on?"

"Not unless it's bigger than it sounds. Even then, I can gloss Parson's sketchy employment circumstances if he's worth writing about at all. When did you hire him?"

"Just after the two Sturdevant car accidents. We have our own repair set-up here, and Max was pushing us hard to get them back on the road. Vinny fit right in."

"Was that before the fire?"

Waller stubbed out his cigar stump and gave me a long look. "Yeah, it was. And come to think of it, he was here the day my car battery went dead. When it was recharged around midnight, then that car coming out of the mall parking area tried to push me off the road. That was a close one. Nearly went over the guard rail and down the hillside."

He rolled open the top drawer of his left side filing cabinet. Paper evidence, I hoped. Nope. He plucked out a fresh cigar and began to roll it absently between fingertips. "Know something else? Vinny was here the day before that D-8 went into Lake Linden. Worked late. He was still in the shop area when I left."

"You think Vinny was capable of screwing up the D-8's controls?"

In Waller's restless fingers, the cigar twirled. "I guess I did, because the next day, I canned him. Told him we had a new full-timer, which we did, and Vinny was no longer needed. I hope to hell you don't need all this detail for your damned history. There wasn't any big, dramatic 'scene.' He just shrugged and walked away."

Apparently, far enough to get his hands on a flare gun. All my probing to date pointed straight at Vinny Parson. With luck, I thought, the county cops will nab him, or his close escape from Sgt. Stoddard and me has scared him out of town. All I have to do now is write up a report for Max Sturdevant, collect any pay still due, and head back to good old Philly.

Oh, sure.

10

Harvey Amerman, fat, florid and fifty, lit a fresh unfiltered cigarette from the glowing stub of the previous...coffin nail, his mother used to call them. Maybe the cigarettes will kill me before the Keystone project does, he thought. I'm a long way from Hardington now—well, a couple hundred miles—but the potential for disaster hangs over me like a god-damned black cloud.

He swung his swivel chair around to gaze out the picture window at the sixth-floor view of the Camden waterfront with the Delaware River's sluggish flow separating New Jersey from the distant Pennsylvania shoreline. Lots of memories over there. Some exhilarating; others...well, not so.

He'd been barely out of Hardington High and already a beneficiary of money-hungry classmate Mateo Cassina; "Monte Cassino," as Mateo had been dubbed by a history-wise nerd of their class of '85, "and you know what happened to Monte Cassino. Bombed flat." To which wiry and crafty-eyed Mateo would only smile.

Cassina had a future in mind, not in his father's tiny one-house-at-a-time construction operation, but as a big supplier to such companies. He'd worked summers for an unimaginative small supplier, learned the ins and outs—especially the potential of importing building materials from China.

A month after graduation, Mateo came to his compliant and more affluent front man, Harvey Amerman. Together they'd set up a small building supplies operation along a county road winding out of Hardington into the Pocono foothills.

Chinese prices let them undercut the sparse local competition, already burdened with soaring costs from U.S. manufacturers, and with frequent minor mishaps that never seemed to afflict Amerman & Cassina—because Mateo turned out to be as proficient in subversion as he was in purchasing-smarts. Often Harvey felt he was more of a passenger than a co-operator of a fast ride, but its substantial financial yield numbed his conscience.

When the tsunami paperwork threatened to overwhelm their struggling clerical staff, they hired an office manager, a tiny red-headed Irish dynamo named Mary Louise O'Brian. Their perky little Colleen was the first to detect the rumblings of an on-coming debacle.

Still chilled by that memory, Harvey took a deep drag, coughed out a cloud. What a gut twister that turned out to be. Cheap Chinese drywall, way under the cost of U.S.-made wallboard, was Amerman & Cassina's major seller. The company was built on it. This stuff had boosted builders' profit margins up and down the East Coast. But while the partners were busy closing sales, Ms. O'Brian delved deep into the wallboard rumors. She came up with a report that curdled their guts. The high sulphur content of Chinese drywall, Mary Louise told them, was suspected of causing homeowners' respiratory problems, nosebleeds, asthma attacks, and the corrosion of pipes and wiring, plus a rotten-egg smell pervading homes—almost entirely in the U.S. South—homes built with precisely the same product that had built Amerman & Cassina. Now, she warned, studies are underway that could threaten the company's survival.

On a day he wished he could forget, Mateo was out of town on a round of sales calls, so the impact of Mary Louise's findings fell on Harvey, and he ordered her to file the report. He meant file it until Mateo returned, but she took that as "bag it." And she turned into an instant hands-on-hips, jaw-jutting bitch.

"You idiot!" she screamed. "You're putting our money — *our* money! — into a disaster waiting to blow up in our faces. If you won't do something about it for the good of the company, I will! For God's sake, it's a *health* issue!"

Yeah, he thought. The health of Amerman & Cassina.

Then, Harvey recalled, as he brushed a splat of ash from his Armani trousers, another shock. Right after Mateo agreed to suppress her report, their newly aggressive office manager was invited to speak at the annual convention of building suppliers in Phoenix. God only knew what she was planning to spill out there.

But on the day of Mary Louise's departure for Arizona, Harvey's chain-smoking trepidation and Mateo's raspy throat clearing (when the hell had he acquired *that*?) were both obliterated by late afternoon word. Mary Louise's car had made it to the down-valley regional airport, but there was no record of her boarding the westbound 707. She was never seen again

Harvey Amerman attended the memorial service in Hardington's St. Francis Church. And he made all his expected condolences to her extensive family, successfully suppressing his feeling of relief. Her inevitable Chinese drywall report at the Phoenix convention surely would have propelled private rumor into public alarm. Now, though, Amerman & Cassina could dump the balance of their drywall stock into the still-innocent northern markets, close the business in Hardington before the coming Chinese-made scandal closed it down for them, then get the hell out of town.

They set up shop as A and C, construction consultants and suppliers in Camden, New Jersey, offering "progressive" advice to building enterprises, plus construction materials. Those who signed on found their businesses sailing smoothly. Those who turned them down: not so smooth. That was Mateo's side of it. Within two years, A and C morphed into a major supplier of building materials.

As Harvey watched the afternoon haze obscure his river view, he remembered the morning weeks ago—the morning the Associated Press article announced that except for a row of lake cottages and one still-occupied holdout, initial construction on Keystone City was imminent.

Harvey's heart had turned to ice. He grabbed his phone. Mateo rushed into his office, snatched the paper, scanned the piece, stared at Harvey. "We gotta do something."

The "something" was an on-call bundle of not-always-savory action going by the name "Vincent Johnson." Lots of wiry muscle on a deceptively average frame, with a knowledge of auto mechanics. Addicted to turtleneck sweaters. His assignment: Get on out to Hardington, find ways to slow down the project—at least. At best, nix it altogether. Big assignment with a fee to match.

As "Vinny Parson," he got himself hired by Susquehanna Contractors, and in A and C's view, began his work competently. The car accidents. The motor pool fire. All neatly engineered. Then the out-of-control bulldozer that killed the driver. "Not in the plan," Mateo had commented, "but it does boost the project's negatives."

***

Now Harvey fired up his fifth cigarette since lunch. Puffed, coughed, puffed again. Then he picked up his phone and stabbed Mateo's extension button.

In three minutes, his partner appeared, his eyebrows high in his narrow foxlike face. "Yeah?"

Harvey shoved the paper across the desk. "Read the lead story on page two."

Mateo scowled, read, then looked up. "So they've broken ground."

"That's almost beside the point."

"What point?"

"I'd say Vinny has gotten too damned wrapped up in his work to think straight. A flare gun into helium, for God's sake—with him right out in the open firing it. Result: a dumb-ass car chase, for God's sake. With a cop and some overeager bystander damned near nailing our man in a blocked alley."

"I didn't see that part in the paper."

"Vinny told me that part. He called this morning. So now the cops have his description."

"And his car. Fingerprints."

"Stolen car. And he wore gloves. The problem is Vinny's gotten careless. We can't afford careless."

"So," Mateo said, "what'd you tell him?"

"I told him sit tight, we'll be in touch. You got any thoughts on what we do about that klutz?"

"It doesn't take a genius, Harve. He's gotta go. We'll still have our in-company contact in place. And we can reset from there."

11

Somewhere I'd read, "A body in motion tends to stay in motion until it attends a meeting." This morning I was not in motion.

I was one of seven grouped around a table in what passed for a conference room. Nothing on the walls. The single window looked straight into the rocky hillside of Hardington's north slope. Like all the Maximall's second floor offices—except for Max Sturdevant's—this conference room felt temporary. Because it was. As soon as Keystone's Town Center was habitable, Sturdevant Developers planned to move into its top floor. Where we now sat would become one of the many shops in the Maximall's upward expansion.

Five of us here were Sturdevant's top officers. Max's buzz-cut brother Cliff; curly-haired, fortyish Chief Planner Marty Elman; and CFO Ed Fletcher, bald and squinting through his wire-rimmed specs, sat across from me. To my right perched tall and hungry-looking Director of PR Mitch Newman. On my left, though she was not a company big-wig, Priscilla Killian opened her laptop, ready, I assumed, to take notes.

A shirtsleeves and tie meeting, except for Pris. She wore her customary drab knee-length gray skirt, white blouse, heavy glasses. Her no-nonsense uniform.

Styrofoam cups all around, filled with bitter brew from a Mr. Coffee dripper in one corner of our echoing chamber. I took a sip, opened my prop notebook to a page where I'd actually scrawled notes during my visit with Ivan Sikorski – and wondered why I had been asked to attend this meeting.

At the head of the table, Max Sturdevant, his surely-dyed coal-black hair neatly parted in the middle in his way-out-of-date style, shuffled paper. Then he looked up, tapped the table with the blunt end of his ballpoint pen. Cleared his throat.

"I thank you, Cliff, Marty, Mitch, Ed, for submitting these written reports on what you planned to say this morning. Well done, so now you don't have to say it. I'll have copies made for all of you."

I got the feeling Max had called the meeting less to transact business than to impress us he was still on top of things.

"I'd like to make one addition," Chief Planner Elman said. "When actual construction on Town Center begins, I suggest we hire security."

Again, Max's annoying throat-clear. "Good point, Marty. Already under advisement." He glanced at me. "I've asked our historian to attend today because we have reached a... a pivotal point in Keystone City's development."

Oh, so that's why I'm here.

"TV and the press are having a field day over the groundbreaking mess. 'Keystone's balloon bust,' one headline called it. Local TV reveled in 'A flare for publicity.' We'll survive all that unhelpful glee, of course."

Max's eyes swept the table and stopped on me. "I want to thank you, Rod, for your quick response at the groundbreaking. I hope one Vinny Parson will soon be found and brought to justice for all the delay and damage he has caused."

"And apparently," PR man Mitch added, "for killing that poor guy on the D-8."

"Yes. Of course," Max scowled – not for the interruption, I suspected, but for having to be reminded of that deadly incident. He seemed to be forcing optimism as a cover for apprehension. "And now," he said, "we are on the verge of beginning construction on what will be Keystone City's central building, and" — pause for effect — "the new national headquarters of Sturdevant Developers."

"Hear! Hear!" PR man Mitch cried, raising his cup. "A toast!" We all joined him in a Styrofoam salute. Max gave us a couple more gung ho-ers. Then he asked, "Any questions?"

Planner Marty Elman raised a forefinger. "I got one. What in holy hell was our *historian* doing chasing that guy?"

Six pairs of eyes swung my way.

"It was my 'send in the Marines' reaction to a situation that shocked all of us," Max admitted.

Marty's eyebrows arched. "I hope it scared that idiot away permanently. Otherwise — "

"Meeting adjourned," Max rumbled. "Rod, see me in my office."

Minutes later, I stepped into Max's plush bailiwick.

"Close the door behind you, Rod. Take a seat."

I took the offered chair in front of Max's huge desk and admired the panorama beyond the broad window behind him. I assumed this upscale office in our otherwise bleak second level hinted at what he planned for the company's future digs atop Town Center. He click-clicked his sterling ballpoint pen then glanced at me. "My crack about sending in the Marines ..."

"Actually, one Marine. I put in a hitch more or less between wars. No glory. I served most of those years as one of the security guards at our embassy in Moscow. But that's another story."

Max swung his chair around, stared out his big window for a long moment then swung back. "Your thoughts on — what's the guy's name...Vinny. Your thoughts on the Vinny thing?"

"A classic case of a saboteur getting so wrapped up in his work, he undoes himself by overdoing it. Until that dumbness at the groundbreaking, he'd managed to do a pretty slick job."

"The car accidents. The motor pool fire. The runaway D-8." Max fiddled with his pen. "At that point he was still well undercover."

"Until he got carried away with himself."

"Right. Now put yourself in his place, which will be a stretch because I think you are a smart guy, and he's just a crafty one. Does he stay on the job or run?"

"You're thinking like I'm thinking, Max. He's not in this all by himself. Where's the profit in that?"

"Wild thought. Could he possibly have been hired by your friend Sikorski?"

Friend? Cliff and Max must have been ruminating about my report on my visit to the holdout homestead.

I let that pass. "He hates the project, but I can't see him actually hiring somebody to stall it. He's more of a let's-go-to-court type than a burn-down-the-house whacko."

"I think I agree, Rod. And maybe you'll agree that the motivating force behind Vinny-boy logically has to be money from some source pretty well determined to head off the project. Somebody is underwriting these disruptions."

"I think so. And the problem is to find out who and why." As I said that, I realized it sounded like a guy trying to extend a well-paying contract. "Look, we have a verbal agreement. You can cut me off anytime."

"I'll tell you something, Rod. The way you jumped in your car and got on that guy's tail — no hesitation, just *get him*. And you got him."

"Almost got him. The cop would have tailed him if I hadn't."

"The cop was after you, Rod. I don't think he realized you were chasing somebody until you both hit the straight stretch past the mall entrance. I want you to stay on the case."

At the moment, he had more faith in me that I had. "Thank you," I said. And our aura of frankness prompted me to broach a question I hadn't felt broachable until now.

"Have you considered — and I'm not implying anything specific — considered the possibility of someone in Sturdevant Developers — "

"That's the last thing I've wanted to consider, Rod, but..."

"It might be easier to look at...uh, a perusal of personnel records as a way to clear everybody in the company." I'd swung so easily into cop mode.

"I've got more than fifty people on the payroll."

"Let's start with the supervisory list."

"It'll take a while. I'll put Priscilla on it. She'll give you a call."

In fact, I saw Pris before Max did. I found her waiting in my temporary office when I walked in, adaze with the potential of my just-ended Max meeting.

"I'm starving," she said.

"Our luncheon trysts are getting to be a habit."

She gave me a conspiratorial smile. "They *are* a habit, Rod. A habit I don't want to break."

12

Cruising north on U.S. 476, the Pennsylvania Turnpike's Northeast Extension, Barton Krag gunned his Amerman & Cassina-supplied Ford Escape toward Hardington. He knew the SUV's license plate had been stolen from a vehicle in the Philadelphia Airport's long-term parking area. And the registration paper would lead any investigator to a fake address in a remote New Jersey town.

Krag liked the car's color—black, and its name. "Escape" could describe this job: escape from sitting around his dreary Camden apartment hoping for a call needing his...services.

A hulking man with chubby cheeks, bright blue eyes, and curly blond hair, he'd been called "Baby Face" as a kid, each caller doing it just once—with a painful result. With a wrestler's body and a thirst for proving he was a hell of a lot more...well, capable than the people he encountered in his on-call assignments, this afternoon Krag found himself wearing an unaccustomed smile.

Blessed are the meek. He remembered that from Sunday school before he was asked not to attend anymore. Blessed are the meek because they're easy to get out of my way.

He had bullied through grade school and high school before bullying became a national concern. Now it still paid off. His mission — he liked to call these jobs "missions" — was to make sure Vinny understood he was off the job and Krag was on it. "Vinny did manage to become fairly effective," Cassina told Krag yesterday in their presumably secure landline phone conversation. "But he got carried away with himself. Damn near got caught. Get him out of the picture then take over the assignment. That city project has to be stopped — or at least delayed until we can negate the threat."

Whatever the hell that meant, Krag had no idea. But he did have a clear idea of his immediate purpose. Cassina had given him the cell phone number for Vinny "Parson" and his last known address: 221 Ash Street. The Hardington map Amerman had supplied put Ash Street in the city's southwest fringe.

After more than a hundred miles of four-lane monotony, and with the afternoon sun now glaring through his left side windows, Krag swung onto an off-ramp in Hardington's southwest suburbs. Convenient positioning, but then he spent nearly fifteen minutes finding Vinny's address.

Ash Street looked like a Hollywood back-lot version of the 1930s. Gray two-story houses along neglected frost-heaved sidewalk slabs. Vinny's boarding house was a three-story exception. Two outdated cars cluttered the gravel lot that once could have been a lawn. The big asset here, Krag realized — with the glimmering of an idea — was the house's location on the southwest corner of Ash Street's intersection with Maple Street.

"Get him out of the picture." Cassina's exact words. Coupla ways to take that.

The simplest solution was often the best solution, and this intersection offered both simple and best.

Heading southwest, Baby Face Krag cruised through it. Two blocks further, he turned northward until he found what looked like a major avenue back toward Hardington's center. A few minutes later, he spotted what he was looking for: a small motel, possibly once a Howard Johnson or Motel Six, now the crestfallen Snooze Inn, with "Hourly Rates" on its plastic sign. A place that asked no questions.

Krag pulled the Ford into a space away from the office, stepped out carrying a worn black travel bag, and registered in the name on his A and C-supplied credentials: "Leonard Lewis." The spidery desk clerk barely took his spectacled eyes off his tattered copy of *Playboy*, reached for one of the keys hanging on the wall beside him, muttered, "Third unit down on the left," and tossed the key on the counter. Krag picked it up without a word—the less said, the better. Always. He grabbed his bag, walked back to the Ford, and drifted it down to unit 7. Not too bad a room, considering appearances out front, and that "Hourly Rates" sign. He used the bathroom, plunked down on the rock-hard double bed. Pulled his cell from his shirt pocket. Punched in the number Cassina had given him for contacting Parson.

"Yeah?" Vinny sounded as if he had just woken up.

"'Lenny Lewis,' Vinny."

"Len—Oh, yeah. They told me you'd be in touch. You in town?"

"Just got in. We gotta meet, and quick. Boss's orders."

"Anytime, Len."

"Say at nine tonight?"

"Good. Where are you?"

"I'll come to you," Krag told him.

"Fine. I'm at Two-Twenty-One Ash Street, southwest corner of Ash and Maple.

I'll be waiting. It'll be good to know what I'm supposed to do next."

"Nine sharp." Krag clicked off and glanced at his Timex. Now to find a crowded restaurant.

***

A few minutes before nine, he wound his way back to the Ash and Maple intersection. A half block away, he shut off the Ford's lights and glided to a stop at the northeast corner.

He peered diagonally across the unlighted intersection. Dark over there, except for a glimmer at the edges of a poorly-fitted window shade.

Then the front doorway of the boarding house glowed briefly as someone stepped out and shut the door behind him. In the scant starlight from a crystal-clear sky, Krag watched the guy stand on the sidewalk and peer into the night. Vinny, on the dot? Had to be.

Krag blinked the parking lights, one quick flash, and watched the not-quite-short guy stride diagonally across the intersection toward him. A guy sure of himself, approaching a dark car on a dark street in this down-trodden suburb.

The guy stepped around the front of the SUV. As he deftly slipped aboard, the overhead light flared briefly. In its quick glare, Krag checked him out. Early thirties, narrow face, long sideburns, dumb little goatee to hide a receding chin. Brown turtleneck sweater. Yeah, he was Vinny.

"Lenny Lewis?" Vinny stuck out his hand.

Krag kept his hands on the steering wheel. "Yeah. Sent by A and C. I'm taking over. You're no longer needed here."

"The hell with that. I'm just gettin' started."

"No, you've just finished."

"Now hold on a sec, Lenny. I started with hit-and-runs that slowed the project a couple days. Then played arsonist at the motor pool. That held 'em up more'n a week. Then fixed the D-8. You know about that?"

"I know you killed its driver. That wasn't smart."

"That wasn't part of the plan."

"And it brought in the Feds." Krag began to drum his fingers on the steering wheel.

"Hell, the Feds coming in was a bonus. Tied up things for days."

"But the groundbreaking went on anyway, didn't it? And that was a disaster."

"I wanted it to be a disaster. The papers, the TV—"

"I mean it was a disaster for you, Vinny. I don't know what you were expecting. A hydrogen blast? Don't you know non-flammable helium is the law now, even in party balloons?"

"I just wanted to bring down the damned balloon. It was — whatchu call it? Symbolic. Dontcha get it?"

"The disaster I'm talking about was for you personally, Vinny: the car chase."

"But I got away."

"Not clean away, Vinny. Your damned turtleneck ID'd you for them. So now you're useless here."

"The hell I am! I can do a lot undercover. I can — "

"Amerman and Cassina want you out of here."

"No! I'm gonna show 'em what I really can do. I gotta couple ideas that'll surprise everybody. I'm gonna start with — "

"They're *ordering* you off the project, Vinny. They want you out of town, out of state."

"Hell no! I'll keep going here. After they see what I really can do, A and C will give me a goddamned bonus!"

"They want you *gone*, Vinny. So, shut up, pack up, and get out of town."

"*No!* I'm staying. Go back to Camden and tell 'em *that*, messenger boy!"

He threw the door open and shoved out, slammed it in Krag's face and strode into the intersection.

You had your chance, asshole. Krag started the engine. Glided away from the curb. Watched Vinny's dim form head back toward the boarding house. His angled return took him toward the middle of the intersection.

Krag floored the pedal. Hung a left. Vinny's face whirled around, pale in the starlight. He lurched forward. Too late. The Ford's front right fender hurled him hard sideways. He sprawled on the pitted pavement. Surely busted up. Maybe dead. Either way, Vinny was "out of the picture," as Amerman had put it.

The deft sideswipe, Krag thought, had rammed Vinny hard but shouldn't have damaged the fender much—if at all. He rushed the Ford down Maple for three blocks, then turned left into a cross street to head back to the Snooze Inn.

He settled back and compressed his wide mouth into a hard line.

Messenger boy.

13

I rinsed my razor, dried my face, and wondered what the heck I could do today to justify the weekly check Max slipped me yesterday. Stepped out of the porcelain-bright bathroom and switched on the small, flat-screen TV, the bedroom's only modern concession in its 1930s-retro styling.

On-screen, a middle-aged fellow grinned at his medicinal rejuvenation while the pitchman's voice-over gave me the reason why I should take the stuff, then ten reasons why I shouldn't. As I buttoned my shirt, the local news resumed.

"A pedestrian crossing Ash Street was found severely injured early this morning. He was discovered sprawled in the intersection of Ash and Maple just before dawn by the driver of a delivery van. Taken by ambulance to Hardington Health Center, his condition is reported as critical. We will stay on top of this—"

While I waited for pictures, my cell phone rang its first four notes of The Marine Corps Hymn. I picked it up from the night table. Thumbed it on. "Rod Stevens here."

"Sgt. Ben Stoddard, County Sheriff's office. You remember our agreement?"

"Sure do, Ben." I was surprised he apparently was living up to it.

"You got the news on?"

"Yeah. What—"

"The guy in the street was wearing a brown turtleneck sweater. Had a driver license on him, name of Vincent—"

"That's our guy."

"But that's about all we got from the city cops who responded. They haven't dug up anything more on him. Neither can we. Had a throw-away cell in his pocket. Nothing on it. His driver license turned out to be a fake. Non-existent address in some remote New York burg. No police record for any Vincent Parson. We checked out the name. Got lotsa 'V. Parsons' with an ess, just two without it, both in the far west. One's an eighty-two-year old in California. The other is mayor of some dinksburg in Oregon. Not likely suspects."

"TV said he was lying in the street. I assume he'd been hit."

"Out like a light at Ash and Maple. Broken hip and left leg. Head trauma. He's still out of it. They're working on him. No tire marks on the street, but they assume hit-and-run. No surprise there. That intersection has no streetlights. One of the mayor's bright—" I heard a muffled chuckle. "Sorry. Part of the mayor's austerity program. Lights off at minimal traffic count intersections. Us county cops fought that idiotic policy. The city cops' union got a threatened salary 'notchdown' cancelled in favor of the brownout. So we lost."

"And so has Vinny Parson. Hey, I appreciate your calling me on this."

"It's not a one-way call, Rod. Now you owe me whatever you got on 'Parson.' If you've got anything at all. Per our agreement: Give."

"All I have so far are the details of what he did in his klutzy efforts to hold up the Keystone project. Not even a hint of why."

"Not even a guess at a motive?"

"Barring some long-festering grudge against Sturdevant Developers, I've come up with just one—"

"Money."

"Right, Ben. But who or what would go that far? And why? There's been a man killed."

"That," Stoddard said—almost reluctantly, I thought—"could have been an unintended consequence."

"True. Vinny seemed intent on delaying tactics."

"With a fatality here and there."

"Yeah," I said. "Somebody sure doesn't want Keystone City built, but I can't come up with one plausible reason."

"I'm a lot more familiar with local cross-currents than you are, Rod, but I'm with you on that. If you do come up with— hell, with anything at all, stick to our agreement."

And he hung up. At least he didn't say, "Over and out."

TV was back to take-and-maybe-die medicine plugging. I sat on the edge of the bed to ponder. Fake name Vinny creates an ultimately blundering trail of sabotage then takes a midnight walk and gets clobbered in the middle of a dark intersection. Ash and...what was the other?

taken notes, you ass. Call Stoddard? Hold on. Hadn't Max Sturdevant given me a city map? I rummaged in my travel bag. Good thing I have a map...map...Maple. Ash and Maple. I headed out the door.

***

Hard to decide whether the neighborhood was working its way up from collapse or sinking toward it. I slowed the Jeep then stopped by the curb on Ash Street's northeast corner. Among all these faded or totally neglected homes, just one stood out: the three-story house diagonally across the street. I squinted in the morning's glare. A sign nailed beside the front door read: ROOMS FOR RENT. I dismounted, walked over there. In the cramped little parking area, I edged between a multi-dented Chevy and a mud-spattered Kia. Both seemed to be in defensive crouches.

I climbed two wood steps to the front door's square-yard landing, thumbed a tiny pearl button, and heard an aggressive buzz inside. Then shuffling steps. A curtain over the door's little eye-level window edged aside a finger-width. Nice, trusting neighborhood. A suspicious brown eye under a curly white brow studied me, unblinking like a camera lens.

The door grated open a few inches. "Yes?" A female voice.

"Rod Stevens, ma'am. I'm writing a history of the Keystone project. Thought you might be able to help me out."

"You ain't another damn reporter from the *Times*? Or one of them TV people. They all like to drive me nuts earlier."

"No, I'm working on a book."

"Oh? Never met a real arther before."

"Author, ma'am."

"Spell it."

"A-U-T-H-O-R."

"*Auth*-or. That's a funny word."

"Are you from here?" I wondered.

"Born in Balmer."

"Balmer, Merlin?"

"Oh, are you from there, too?"

"Spent some time there years ago."

That melted her ice. The door opened wider. "Come on in, Mr. Auth-or. Though I don't know what I can tell you about anything fit for a book."

The big front room looked like a Goodwill display, mismatched but serviceable. Short, heavy, and durable, she fit right in. She fluffed her pinkish cotton candy hair, straightened her flowered dress, and pointed at an overstuffed green armchair. "Sit."

Mostly for show, I opened my notebook. "Your name, ma'am?"

"O'Boyle. Betty O'Boyle. You want coffee? I don't serve nothin' any stronger."

"I just had breakfast, Betty. Thanks anyway."

With a huge sigh, she sank into a rust-colored sofa near my pudgy green-and-white-striped armchair.

She peered at my prop notebook. "Like I said, I never met no auth-or before. How does it work?"

"It's easy. I'll ask some questions and you answer them in your own way."

She folded her plump arms across a bosom the size of a Navy blimp. "Shoot."

"You saw all the excitement out there this morning?"

"How could I not? Woke me up. Rushed down the hall to a front window. Police cars, ambulance. Then, sure enough, reporters and TV. All that before the sun came up. It was still dark out there."

"You didn't hear anything before all that?"

"Heard Mr. Parson go out around nine or ten."

"Wait a minute. Parson was *here*?"

"He had a room here."

I felt the hot wave of eureka. "For how long?"

"Weeks. Then one day his car is gone, but he stays. Walks the six blocks down Maple to Burger Haven. I used to serve meals here but then I got the artheritis. Had to change the sign from BOARDING to ROOMS. Would have been in a pickle, 'cept for Larry's pension."

"Larry?"

"My husband. He passed, but his pension benefits keep coming."

I decided not to ask whether the checks were made out to him or her. Settled for: "Larry was...?"

"A 'sanitation specialist,' he called it. Garbage man. Not pretty work, but steady. And risky. One of them big, heavy old TV tube sets slipped off the truck and fell on him. End of story."

"Sorry, Betty," I managed. "Tell me about Parson."

"Not much to tell. Sure you don't want coffee?"

"Thanks again, but no. Did Parson tell you where he worked?"

"Didn't tell me much of anything. But, yeah, said he worked with the contractor on the new city project."

"Know where he was from?"

"Jersey, he said, but his car had a Pennsylvania license."

His stolen car, now impounded, and surely dusted for prints. But if they'd found anything, Stoddard would have told me...wouldn't he?

"After his car was gone, what did he do other than walk to the hamburger place for meals?" I asked her.

"Waited. Mostly in his room. Like he expected something. I'm sorry I don't know more about him." She dropped her hands to her lap. "You know, maybe what he was waiting for came true."

"Oh?"

"He got a call last night. I have the room next to his. I couldn't make out what he was saying, but right after the phone call, I heard him leave his room and go outside."

"What time was this?"

"Around nine, I think."

"Did you hear anything after that?"

"Only a kind of squeal. My room's in the back. Can't hear much going on out front. Fact, nothing much at all goes on out front."

"Except last night. A lot went on, and Parson ended up in the hospital." Another thought. "After they carted him off, might you have checked his room?"

"Well...yes. But all I found was clothes, shaving stuff, and some car magazines. That's it."

Not one damned clue. I stood, thanked her, and walked to the door.

"Will I be in your book?" Her voice had an almost plaintive tone. Poor soul, isolated in life's by-way, hoping for a grain of recognition.

"If it ever gets published." A hedge of mercy. What book? Or maybe...?

I stepped out of the gray of poverty into the gold of the late morning sun. "A kind of squeal," she'd said. Had to be the tires of a quick stop, a stop not in time. Then the panicky acceleration of a hit-and-run getaway. Around nine last night. That would mean Parson lay out here for hours on a street with no traffic until that pre-dawn delivery van appeared.

I walked back into the intersection, eyes on the age-faded macadam. "In the middle of Ash and Maple," Stoddard had told me. I stepped out there. Stopped where I judged the centerlines of the two streets crossed. I searched the old macadam. A few oil stains. No tire marks. I moved around to check the area from a couple of angles. Not a mark. I walked back to my SUV rental. Something ventured, nothing gained.

Then I did notice something. Right under my nose...well, the Jeep's nose. I could see how they'd missed this in the pre-dawn gloom. A pair of tire marks curved away from the roadside then faded into the intersection.

I slid into my Jeep, started it up, put it in reverse, carefully backed up a few yards, stepped out, and — *Yes!* The twin tire scuffs started heavy then faded out as they curved into the intersection. And in the dust that lay along the foot of the concrete curbing, the track nearest the curb showed the sharply imprinted tread pattern. These tracks were new.

A driver suddenly spotting someone in the road ahead of him would ram on the brakes, leaving twin tire scuffs light at first then darker as his brakes took hold and locked. The scuffs I looked at began heavy then faded. They were the tracks of a car at curbside suddenly fed full throttle, leaping forward with tires shrieking until the driver eased up as speed built up.

Educated guess: Somebody had waited for Vinny to step into the intersection. Speculation: Whoever made those tire tracks knew Vinny was coming. Betty O'Boyle had heard Vinny on his cellphone just before he stepped outside.

"I'm here, Vinny. Come out and die."

14

Parked at Ash and Maple, I called Sgt. Stoddard. My "give" in response to his.

"When the city police sent Parson off in the ambulance in the wee hours," I told him, "they missed something—not surprising in the darkness."

"And?"

"And in daylight, I just found it. New tire tracks curving away from the northeast corner into the intersection. You may want to check them out yourself, but I'd say somebody waited for Parson—he got a phone call before he stepped out—"

"Stepped out of where?"

"The rooming house at the southwest corner."

I heard Stoddard's frustrated exhale. "City cops' report doesn't say a damned thing about that."

"Here's your chance to one-up them, Ben. I talked with Parson's landlady. Nothing of any use in his room. Told me that after his car disappeared, she wasn't aware he did anything but sit around. Waiting, she thought, as if he expected something."

"And he got something, but I doubt it was what he expected."

"That's for sure, Ben. You thinking what I'm thinking?"

"He was waiting to be told what to do next."

"And all of this tells us he's been superseded the hard way."

"What the hell do you think we are up against, Rod?" I liked that "we."

"Top of my head, I'd say Parson has been replaced by somebody a couple steps up the action ladder."

"One guy killed, another in the hospital, and you think they — whoever 'they' might be — don't think that's enough?"

"The Keystone project is still on track, Ben. But it's pretty evident to me somebody wants to do more than just slow it up."

"Yeah. Kill it altogether. I'm not sure I — did the landlady say anything at all that could be useful, other than Parson was just sitting around? Anything he might have said?"

"Not a clue, Ben. Anything new, I'll get back to you."

"'Preciate that." Click.

I fired up the Jeep, wound back through Hardington then climbed the slope to the Maximall. There I found a fat folder on my usually bare desk. The files Max had promised on his officers and department heads.

I spent the next hour poring through educational backgrounds, employment histories, interviewers' comments — none of it naughty; all of it numbing. If there was a devil in the paper pile, he was well underground. I hadn't even scratched through the topsoil.

I piled the fourteen folders on a corner of my desk. Max had told me Sturdevant Developers had fifty-plus employees. That left thirty-six-plus to go. Based on no revelations so far, I decided perusing employment records was a desperate stab with no cutting edge.

At this rate, I'd be on the Keystone case until the ethanol content in my inert old Dodge back in Philadelphia reverted into corn kernels. What was my next step? Well...uh —

"Morning, Rod." Corporate president Max walked in and sank into the hard chair across from me. He cupped his hands on his knees and gave me a hard look. "Tell me what the hell is going on."

"Vinny Turtleneck was run down last night. He's in the hospital."

"I got that much from early morning TV."

"I drove out to the intersection where he was hit, interviewed the landlady of a nearby rooming house. Lucky shot—it turned out he's been living there. She told me he got a phone call around nine, walked out and got run down in the street. What TV didn't tell you is my guess—based on tire tracks the city police missed in the darkness and I found in daylight—is that Parson was the victim of a set-up."

Max tented his fingers, studied them then turned back to me. "So he's out of it. And somebody else more organized is taking his place."

"Your opinion is my opinion, Max."

"You suggested security at the Town Center building site, once construction gets underway. I've hired a rent-a-cop agency to keep things intact up there. In the meantime, I'm counting on you to do whatever it takes to find out what we're up against. And why. Tall order?"

"Until you have to get martial law declared—"

Got a laugh out of him on that.

"—I'm one hundred percent on this case."

"Right." He pushed to his feet. "I don't mean to pressure you, but..."

"Pressure is my business, Max."

He nodded and walked out. I hoped that sounded confident, but to be honest with myself, I knew I was looking for a straw to clutch. Was there anyone—anyone at all—who I knew hated the Keystone project? ...Yes. Ivan Sikorski.

I thought he was an unlikely suspect for committing sabotage, but had I misread the guy? Ten minutes later, I pulled out of the Maximall's parking area and turned left to head further uphill to the Keystone acreage.

The woods behind the Town Center building site were a bright green contrast to the leveled farms beyond, but the woods, too, were slated for destruction when construction began on Keystone's central city area. At the Y intersection, I took the left fork. In a few minutes, I passed the side road to Lake Linden where the rigged D-8 had killed its driver. All the lakeside cottages on the Sturdevant tract were gone now. Couple miles later, I pulled into Susquehanna Contractors' motor pool.

Operations Manager Jake Waller, his gray forelock shading his tired eyes from his barren office's overhead bulb, looked as if he hadn't moved off his folding chair since I'd been here days ago. The office reeked of cigar. I walked in through an alto-stratus layer of smoke.

"Rod Stevens, Jake. Back again."

"The history writer. What brings you up here now?"

"Just passing by, Jake. You heard about your day worker?"

"Vinny? Yeah. Got it on the TV this morning."

So, I thought, he actually does leave this smoke house occasionally.

"TV says it was an accident, Jake. I took a look at the scene. Seemed to me like a set-up."

"Set-up? What the hell are you talking about?"

"Just my opinion. But I suggest you be careful about any new day job applicants. My opinion includes the possibility Vinny was taken off his real job so somebody else could be put on it."

"You gotta be kidding."

"Wish I was, but too much caution can be healthier than too little. Tell you what. You get somebody else out of the blue who wants undocumented day work, give me a call." I wrote my cell number on a note pad amid his desk rubble.

"With an imagination like yours, Stevens, that should be some wild history you're writing."

"That's what I'm beginning to think, Jake. And you're a sure bet for a cameo role."

I left him with his cigar suspended between ashtray and mouth, stepped back into my rental, and drove on to Sikorski's defiantly still-standing mansion. I noticed his Hummer was positioned right where I'd first checked it. Since I'd been here, he'd apparently driven nowhere.

I parked, walked up the five marble steps, and the big front door swung open.

"Mr. Stevens. Again." Not exactly a friendly tone from Ivan, two hundred pounds of aging muscle without a smile.

"Just passing by. Thought I'd see how you're doing."

"Yeah, I'm still here. To your company's dismay, of course."

"You heard about one Vincent Parson?" I watched him closely, but all I saw was a slight shrug. "Last night's hit-and-run victim. It's all over TV."

I'd been kicking around a long shot. Could it be possible Sikorski had hired Vinny to do what he could to slow down Keystone's progress? Then when Vinny was ID'd in the car chase, he became a liability. So Sikorski and his Hummer—

Ivan gave me a hard squint. Then he shrugged. "What the hell, Stevens. Coffee's on. Come in."

As we walked through the impressive living room, I took a pseudo-admiring glance around. The incongruous souvenir M-14 was in place over the entrance doorway. But it still looked ominous. If it weren't for the damned gun, my little thread of suspicion would have raveled away days ago.

At the kitchen table, he poured and we sat in silence until he said, "You thinking I had something to do with all the stuff that's been happening on the friggin' project?"

I nearly choked on my coffee. Was I that obvious?

"Well, Mr. Historian, I don't work that way. I'm about to file a legal protest against Sturdevant Developers' knocking down my house. This house. Get it officially declared a national historical site. Law firm is working on that right now."

"You think you can actually win that in court?"

"It'll tie them down until I think of something else."

I didn't like what I was hearing. Suspicion revived. Stoddard and I both felt someone had hired Vinny then didn't like his klutzy work. Sikorski the financier and boss of a sabotage campaign? With necessities delivered, he wouldn't have to leave this house.

Thin, Rod. But for the moment, the only straw I could grasp.

15

I stared out my office window, increasingly desperate for investigation inspiration. Translation: What the hell can I do now? Down in the valley, Hardington baked in early summer heat. Up here, my so-called case had gone stone cold. If I couldn't do any better than sit here and stare downhill, I would have no excuse for—

My cell's four notes broke the barren silence.

"Ben Stoddard, Rod. Just got word Vinny's conscious and mumbling. I'm heading for Hardington Health Center. You show up there and we'll see what he's mumbling about."

"I'm on my way!" Then I asked him, "How come they're notifying you? Wasn't he picked up by city cops?"

"Yeah, but he committed his crime in the county."

"The rigged D-8?"

"Can't prove that one yet. He's charged with willful destruction of private property—"

"Don't tell me he's being nailed for his dumb-ass balloon busting caper."

"Yep, plus leaving the scene. All that happened in the county. So, it's the County Sheriff Department's responsibility. See you at the hospital ASAP."

He clicked off and I jumped up to unfurl my Hardington map. The Health Center sprawled along Laurel Boulevard in the northwestern suburbs. In four minutes, I screeched the Jeep out of Maximall parking and rushed downhill into the city.

Hardington Health Center turned out to be a multi-building complex, a startling contrast to what I'd seen in this once-great anthracite center slowly groping its way into the age of technology. I found the parking area for the main building and turned in. Near the hospital entrance, I spotted a county blue-and-white. I parked near it.

Big Ben Stoddard shouldered out of his cop car. I met him halfway. Shook his meaty paw. "Appreciate your calling me in on this, Ben."

"Owe you one for the tip on the tire tracks. I checked them out and I agree. It looks like a planned hit."

The hospital's entrance door slid open, and we walked into an extravaganza that could have served as the plush lobby of a major hotel. I heard a piano tinkling somewhere among the potted plants. A row of busy shops brightened the back wall, and the bustling cafeteria to our left had to be the source of the pervasive roast beef aroma.

"Hard to believe what goes on upstairs," I said. "Down here looks like a hotel."

"Designed to. Story is, the investors wanted it convertible in case it flopped as a hospital." Ben stepped over to a reception desk just inside the entrance. "Sergeant Stoddard and Detective Montgomery to visit Vincent Parson," he told the gray-haired woman wearing a VOLUNTEER badge.

She consulted a three-ring notebook then frowned at us. "He's in ICU. Only close relatives are permitted to—"

"Already have police clearance, ma'am. Check again."

She shuffled through some loose papers. "Here it is." Her eyebrows arched. "Oh. You both *are* cleared. The ICU is on the second floor. Elevators are back there behind that row of palms."

Palm trees in northeast PA?

We took one of the three elevators and zoomed upward in silence. When the door slid open, the lobby's welcoming cafeteria aroma was replaced by the stomach-tightening reek of medicinals.

We stepped up to the nurses' station. "Stoddard, County Sheriff's Department, and Detective Montgomery, cleared to visit Vincent Parson."

Each time he referred to me as "Detective Montgomery," I thought: There goes my "history writer" cover. But we were almost a full city width from the Keystone project, so maybe my concern was more procedural-bound than security-essential. I'd begun to think the history-writer cover might not be all that vital, but now with a man in ICU from an apparent attempt on his life, I was rethinking my rethinking.

A chunky blond nurse who looked like she needed a week of sleep ushered us three doors down the hall then into an all-white room crammed with humming and dinging electronics. Amid all the looming science, the single bed seemed an afterthought—until I looked at the heavily bandaged body in it. Left leg and left arm in casts, with the leg pulled high by a complicated pulley and cable system hooked to the overhead frame. Head swathed in bandaging. Purple smudging around both tightly shut eyes gave his narrow face a raccoon look.

"Vinny?" the nurse murmured. "Vinny, you have visitors."

"We were told he's been mumbling." Stoddard's voice was almost a whisper. "Could you make anything out of what he said?"

"Just the same word over and over." The nurse shrugged. "Didn't make any sense to us. Something like...'antsy.'"

"Antsy?" Stoddard turned back to the bed and bent down. "Vinny?" Then louder: "Vincent Parson?"

The blackened eyes slitted open. Unfocussed. The cracked lips moved. "An...see," he whispered.

"What, Vinny?" Stoddard leaned closer. "What was that, Vinny?"

"Aaaan...an...ss..."

Then the electronic watch group suddenly went into what sounded to me like *uh-oh* mode. I glanced at the screen that monitored his heartbeat. The green line raced into a profile of the Alps.

"Out, gentlemen!" With surprising strength, the no-longer-sleepy nurse grabbed both of us by the shoulders and steered us out the door.

Then she shouted "STAT! Room three!" And the placid hallway burst into professional pandemonium.

Stoddard and I got the hell out of the way and took refuge at the elevators.

"You make anything out of that mumble?" I asked him.

"'Ant-something,' like the nurse told us. You?"

"'Antsy,' I thought."

Stoddard shrugged. "What kind of sense does that make — if any at all?"

We stood there a long moment. Then I turned and pressed the elevator button. "Nothing more we can do here."

As I said that, I sensed a sudden ease of tension in the hall. The whitecoats emerging from Vinny's room looked like a favored team who had just lost the championship. As the blond nurse strode by, she shot us a look as if we'd killed the guy. Maybe we had.

I caught Stoddard's grim expression. He nodded. "Yeah. He's gone."

"The head injury, I'd guess."

"'Antsy,' he said, scowling. "Not exactly an inspiring last word, was it?"

16

At the Snooze Inn, Barton Krag carried his take-out breakfast to his room. Four scrambled eggs, double rasher of bacon, three slices of toast, a pint of O.J., and an extra-large coffee. A celebration breakfast. When last night's TV reported "The hit-and-run victim found at Ash and Maple has died," Krag felt a surge of elation. No worry now about Vinny talking. Better among the angels than shooting off his mouth in the hospital about being suckered into the street as a target.

Krag set down his carton, pulled the rolled copy of the *Hardington Times* from under his arm and settled into the room's only chair — blond wood back and arms, but the seat was padded leather.

KEYSTONE HOLDOUT FILES SUIT, the page-1 headline shouted. Some guy named Sikorski was going to court to get his house named a national historical site. That, the paper reported, might hold up the development of Keystone's proposed Village of Stag Run, but not the entire new city project.

"Dumb," Krag muttered around a mouthful of scrambled egg. Like Parson's feeble car accidents, motor pool fire and groundbreaking crapola. The rigged D-8 came closer to Krag's approval level. At least the driver was killed. Bet that sent a chill down some Hardington spines.

But it hadn't stopped progress.

Krag chomped three bacon strips, end-to-end. "Something significant," fleshy-faced Amerman had told him, with wiry, slit-eyed Cassina nodding like one of those head-bobbing car toys. "Something that puts the kibosh on the whole damned project. Or at least significantly delays it. You get that?"

Now Krag bobbed. "Something big, really big."

"Yeah, you got it," Cassina chimed in from the purple sofa in Amerman's office.

Harvey Amerman, Krag thought, looked like an over-dressed bear in his dark blue business suit. Cassina? He'd make a convincing mop-up man under Capo Amerman in a Mafia movie.

Something big. Like burning down everything in Keystone City. Except the paper said there wasn't anything out there but the motor pool and the Sikorski house. Vinny had flamed one of the motor pool's sheds, but it had promptly been built back up. And putting the torch to Sikorski's place would actually be a gift to Sturdevant Developers.

So Krag's project had to be something other than fire-starting. Something mind-blowing... Or at least something seriously damaging. From desperation, an idea began to form.

Problem. This curly bright yellow hair. Like a beacon in a crowd. Brown or black dye plus hair straightener? That could do it, and he'd seen a drugstore a few blocks away.

Never tried anything like that. Hadn't needed to... Problem. Had to buy the stuff, and whoever sold it to him would be a potential witness if everything fell apart. Too complicated, and —

Hell, what was he thinking? Bare skulls were in fashion. Shave off the damned curls. Then even with change in place, could he really pull this off by himself? With the right preparation, a strong maybe.

Step one: Get seen here as the curly blond guy. Then check out. Tell 'em I'm leaving town. Next: Wearing a baseball cap and dark glasses, move to a different motel, well away from this area. Then shave bald and never go out without the glasses. All this would be risky as hell, but wasn't that why Amerman & Cassina had sent him?

The next morning, Krag went into action. "Gotta move on to Pittsburgh," he told the clerk as he checked out of the Snooze Inn. In a crowded east Hardington strip mall, he found a sports store, bought dark glasses and a Phillies baseball cap. Even this was risky, of course, but two new appearances — bald head bared or with cap — would surely be less conspicuous than a head of lemon curls.

Just before noon, with the damned curls tucked under the cap, and at least a third of his face obscured by the oversize, thick-rimmed dark glasses, Krag checked into the East End Economy Court. The parking area was sufficiently occupied, he hoped, to make his arrival part of the midday routine.

The red-headed kid desk clerk glanced up from his iPad long enough to nod at the registration forms on the counter. Then he hunched back into tech world.

Elliot, Krag scrawled. Liked that name since he'd seen "The Untouchables" on late night TV. He glanced around the scruffy office. Elliot Calendar, he finished. No credit card this time. Though its address was phony, a computer search would tie into its use at the Snooze Inn by "Leonard Lewis," a finding sure to excite even the dullest detective.

"Like to pay in advance," he told the iPad Kid. "Say, for a week."

The kid shrugged. "That will be..." Back to his damned pad. He clicked away then looked up again. "Three hundred eighty-nine, including tax."

Krag peeled eight fifties off the roll Amerman had supplied for just such anonymous-imperative eventualities. "Keep the change," he told the kid and could see he'd just bought a friend.

***

His room was squeaky clean and graced with all-in-one-package discount store bed, bureau, chair, and small table. He tossed his carryall on the bed, pulled out his shaving gear, stepped into the tiny bathroom and yanked off his cap. Lotta hair to get rid of. With his Atra razor looking puny to do the job, he squirted a handful of foam out of his Barbasol can and set to work.

Shoulda bought a scissors, he realized too late. This was going to take a lot of work. At frequent intervals, he flushed the soapy locks down the toilet. What he sure didn't need was a blocked crapper. When he became more adept with the razor, he did manage to block up the flush, but an arm plunged elbow-deep shoved the wad of hair on down just before the bowl would have overflowed.

Forty minutes later, he emerged from Unit 16 appearing the same as when he'd entered—except under the cap. But the desk clerk hadn't seen Krag's goldilocks crammed under there. In what must have been a couple hundred razor strokes, Barton Krag's "Leonard Lewis" had become "Elliot Calendar."

17

I was at rest again—another meeting: Max, with his blue eyes unusually alight, I thought; brother Cliff, his mustard-colored hair newly buzzed; Chief Planner Marty Elman, looking a touch disturbed; PR man Mitch Newman in his usual pins-and-needles mode; finance chief Ed Fletcher chewing nervously on an earpiece of his wire-rimmed glasses; and Priscilla, Max's administrative assistant, looking downright appealing in her snowy white blouse and sky blue skirt—especially when she flashed me a quick smile and a wink. Downright suggestive, I thought. Control, "Rodney," control.

With the blunt end of his ballpoint, Max tapped for silence.

"I assume all of you have heard about the death of a Susquehanna Contractors' motor pool employee, apparently another of the unfortunate incidents plaguing our project. Sorry about anyone's death, of course, but especially this second one linked to Keystone."

Max scanned the assemblage. "Now I know a Friday meeting is unusual, but after a careful review of the entire project with Marty, I've decided to make a significant change in the original progress sequence. Instead of initiating construction of Heron Glade Village concurrent with the construction of the Town Center office building, we will build not just that office structure. We will complete the entire Center area before developing any of the three projected villages."

Again Max glanced around the table. "Questions?"

Up went PR Mitch's hand. "Just one, Max. Why?"

"Our original plan to move into the main building as soon as it is completed still stands. But Marty and I have come to the conclusion that doing so would isolate our offices – all our people – from the conveniences of the Maximall and other services down in Hardington. So our revised scheduling calls for development of that entire complex concurrently with its main building. Then, when we move up there, we will have Town Center services available to our staff."

"Develop the whole Town Center before we move in?" money man Fletcher asked.

"At least a restaurant, possibly a branch bank to start with."

"That'll take some selling," Marty Elman said, "but it'll beat our commuting back here or down in Hardington for services like that."

"And a new opportunity for you, Marty. Should be a big story in the *Times*."

"True. And I can drum up a TV interview for you, Max."

"Always ready, Marty." Another glance around the table. "I'm sure there are more questions about this. So on Monday, I'll have Priscilla give each of you a copy of the study Marty and I made for this change."

I gave Max a "me too?" look.

"Certainly, Rod. You especially. This will be an important change in our overall plan. An interesting part of your historical narrative."

He slapped the table. "Okay, everybody! Thanks for your attention, and have a nice weekend – despite the ominous weather prediction."

"Ominous?" I asked Mitch as we walked into the corridor.

"TV's been yakking up a cold front coming east and a possible nor'easter coming west. They're expected to collide over good old PA. So it looks like indoor sports over the weekend."

"Yeah. Me and my notebook."

***

In what had become "our" booth in the Maximall's Ye Olde London Pub, Pris took a long pull on her iced coffee. "I'll get you a copy of the study Max mentioned as soon as it comes out of our repro room."

"Thank you." I glanced around the crowded restaurant. "Looks like almost half the people in here are Sturdevant employees. You think they'll be enough to support a restaurant up there until the villages are ready for a population expansion?"

"Whatever is built in the Town Center will be rented from Max, and he can keep the rates low, raising them as the villages build the customer base."

"Ah, spoken like a dedicated corporate insider."

She grinned. "I am a corporate insider."

And I realized that was nearly all I knew about her. Once we passed the "No rings — you ever married? — Long ago. It was a disaster" — stage, I could coax only a few bits out of her personal past. Born in Asbury Park on Jersey's shore. Father managed a fast food store until the chain downsized him. Family moved to sparser digs in Camden, where Pris helped them survive via clerical work that led to her administrative assistant spot with Sturdevant. "Answered their want ad, and here I am."

And here we were. I wondered where we were going.

"Know something?" I said as our sandwiches arrived, "You've given me an outline, but most of the details are missing."

"Well, Mr. Historian," she said, those hazel eyes flashing over a half smile, "I've heard only an outline from you, too. Enlisted in the Marines after high school, served as a guard at our Moscow Embassy. But you weren't a career Marine, so that leaves a gap, doesn't it?"

"A gap? I got married."

"That's not a career gap filler—unless she was supporting you."

During our lunch break chats, Pris must have paid closer attention than I thought. Gap? My years as a Philadelphia detective had been one hell of a gap filler, but as "Rodney Stevens," I shrugged. "Oh, I did this and that, knocked around while I worked on books that didn't sell until I discovered there was money in writing annual reports."

Did she buy that? She gave me a bemused smile. Took another long sip of her coffee. "Was that 'knocking around' what led to your divorce?"

"Yeah, but it was her knocking around that did it." I had an unsettling feeling we both were stretching or compressing the truth. I knew I was, but maybe she was simply lobbing back my not exactly crisp serves.

"Plans for the weekend?" she asked as the food arranger held out the check.

"My turn," I said, as I grabbed it. "Weekend plans? I'm going to hole up at the hotel and work on turning some of my notes into narration. You?"

"Reading, letter writing."

We strolled through the mall's afternoon shoppers. "I don't have any reason to go back upstairs," I told her, "so I'm heading to the hotel. See you Monday. Have a nice weekend, readin' 'n writin'."

I walked into the dead calm but ominously darkening afternoon. Looked like I'd picked a glum half-day to play hooky. As I stepped into my Jeep, a thunder rumble confirmed that.

***

No sunrise Saturday. Old Sol was well hidden up there behind a roiling mass of sooty cumulonimbus. After my western omelet breakfast, I spent the morning in my room. Made a token effort at writing "Keystone City, Chapter 1"—a demo, in case somebody insisted on seeing progress on my purported historical epic. This Chapter 1 effort would be the only writing I'd ever done, other than my case reports as a Philadelphia detective.

As I scrawled into page 4, a thunder mumble escalated into a flash and crash. A look out my window told me this thing was getting serious. I flipped on the room's TV.

"...gale force winds are predicted late this afternoon in advance of a line squall as the eastbound cold front collides with a fast developing nor'easter over southern New York State. Local residents are advised..." The rest of the meteorologist's dire dialog was drowned out by the jangle of the phone on the room's night table.

"Rod? It's Pris. I'm down in the lobby. I brought your copy of Max's study on the project change."

What the hell? "You're here, in this weather?" Or here at all? "I'll be right down."

As I stepped from the elevator, I spotted her near the registration counter shedding a bright yellow hooded rain slicker. She handed it to the crusty old bellman as he emerged from his counterside cubby. As I crossed the lobby, she gave me a finger waggle.

"Hi!" She held out a big manila envelope. "I thought this would be useful to a holed-up historian on this miserable afternoon."

Well, yeah, I thought. And just as useful, delivered to my Maximall desk next week. But I said, "Such devotion to duty on a storm-lashed Saturday deserves a drink."

At the hotel's dining room bar, we ordered mai tais. Mai tais here, palms at the Health Center — wistful touches of the tropics in this bleak coal valley? While I fidgeted about the storm's predicted increase, Pris sipped and smiled. "I'm waterproof. Weather never — "

A sudden flash wiped out the dining room's gloom. The whole building shook in the following thunderblast.

"Close!" I dabbed at a splat of mai tai on my shirt. I peered across the dining room to its windows. "Like a monsoon out there. Look, it's almost suppertime. Why don't we dig in while we wait for the monster to moderate?"

After chicken l'orange for her, sirloin for me, and an hour of pleasant vocal...well, sparring, neither of us knew much more about each other. What in her background was she hiding, if anything?

The only change was in the storm. The flashes and bangs had faded, but now sheets of wind-driven rain cut visibility to mere yards.

In the lobby, I peered out at the whirling rain. "You can't possibly drive home in this. And I doubt it's going to let up soon. A cold front and a nor'easter—better stay here, then drive out in the morning. Let me get you a room."

"Oh, Rod..." She looked stricken.

"What's the problem?"

"I don't...I can't. I had a terrible experience staying alone in a hotel room twenty years ago when I was...I just can't."

I nodded toward the entrance. "You sure can't drive off in that mess. That'll be a lot worse than a twenty-year-old memory."

She looked at the floor. Then she looked at me. And said, softly, "You have a room."

"Yeah, I do. But..." But what, you idiot? Here was a not-gorgeous but sure good-looking woman asking to share my room.

"Seems there's no reasonable alternative. Welcome to Room 301." Nice recovery?

She looked toward the row of lobby shops. "I'll have to pick up a few things."

"I'll wait. Where's your car, by the way?"

"Down in the hotel's parking level." She turned toward the shops. "Be right back."

I sank into one of the lobby's armchairs. I hadn't been in a bedroom with a woman since Leahla moved up the street two years ago. I determined not to make a sex-starved ass of myself.

Ten minutes later Pris reappeared, carrying a couple shopping bags. "Storm's still raging," I told her. We walked to the elevators. "You all set?"

She gave me a little smile. "All set."

The elevator door slid open.

***

We watched the room's TV for an edgy hour, at least on my part. I wondered what was going through her mind. I barely knew what was on the little TV except when the program was interrupted for storm bulletins. Rain cascaded against the window, sometimes loudly enough to drown out the TV's sound.

When CSI finally solved its complex crime, Pris stood and stretched. "I'm beat. Time for bed."

I flipped off the TV.

"You first," she said. "I'm a dawdler."

I grabbed my pajamas off the closet hook and shut myself in the bathroom. Emerged a few minutes later. "Your turn."

Yes, she was a dawdler. When she finally stepped forth in her newly-purchased flamingo-pink shortie nightgown, I was under the covers. I'd turned out all the lights except the bed lamp. In its glow, she looked absolutely dazzling. But I figured at that point in my long-term bachelor mode, any woman in a shortie nightgown would look dazzling.

As she slipped into the room's only bed, Pris's hair shimmered in the lamplight. Her hazel eyes met my "now-what?" expression. Was I staring? How not?

"Good night," she said pleasantly. And turned toward the wall.

"And good night to you," I managed. I had her back, so to speak. Talk about anticlimaxes...

Five minutes of absolute silence.

Then she said, very softly, "Well, you certainly are a gentleman."

"And you are a—" I felt fingers gently touch my thigh.

"The guy I was married to—'way back, and briefly, thank God—he treated me like I was still his bookkeeper." Her hand began to caress gently.

"He was an idiot. Hey, remember I'm two years behind in this category of athletics. Don't expect the moon."

"I'm already on the launch pad."

Glorious minutes later, near the height of festivities, she whispered, "Tell me why you're really here."

"Here?"

"With Sturdevant. Is he actually serious about a project history?"

What kind of love talk was this? "Pay attention to this chapter," I urged.

"Oh, I am, I am."

And, movie style, the storm raged on.

***

Later, and I don't know how much later, I woke up muzzy with bliss…and in the room's gloom, squinted toward motion at the nearby chair. I propped up on an elbow.

"Oh!" she said. "I was just heading out of the bathroom. Saw your pants had fallen on the floor."

"Thanks," I mumbled. A neatnick in the aftermath?

She slipped back in bed, caressed my back with fingertips until I was a few winks from back to sleep. "So fill in the gap," she murmured. "The time after the Marines. Your 'this and that' time."

"Oh," I said, groggy with her fingertip finesse, "I was—" In my rapturous fog, I almost blurted, "a cop." Caught myself in time. "I was a truck driver, bartender. Short term stuff."

"Sure," she said.

***

I ordered room service breakfast for two: orange juice, scrambled eggs, toast and coffee. The storm had diminished to a spring drizzle with the sun occasionally peeking through thinning clouds.

"I'd better get going," she said as she finished her last slice of toast. Not a damned word about last night.

"I thought maybe—"

"Nope. Gotta go." She wadded her rumpled nightie into one of the shopping bags and walked to the door. Paused.

"Thanks for having me," she said with a little smile.

And she left.

18

F ive feet from the cup, Harvey Amerman surveyed the gentle leftward slope of the ninth green. Give the putt a little angle to the right to compensate, and he would chalk up his second birdie of this bright Sunday afternoon.

He glanced at Mateo Cassina leaning on his putter at the edge of the green. A good two putts for him, maybe three, with the close-clipped grass still soggy from yesterday's deluge. Their weekend golf duel on gated community Maple Glade's private nine-hole course was about to end in another Amerman victory.

He stepped up, took two practice swipes, sucked in his gut, and addressed the ball.

In his pocket his cell phone buzzed. Amerman stepped back, pulled out the cell. Checked Caller-ID. Barton Krag. What in hell could Krag be calling about on this serene Sunday?

"Yeah?" Though the phones were supposed to be secure, names were never used.

"Just saw it on TV. They're changing the schedule. Gonna build the whole Town Center before they start on the villages."

As those raspy words sank in, a sweaty twinge of apprehension swept down Amerman's spine. Despite the groundbreaking for the center's office building, he'd been certain he and Cassina had at least a year more, even two or three, before work on the Town Center itself would begin. Plenty of time to come up with an effective means of killing the damned project. Or failing that, gain enough time to sell Amerman and Cassina Company at a considerable profit, then disappear.

God! This call from Krag means the time is down to... weeks?

"There's gotta be something more we can try." He tried to keep his voice from quavering. His brain had gone numb. "I'm...out of ideas." Jesus, Amerman, get a grip. Never thought I'd hear myself say a thing like that.

"That's why you have me," Krag snapped. "I know how to bring Keystone to a screaming stop."

"And that is?"

Krag gave him two words. Two words that sent an icy ripple across Amerman's shoulders.

"You have a problem with that?" Krag prompted. He was beginning to sound like a man in charge. Amerman knew he should nail the guy for that kind of smart-ass attitude, but the potential consequence of the scheduling change made Amerman's knees tremble.

"Can't you can come up with something—" His voice stalled. He cleared his throat. "Something less...uh... drastic?" he managed.

"Damn it, you told me to find a way to kill off or seriously stall the project. Killing it has gotta be something political. Not in my bag of tricks. Seriously stall? Yeah. So, you with me on this?"

Amerman swiped at the cold sweat that beaded his forehead. Hesitated.

"Well?"

"Looks like no other way," he blurted. Clicked off. Took two deep breaths. Stuffed the cell back in his pocket. And tried to concentrate on his putt. Ease trauma with trivia.

The ball rolled off to the left, missed the cup by more than a foot.

Cassina grinned. "That must have been one stinker of a phone call. Worst putt you've ever blown."

"Shut up and putt out." That got him a hard look. "I'll fill you in on the cart."

Cassina sank an eighteen-footer, his best putt of the entire month. No reaction from Amerman. Numb with the import of Krag's call, he herded him back to the golf cart on the path near the green. They stowed their putters and climbed aboard.

"What the hell is going on?" Cassina's vulpine face wore a look of bemused concern. "It's gotta really be something to make you blow a five-foot putt that bad."

Amerman didn't answer. He jerked the cart into motion, drove it up the path toward the clubhouse then pulled off the sandy gravel to park beneath a stand of sugar maples.

The damned phone call had changed everything—everything that had gone so smoothly, from the day Cassina had laid out his idea of setting up a company to wholesale building supplies. A swaggering wannabe from Hardington's unsavory Southside, Mateo had worked a few summers in his father's tiny construction company and thought he knew it all. Amerman had let him feel like he was the man in charge—from their Hardington Chinese drywall bonanza-then-getaway to their big-time ops in Camden.

While he'd let Cassina think himself boss, Amerman established contacts in upper-level circles, maneuvered both of them up to Maple Glade level and the social acceptance that came with it. Amerman watched Cassina's arrogance slowly dissolve into his passive enjoyment of luxury. Mateo was still their essential recruiter of certain talents—such as Krag's—while acknowledging Amerman as top dog.

"So?" Cassina prompted.

Amerman took a shaky breath. "When we set up the company in Camden, we figured we were in the clear."

"Yeah, yeah."

"Then came the goddamned Keystone project. Hit us like a tornado—well, a potential tornado."

"Where you going with this?"

"We figured we had lots of time left, Mateo—depending on the Keystone development sequence. Town Center office building, then the three villages, then the Town Center shops, eateries, and stuff last. Coupla years at the minimum before that last phase got underway. Well, our new guy in Hardington just heard from our Sturdevant mole that the plan has been revised. They're going to build the whole Town Center before starting on the villages. You got any idea what that means?"

"It means we gotta go to Plan B pretty damned quick."

"No, Mateo. It means we gotta go to Plan B *now!* Sell out and move out."

"Whoa! Not that easy."

"It won't take much time to get out of our leases here in Maple Glade. Sell the company at the best price we can get in this damned recession. And get the hell out of Camden—out of the country."

"Only easy part is we got no wives to gum up a fast exit. Good play there, Harve."

"When you got the money, you can buy the honey."

Mateo peered at the golf course then at the luxury units beyond the trees. "Sure hate to give up all this gated community living. High style for a coupla guys from coal town."

"Yeah, we've done okay. Now we gotta make sure we can get outta this with enough scratch to keep doing okay someplace like…uh…Belize or Aruba." Easy to say, Amerman thought, but Mateo was right. Dumping this easy all-services-included life… Never dreamed that one day—

Mateo shot him a sour look. "Pull yourself together, Harve. I know my people."

His people. Mateo's solution to serious problems. Their pressure-supplied extrication from the Chinese drywall business when it went sour; the derailing of a potential major competitor in Camden; and now the Keystone City threat.

Worse than any of the others.

19

Below my Maximall office window, the valley seemed to be snoozing in Monday's late morning haze. After my… uh…adventuresome weekend, I tried not to snooze along with it. Celestial fireworks outside, intimate fireworks inside — then she walked out. But with a smile, apparently hoping to leave me with a warm glow.

I rated her little play an A for performance. But the script was transparent. I'd had no urgent need to see Max's report on Saturday. Her handing it to me today would have been as acceptable. I had to admire her weather timing. Stuck at the hotel just as the incoming near-hurricane storm hit. Her story about the years-ago hotel room incident still haunting her? Uh huh.

Her out-of-context questioning when I was sex woozy? I gave her points for a technique a lot more imaginative than anything I'd ever tried. Her explanation of a neatness attack when I caught her picking my pants pocket? Quick thinking, but before I'd emerged from the mists of sleep, had she taken my wallet into the bathroom and eyed my Elrod Montgomery PI license? I had to assume she'd done precisely that.

Here's how the weekend's events shape up: She knows who I am, but she doesn't know I know she knows.

Glad I got that straightened out. Now, do I make her a confidential part of my "Rodney Stevens" effort to find out who is so damned intent on derailing Keystone City?

I don't think so. Not after all her obviously well-planned bedroom craftiness. Instead, I —

"Lunch?"

I swiveled around. She stood in the doorway. Business-blue skirt, creamy blouse, lustrous mahogany hair in a saucy teen-age-like ponytail. Her half smile and hand-on-hip stance hinted at playfulness.

Had I read her all wrong?

"Unless Ye Olde London Pub has run out of BLTs and French fries, let's go." I can play-act, too, Ms. Killian.

A starchy-looking admin assistant from Finance joined us in the elevator. In silence, we sank to the Maximall's retail level. Sparse Monday attendance at the Pub got us seated in our preferred corner booth where an angular blond girl announced, "I'm Carly, your table attendant."

Food arranger. Table attendant. Political correctness was becoming ludicrous.

"The usual?" she asked. Good lord, had we become that well-known to the whole...uh...wait staff?

We ordered — yes, the usual — and Carly strode off to attend to it. Pris plucked a roll from the plate already on the table, broke it and buttered one of the halves. "Anything new on the historical front?" she asked without looking up.

What? Not a word about the weekend's delight? I'd expected at least a secret smile. A pantomimed kiss, maybe? No warm memory of our midnight merging? Well, okay. Have it your way.

"Nothing new since Vinny Parson's hit-and-run demise," I said. "Looks like he was some kind of a nut who hated progress." How's that for apparent naivety, lady? Rodney-the-bookworm in character. I still wasn't certain she'd conducted a dim bathroom-light review of my wallet cards in yesterday's pre-dawn pants pick-up.

"If that's all Vinny was," Pris said, "his death could end all the clumsy efforts to stall progress. Assuming he was the only one involved. What do you think?"

"Wish I was less of a writer and more of a Sherlock Holmes."

The quick flick of her eyebrows gave her away. Yeah, she'd seen my PI card.

"You think with Vinny gone, that's the end of it?" she asked.

"Of what, the series of accidents?" I took another bite of my sandwich, still playing my dodo role.

"The flare shot at the balloon was no accident."

"True. But the motor pool fire and the runaway D-8 could have been." I hoped my Rodney Stevens character act had her convinced I was one of the dumbest private detectives ever given a license.

Vinny's "accident" had been a set-up. That told me he'd been replaced. By whom? And why was Pris concerned about me in the first place? What would compel her to check out my wallet? Simple curiosity about the guy she had just slept with? Or something well below that surface possibility?

Max certainly hadn't assigned Pris to spy on me. Someone else in the Sturdevant roster? Too much of a stretch?

Whatever the purpose of her probing, it didn't strike me as a positive character trait. Not from my newly acquired point of perception. But I couldn't just let this ride.

Now for a plunge into the deep end.

I took a quick swig of my iced coffee. Set it down. Looked Pris in her hazel eyes. "Does it seem logical to you that a part-time handyman type would be personally interested in sabotaging a major project like Keystone?"

Her eyebrows arched. "You think handyman might have been a cover? That he might have had some serious concern about the project's progress?"

"Like what?"

"Oh, I don't know. Maybe he owned some business that would be—"

"More likely, Pris, Vinny was being paid by someone seriously concerned about Keystone City's development schedule. He fumbled the ball, and now what?"

There you are, too-smart-for-your-own-good lady. Had I put my uncertain foot into something I was beginning to fully grasp? Either this attractive, purposeful woman was simply curious about me—or she worked for someone desperate to undermine Max Sturdevant's signal achievement.

I waited for a revealing reaction, but all I got was a tight little smile.

20

In his underwear, Barton Krag peered into his East End Economy Court bathroom's mirror. He ran a hand over his shaved scalp. Somewhere he'd read that hair grows six inches a month. Didn't feel like he needed another scalp shave yet. The blond stubble on his cheeks and jaw had to come off. A golden beard would be too easy to remember. He picked up his Barbasol can and got to work.

Odd how a shaved head looked like...power. At least in the mirror. Maybe if he'd shaved it back in his Jersey City high-school days, he wouldn't have had to use his mouth and fists so much. And if he'd come from any other part of the city than the "hind end," as one of his derisive classmates called it—until Krag fed him a fist—maybe he'd be a nine-to-fiver now.

His father had the right idea. "Never call me by one of them sissy names like 'Daddy' or 'Pops.' You call me 'Boss.'" And Boss cuffed him when he didn't.

With his left hand, Krag stretched the skin of his throat for a smooth razor swipe. He'd done well in high school. Not in classwork; barely passable there. But he'd rated an A+ in, well, call it leadership.

Couldn't have done it if he'd been a skinny nerd or a pudgy wimp like many of his classmates. Gutless, all of them. But he'd been "Muscle Kid," the nickname his father gave him as a reward for using his guts and fists to "get some respect," as Boss put it. That was in the days before do-gooders called his kind of...leadership "bullying," and made such a public stink about it.

Big deal, he thought, rinsing the razor. By then, he'd discovered his brand of "leadership," as he still called it, had commercial value for certain aggressive businesses. Like Amerman and Cassina.

A phone call from Mateo Cassina had brought him to Camden, where Cassina laid out the problem... Well, explained that A&C wanted the Keystone project stopped altogether. Failing that, delaying the project for several weeks would be acceptable. He did not say why. The "why" was not Krag's business, anyway. The "how" was.

"We already got a man on location," slit-eyed Cassina told him. "A half-ass named Vinny. You get him out of the picture and take over." No procedure details offered, so Krag understood he was to take care of that as he saw fit.

Turned out there was nothing like "initiative." So, when Vinny turned mule-stubborn about getting out of town, initiative got him "out of the picture," as Cassina had put it.

And—Krag felt a glow of satisfaction with this—Camden had approved his inspired initiative. Talk about leadership.

But... Krag rinsed his face and toweled it dry. But now he had to figure how to handle his main purpose here. Vinny was supposed to do that, but he'd blown it. Nothing he'd done had held up progress for more than a day or two. He'd just winged it.

That was about to change. Krag had a plan. Step one: find the place. Somewhere away from prying eyes. An empty warehouse maybe. Time for a recon of Hardington's industrial section.

He pulled on his rumpled jeans, black sweater, and ankle boots. Slapped his Phillies cap on his bald dome and stepped into a morning still murky from the weekend's gut-rattling storm. He climbed into his Ford Escape, fired it up, drove out of the motel's lot and headed for southwest Hardington.

On Ash Street twenty minutes later, he drove back through the Maple Street intersection. Returning to the scene of the crime, he thought. Or at least through the scene. Hell, Vinny deserved what he got, dumb bastard. He never would have come up with anything like this. It's gonna shake up the whole damned city and put Keystone on hold for at least a coupla weeks, like Amerman and Cassina want.

A mile or so farther, the downscale housing dwindled into rental storage unit, and a shoddy used car lot. Then he passed through blocks of warehouses, all well-kept, most of them with cars parked out front. None of these fit his plan. What he needed was—

As Ash Street's pavement gave way to packed dirt, he spotted an obviously abandoned flat-roofed, one-story, windowless storage building huddled at the foot of a wooded slope. Weeds studded its parking area. Obviously abandoned, it was ideal.

He bounced onto the parking area's cracked concrete. Not a sign of life. He reached for the door handle. Then froze.

A hundred feet up Ash Street's dirt track, a string of bicyclists rolled around the street's rightward curve. They pedaled on by, almost a dozen cyclists, men and women. A couple waved as they passed.

He thought he'd found the perfect place for his plan. Isolated, with only vacant lots opposite. But judging by the age of the riders, this area could be on a bicycle club's tour route. He sure didn't need passing parades of witnesses on wheels.

Damn! The only thing he feared was witnesses. The bikers had told him something. Here he would have to park in front of the building. Thick brush on both sides blocked access to concealed parking in the rear. A car out front at an abandoned building with bikers rolling past—what was he thinking?

For a sweaty few minutes, Krag realized he had trapped himself. Made the proposal to Amerman & Cassina. Got the okay. All that before he thought the thing out in detail.

He gunned the idling engine and bounced out of the decrepit parking area back into Ash Street. He'd blamed Vinny for acting without thinking. Now he was thinking without acting.

He meandered back on Ash, central Hardington off to his left, Pocono Mountain foothills to his right. Then he noticed a narrow road winding up the hillside. Looked like an extension of Maple Street. Back to the scene of the crime. Twice in one day, he thought, as he swung off Ash into Maple. He rolled generally southward through thinning suburbs. Then the narrow pavement pitched uphill, apparently the mountain-climbing road he'd spotted from Ash Street. Well, how about that, genius?

Soon dense trees and underbrush lined both sides, broken now and then by a driveway he assumed led to houses. The well-maintained driveways thinned out as he climbed higher.

Four miles later, the roadway leveled. Driveways were few, then none. He drove through the Pocono boondocks. Nice scenery, but what damned good was—

He'd spotted a faded realty sign, awkwardly cocked on its angled stake. Faded red lettering: FOR SA E, with a Realtor's name and phone number underneath, mildew-stained and barely readable. Near it, he made out a break in the brush line, concealed by overhanging evergreen branches.

Krag hit the brakes and turned into the rutted dirt drive. Through a quarter-mile of gradually descending lane, the tires crunched fallen twigs, and low-hanging tree branches slapped the car's roof. At one bumpy curve, he had to climb out to lift a fallen branch out of this so-called driveway. More like a hike through the woods by car.

Then he drove into the clear, such as it was. Clear, except for the battered-looking, three-story house looming dead ahead. Lots of fancy woodwork. Well, fancy once. Now gray with neglect. What did they call houses with all these railings and turrets? Victorine...or something like that.

What must have been the parking area near the front entrance had become more of a weed patch, but he pulled in, shut off the engine and clambered out. The four steps were stone. Marble, maybe. And gritty with blown dust. He climbed up, avoiding the splintery handrail. A wood rail on marble steps? An afterthought maybe, to help the last owners, feeble with time. The flooring of the wide front porch squealed under his boots. The big front door was locked, of course. With both hands, he cupped his eyes to peer through its narrow eye-level window. No ghosts peered back at him, but he could kind of feel...Nah. An empty old house was an empty old house—and this one looked to be what he wanted.

He prowled the length of the porch. The three windows left of the entrance fronted what might have been some kind of—what did they call it? Sitting room? Nothing in there. Not a stick of furniture. He tried each of the windows. Locked.

Three matching windows on the other side of the doorway looked into a really big living room. When he pushed at the top of the middle one, it gave about an inch. With both hands, he reached under it and pulled. He was in.

Dust everywhere. On the bare floor. On the empty bookshelves. This room had been stripped, too. He walked into the central hall, clumped down to a naked kitchen, its black-and-white linoleum floor tiles streaked with what could be the scuffs from dragging out the stove and refrigerator. Or icebox? Like the front rooms, this one was empty—except for its stained sink. He tried the cold water tap. Nothing, of course.

Upstairs? He returned to the hall and climbed the broad stairway. Three bedrooms, all stripped bare, with only a few empty hangers in their walk-in closets. A big closet in the master bedroom. Two bathrooms, their fancy fixtures rusting.

He returned to the kitchen, peered at the two doors in the kitchen's interior wall. Opened the one on the left. Must have been the dining room, now naked as a gymnasium. The other door, the one next to the refrigerator alcove, had to be what he was looking for. A cellar access. He yanked it open. Yep, a flight of steps leading down into darkness. Well, not totally black darkness. His eyes adjusted to the dim light from two narrow, high set ground-level windows, one at each end of the murky cellar.

Wary of the stairs' creaking, Krag stepped on down. The cellar took up about half the house's area—the south half. Like the main floor and presumably the second floor, this area had been stripped of whatever they'd kept down here. Empty shelves, a lone chair possibly for a handyman to catch a breather between chores, and a mammoth furnace. Jeez! Coal fired. It was flanked by a little room with an entrance of vertically sliding boards. That puzzled Krag until he realized it was the coal bin.

In the middle of the dismal cellar in an abandoned old house well off a remote road in the Poconos, Krag made a full circle sweep. "Perfect!" he said aloud.

Now for step two.

21

On Wednesday morning after the stormy weekend, I hunched in my Maximall office and stared at my stage-prop notebook without seeing it. Since that weekend's cozy cuddling with Pris, something bothered me.

"Let's take a ride." Cliff stood in the doorway. His blond buzz cut and sky blue sweater made him look like a college kid. His frown told me something bothered him, too. I wondered if it was the same something.

In the elevator down to ground level, neither of us said anything, certainly unusual for Cliff, the boss's chatty brother. Not a word from him as we buckled into his Subaru, backed out of his reserved space and rolled toward the parking area's exit.

As he turned left and headed uphill toward the Keystone project site, he said, "Didn't want to discuss this in the office."

When the road leveled out, he took the left branch of the Y intersection. "Beautiful scenery," he muttered as we passed the side road to Lake Linden. I nodded, but I knew we weren't up here for a travelog.

Then he said, "I wonder if you got the same feeling I did about…Well, I'm not sure."

"That Vincent Parson's death is not the end of the situation?

"Yeah. You, too?"

"Nothing really specific, but yes. The tire tracks at Ash and Maple." The media hadn't made any mention of them, so maybe I was talking out of turn. But Cliff wasn't general public. He was client.

He glanced at me. "What about the tire tracks?"

"To me, they showed Vinny's 'hit-and-run' was a set-up."

"A set-up? Why the hell would anyone want him on a slab? A part-time worker for our subcontractor apparently acting out some grudge against us? He wasn't even good at it. The motor pool fire, assuming he set it, took out a temporary shed. It was back in business in two days. The D-8 accident? That could have been some mechanical fault."

"I wouldn't bet on it. I would bet on Vinny's having a hand—both hands—in it. I don't think he figured on the driver's death. That was a bonus, from his viewpoint. It did stall progress for more than a week."

"So that's what you think is going on? Delaying the project?"

"That, or trying to kill it altogether. But—and this is speculation—Vinny got carried away with himself. Wanted to show what an imaginative guy he was."

We cruised around the loop road's eastbound curve. Our leisurely thirty-five mph told me we were in this sight-seeing isolation to keep Cliff's concerns private. He trusted me more than his fellow staffers?

"So," Cliff said as we rolled past Susquehanna Contractors' temporary motor pool complex, "I figure Vinny's dumbass flare shot at our groundbreaking balloon showed us he was getting carried away with himself as a showman instead of an anonymous saboteur."

"Couldn't have put that better myself, Cliff. And I doubt he was on his own. The tire tracks told me that much. And more, I'm afraid."

"They told you he wasn't working on some grudge of his own? He's gone, but your reading of those tire marks of a set-up tell you he's been replaced."

"And the way Vinny was set up tells me we're not dealing with an over-eager bungler this time around. And I doubt he'll use the same part-time employment cover with Susquehanna Contractors.

"I'll have human resources send me copies of any post-Vinny employment records with Susquehanna or with us. That could —"

"I doubt the replacement will want to be hampered by employment concerns. More likely a freelancer will replace, or already has replaced, all-thumbs-Vinny."

Cliff looked puzzled. "That shoots a hole in what I've been thinking."

"Such as?"

"Such as a company mole. Vinny was a Susquehanna employee. But if someone is desperate enough to sabotage our project, wouldn't it make sense to infiltrate Sturdevant?" He shook his head. "Hell, all this is making me think like Perry Mason. I'm no detective; just a desk jockey helping to build my brother's dream."

I had no answer for that — and he'd come close to confirming a suspicion I'd had since Monday. What kind of a woman says not one word to her partner after their first night of physical revelry? Guess it was our last night of revelry. More than that, her all-business post-passion reaction also told me I'd been seduced — oh so willingly, of course, but that post-coital all-business demeanor of hers told me the whole event had been a set-up.

Why? Two possibilities. Her apparent timing with the storm's predicted arrival, her purported hotel-room-alone phobia, her need for comforting — truth or trap? Was her standoffishness the next day a middle-aged guilt reflex? Shame from a purposeful forty-plus, self-confident challenger type like Pris? Oh, sure.

I was suspicious. Now the question is: do I tell Cliff? If I'm wrong about her, it could ruin an innocent...well, a not-guilty woman's career.

"Can't shake my Perry Mason suspicions," he said. "You got any thoughts on the possibility of a company mole?"

Thoughts? He seemed to be reading them. I parried. "Could be a possibility. Who would...he"—almost said "she"—"be working for?" The "he" could be a misdirection, but I did not have any real evidence to name anyone.

"Good question," Cliff said. "I don't have any idea who would want to interfere with the project, or why."

We neared Sikorski's big mansion.

"Oh, except him." Cliff angled his thumb leftward as we rolled by.

"So far, he's been the type to confront, more than work behind the scenes."

"He has filed that National Historic lawsuit, Rod. So far, it's gone nowhere. Wonder if frustration—"

"Timing's wrong. He filed that after Vinny's bumblings."

"Good point."

At the Y intersection, he turned back into the Hardington-bound road. "Well, Detective, I don't think we solved a damned thing. The only thing we can be sure of is that no one has overheard our speculations."

In the Maximall's parking area, he pulled into his slot, switched off the Subaru's engine and turned to me.

"Maybe I'm trying too hard to be a layman gumshoe when I've got a real one sitting next to me. Could be the sabotage ended when Vinny did."

I couldn't agree with that hopeful assumption, but I didn't want to sound like a consultant trying to extend his lucrative contract. So, I said nothing.

We took the elevator back to the Sturdevant office level. "Thanks for the buggy ride," I quipped with a shrug. I could not share Cliff's more positive outlook: optimism, as we would soon realize, in the face of calamity.

22

B arton Krag set his carryout breakfast on the small table in his East End Economy Court room. He lifted out a stack of syrup-slathered peanut butter pancakes, a rasher of bacon, two biscuits with sausage gravy, pineapple juice, and coffee. He tossed the empty carton on the floor, picked up the plastic fork and cut into the pancake stack.

A celebration breakfast. Step 1 complete: He'd found the perfect place, isolated out there in the Pocono woods. This was his first job that needed real planning.

Until now, he'd always been a pusher, a freelance strong-arm for whoever paid him. Always carrying out someone else's plan. This project, though, would be a big leap past that kind of petty crap. This time, *he* was the planner.

Krag polished off the pancakes and biscuits, shoved the paper plates aside, picked up the pen he'd lifted from the motel's registration counter, and looked around for a piece of paper. Nothing. Then he had an inspiration, checked the drawer in the night table: Yep. He took out the Gideon Bible and ripped out its blank flyleaf.

Water, he wrote. The first item on the list of what he needed to complete Step 2. *Bread, peanut butter...* Took fifteen minutes to draw up the list. And he wasn't sure it included every essential. One item was right here. The extra blanket he'd noticed on the narrow shelf of the tiny closet.

He set the blanket on the floor near the door then checked his pockets. Always checked his pockets...Wallet. The fat roll of fifties and twenties Amerman had supplied. Keys. And knife. Not a dinky penknife or one of those Swiss Army pocket knives with puny blades and a half dozen folding doodads in its fat little handle. No, this knife of his, a freebee that came with the two pairs of bargain pants he'd bought from a mail order house, had some authority. He liked the fancy plastic inserts on each side of the four-inch-long handle: a picture of a bear eating a fish. Seemed appropriate.

But what he really liked was the single folding blade, just short of four inches long, and a full inch wide. Real authority. The one time he'd discreetly flashed it to quiet down a loud-mouth picketer, the silent threat beat the hell out of a panic-producing pistol.

He slid it into his hip pocket, slapped on his Phillies cap, held the tightly rolled blanket under his arm, and checked the parking area. Nobody. He headed for his car.

***

First stop: a hardware store, a big one where he would be a customer among many. He paid cash for a padlock and hasp assembly, a screwdriver, a little packet of a dozen screws, and a roll of duct tape.

Next stop, a busy big-chain grocery store in Hardington's north end. Two gallons of water, two loaves of bread, peanut butter, jar of jelly...what kind? What's the difference? He set a jar of grape jelly in the cart. And... He consulted his list. Oh, a pack of toilet paper and a flashlight. Among the display of new-fangled lights with multi-knobbed lenses, he found a chubby, old-fashioned flashlight that took a pair of D batteries. Dropped it and batteries in his cart. Damn! This was getting complicated. He pushed the cart to checkout and joined the line.

Next, a bucket. Shoulda picked that up at the first stop. Go back there for a repeat appearance as the guy with the Phillies cap? Huh uh. He drove to the city's eastern outskirts, found a dingy little hardware store in a strip mall. He parked close, opened the car door—then shut it again. Remote as this was, it would be his third stop as the guy in the Phillies cap. Something of pattern. He flipped off the cap and dropped it in the passenger seat. Now this would be the first stop by a guy with a shaved head, a break in the pattern. He opened the door again and stepped out.

He'd figured on a metal bucket but had to settle on a gray plastic one. Plastic was taking over, he thought, as he checked out. They're even making plastic cars now.

Back in the Ford, he pulled out his makeshift list on the pilfered Bible flyleaf. Padlock, bread, peanut butter, jelly, bucket...Oh, hell. To make PB&Js, you gotta have something to spread 'em with. Where was he going to get a goddamn table knife?

At a table, dummy. The strip mall had no restaurant. He fired up the Ford, eased out of the lot and cruised the area until he spotted a small eatery named Kelly's Kitchen in outskirt-nowhere. He pulled into one of the spaces out front, locked up and walked in.

Time for lunch anyway. No hostess, of course. No other customers. A solitary waitress lounged at the counter, jawboning with the cook through the opening behind it.

"Take a seat," she called across the empty room. "Anywhere."

He plunked down at a table near the door and took a battered, plastic-sheathed menu from the table's little rack.

"Coffee, hon?" she called across the room.

"Yeah."

When she plunked down the steaming mug, he figured the plump, middle-aged, haggard-looking waitress was probably an exhausted mother forced to hold down an outside job. She wore a name tag: *Emma.*

"I'll have the beef stew, two cheeseburgers" — that got a frown from Emma — "and French fries." Her eyebrows went up, she shrugged and headed back to the counter's kitchen access window.

The table had four settings, each with knife, fork, spoon, and paper napkin. When Emma set down his stew, cheeseburgers and fries, he tucked a corner of the napkin under his chin, dug in, and flicked his eyes to the counter. With her back to the room, she was gabbing again with the cook.

With his right hand, Krag fingered his coffee mug, shielding his left as he slipped his stubby plastic table knife up the right sleeve of his sweater.

He polished off his lunch in minutes. Mopped his mouth, nodded at Emma as she dropped the check on the table. He fished out a twenty and two ones for the $17.95 tab plus tip. Stood, waved a cheery good-bye. "Thank you, Emma!" And he walked out. Shopping list complete.

He worked his way back through the city to Maple Street and climbed its sinuous assent into the Pocono foothills.

He thought he'd be on cloud nine at this point, but all the damned details so far had him already dragging his ass. Come on, Barty Boy — he would have flattened anybody who called him that — get it together. You're on a roll. Found the site, got everything on the list. Step 2 is about to be wrapped up.

Partway up the road's climb, he looked ahead and behind. No other cars in sight. He slowed, eyes raking the right side's tangled shrubbery. There it was — the almost hidden break for the abandoned driveway. He rechecked the road. Still empty. He swung into the narrow drive.

Jolting moments later, as he neared the secluded clearing, he held his breath. Another car or truck parked in front of the decrepit old mansion would blow everything sky high. But when the house reared into view, it looked just as deserted and forgotten as he'd first discovered it. Nerves, Barty. Nerves never bothered you before. But you've never done anything like this before.

He didn't have to climb in through a window this time. He'd left the front door unlocked. Took him two trips to carry everything inside. By the time he'd carried all but the hardware downstairs, he was sweating bullets. The planning had been a kick, but this part was a drag.

Screwing the hasp and plate on the kitchen side of the door and its frame wasn't so easy, either. The ancient frame and door must've been made of ironwood. Shoulda brought a drill.

After fifteen minutes of forcing eight screws into the resisting wood, his fingers and wrists were numb. He swung the hasp into place, looped in the padlock, clicked it shut, and slipped the key on top of the frame's lintel. Done.

"Oh, *shit!*" he muttered. Took the key back down, unlocked the padlock, opened the door, plodded back down, groping under his sweater. He pulled the pilfered table knife from his shirt pocket and dropped it on the cement floor between the peanut butter and jelly jars. Back up the damned steps — this was the sixth time he'd clomped up or down. At the top, he bent over, hands on knees, gasping for breath. This was shaping up as a two- maybe three-man job, handled by one guy with too many pounds — yeah, he admitted it — too many pounds to be humping cargo down creaky cellar steps.

When he'd driven back to the road and turned left toward Hardington, he'd been both planner and doer. And damned good at both, he told himself. Step 2 complete.

Now for Step 3. The big one.

23

Precisely at 8:45 a.m., Max Sturdevant gave his still-in-her-bathrobe wife, Elaine, a peck on the cheek. He picked up his briefcase and opened the kitchen door into the garage.

"Dinner at Zenkie's tonight, Sweets," he called as he shut the door and thumbed a wall switch. The big garage door climbed, and he pressed the remote on his key chain then folded his six-foot frame into the driver's seat of his dark green Lexus. He fired up and carefully backed into the broad driveway. Finding this place in the city's upscale hill section was an unexpected boon for moving Sturdevant Developers from Dixon, Illinois, to Hardington.

The driveway was wide enough for a turn-around with only one reversal, which he executed smoothly, then rolled into Pine Street and headed east. He felt good this bright day. The clumsy sabotage attempts had died along with... What was his name? Parson. That was it. Vincent Parson, killed in a hit-and-run. Bad luck for him, good luck for us.

Waiting for the green at Olive Street, Max drummed his fingers on the wheel.

Impatient to get to work? Well, yeah. Building a whole new city is damned exciting for a guy only in his mid-fifties without a sign of gray in his black hair. So, yes, he enjoyed the hell out of moving the company here and building a whole new city from scratch. Now all that stood in the way was Sikorski's big house. But that was only a temporary glitch in the planning of Keystone's third-to-be-built village.

The traffic light turned green. Foot off the brake, Max rolled on.

Precisely at 9:00, he nosed the Lexus into his reserved space in the Maximall parking area's front row, noticing that the Ford SUV on his left had backed in. Its driver still sat behind the wheel.

Max grabbed his briefcase and opened the door. At the same time, the driver of the backed-in car opened his door. As Max stepped out, so did the other driver. Big guy, couple of inches taller than Max's six feet. Wearing a Phillies cap.

Max nodded. "Morning." Then, as he turned to shut the door of the Lexus, he felt something hard shoved against his lower back.

"What the he—" He twisted around and felt the painful pressure slide to his left side. He looked down.

Jesus Christ! The big bastard held a *knife*!

"What the hell are you doing?"

"Get in the car."

"Okay, okay." Max stepped back toward his Lexus.

"Not your car, dumbhead. *My* car." He reached past Max, slammed the door of the Lexus shut, yanked the briefcase out of Max's hand and threw it onto the back seat of the Ford. "Now. Get. In. My. Car."

This guy sounded and acted like he was damned serious, and the knife pressed deeper into Max's suit coat. Painfully deeper.

He stepped toward the other car. The knife point's pressure eased as the guy moved aside. Max plunked down on the driver's seat, swung his legs aboard. What in God's name was this oaf up to?

"Slide over," Phillies Cap ordered.

Max glanced down. The key was in the ignition. If he could flip on the engine, slam the door, shift into drive, hit the accelerator—

"No, you don't," the guy hissed in his ear.

Screw you, Max thought and reached for the key.

The knife jabbed through his jacket sleeve, through his shirt sleeve. Bit into his upper arm. "*Jesus!* What in hell—"

"I told you, slide over."

"Okay, okay." Max managed to clamber sideways into the passenger seat. He made a quick survey of the parking area. Where the hell is everybody? Looks like no one wants to be late when the boss is noted for being on time. And the mall's shop area doesn't open until nine-thirty.

"You after my wallet? Be my guest. It's in my right-hand hip pocket." He reached for it.

"Hands behind your back."

"What?"

"Put your hands behind your back, cross your wrists, and turn so I can see 'em."

This keeps getting worse, Max realized. If this dodo doesn't want money, what does he want? Then he felt something that came close to terrifying him. The stickiness of tape pulled tight around his wrists. Christ Almighty! A kidnapping? What would be the purpose? Ransom, of course. This big stupe didn't seem likely to work out kidnapping for ransom all by himself. He's got to be working for someone else. The Keystone project's run of incidents might not be ended after all. Could this clod be a big step up in the sabotage effort?

The dough-faced driver twisted the ignition key. They rolled out of the lot onto the Hardington access road and turned south toward central city. Big Stupe wound them through city traffic, headed across town, turned west into Ash Street then south again at Maple.

A few minutes later, the narrow two-lane macadam climbed steeply into the Poconos—and out of civilization, Max thought. Worse and worse. Hell of a way to spend a morning. By now I should be into my second cup of dark-roast coffee from my office machine.

He scowled at the driver. In his thirties, still with the baby face of a chubby adolescent. Eyes intent on the road.

"Somebody paying you to do this?'

No response.

As the road climbed a long hill, the guy began peering to the right. When the macadam leveled out, Max heard him mutter, "Son of a bitch." And he wrenched the wheel into a cramped turn-around. Something to avoid up there? As Chubby Cheeks managed the clumsy reversal, Max peered up the road. Nothing…except some sort of frame tower with antennas poking out of the tree tops a mile or so east.

As they rolled back the way they came, the guy kept squinting to his left. Apparently, he'd missed something on the way up.

"You got a name?" Max asked.

No answer.

"You from Hardington?"

Lunkhead scowled, but his eyes stayed on the roadside tangle.

"Ever been in the military?"

No reaction. Can't work a reverse Stockholm Syndrome on this guy if he won't react at all.

"I was," Max said. "In the Corps of Engin—"

"Shut up! I'm tryin' to—there it is."

There *what* is? Max wondered as the lumpish dodo turned into the brush line and pushed through some hemlock —oh, a driveway. Crumbling, overgrown. In the middle of nowhere. Not good.

Long, bumpy minutes later, Chubby Cheeks rolled the SUV to a stop in front of what looked like a mansion from the

Victorian-inspired nineteen-twenties. Long deserted, from the look of its weather-ravaged tile roof and siding.

The burly driver switched off the engine, shoved his door open and grabbed the edge of the roof to hoist himself out. He walked around the Ford's rear and yanked open the passenger side door.

"Out."

Not all that easy with your hands taped behind you, Max discovered. But he managed to swing his legs clear then stand up on the gritty, weed-choked parking area.

The guy punched Max's shoulder. "Up the steps."

As Max clumped up the first of the four marble steps with his abductor close behind, he realized he could kick back with one leg and send the guy sprawling. Might work—if he had use of his arms. He climbed to the top. Chubby pushed past him and opened the big front door.

"In."

Max looked him straight in the face—and saw brutal hardness in the ice-blue eyes. They stepped into a gloomy central hallway. Hard Eyes, close behind him, shut the door. "Down the hall," he growled.

They walked toward the doorway at the far end. The only sound in this big place was the squeak and snap of the hallway's aged hardwood flooring. The door opened into a big, empty kitchen. Only the sink remained, its faucets dull from disuse. Hard Eyes opened a door on the right, an old door with what looked like a new padlock installation with the open lock hanging on it. From a pocket in his baggy pants, he yanked a flashlight, clicked it on and aimed its beam into the darkness.

"Down." That, with a prod in Max's left side. He had the damned knife out again.

Careful not to trip—with his hands taped behind him, a fall could be a calamity—Max clumped down the shaky steps with the guy close behind. At the bottom, the flashlight clicked off. Two small ground-level windows were set high at each end of the cellar. In their gloom, Max muttered. "Now what?"

"Make yourself comfortable." He gave Max a little grin, the smirk of a guy enjoying total control. A crafty guy, but careless, Max thought. *I'll be out of here with a police escort. I still have my cell phone.* Then he felt hands all over him, patting pockets until Hard Eyes found the cell and yanked it from Max's shirt pocket.

"You going to leave me taped up?"

The guy pulled out his knife again, popped the blade and Max felt him sawing away at his crossed wrists. When his hands parted, and with the knife pointed at his gut, he pulled off the severed strips of duct tape and threw them on the concrete floor. Hard Eyes flicked the knife to his left. "Siddown."

As his vision adjusted to the dimness, Max saw a folded blanket in the far left corner. He stepped over, set himself down easy then worked his right hand down into the jacket's left sleeve. Felt a small patch of hardness in the shirt sleeve. *Congealed blood, from where this bastard pricked me back in the parking lot.*

So now what, you big oaf?

Hard Eyes folded the knife, slipped it into his pocket, walked to the steps then turned back. "Make yourself comfortable. What's next isn't up to me." He pounded up the steps and slammed the door. Max heard the padlock clink into place.

Christ Almighty! A degree from Harvard Business School, two years between wars as an Army Engineers lieutenant, then thirty years building Sturdevant Developers into a national company—none of that prepared him for *this.* Abducted by a loony with a knife. Locked in the cellar of an abandoned mansion in the Pocono Mountains.

Okay, Max, okay. Think. First move: inventory. What the heck is down here? Chair. Empty shelves, but a pile of something in the opposite corner. He pushed out off the blanket and walked over. My God! Two gallons of water. Two loaves of bread. Couple of jars of... He held them up toward the window overhead. Peanut butter, jelly, and a table knife! Hard Eyes supplying the makings for PB&Js? Almost laughable, except for the circumstances—and supplies for what looked like a long stay.

He peered closer at the package beneath the bucket. Four rolls of toilet paper. Oh, crap! Precisely. This stack of basic necessities, Max realized, is here for more than an overnight stay in this musty prison.

The baby-faced thug had said, "What's next isn't up to me." So he wasn't doing this on his own. What possible motive could someone else have...

Yeah, it was obvious now. Vincent Parson's death hadn't ended the attempts to delay or stop the Keystone project. Hard Eyes was his replacement.

But who in hell was behind all this?

24

Another morning parked in my temporary office, wondering whether I still had an on-going "case," or was I wheel-spinning to justify an unjustified fee. Stripped of speculation, I had...what?

One: Based on the tire tracks at Ash and Maple and what the rooming house owner had told me, Vincent Parson had been set up and run down.

Two: Dying in the hospital, Vinny had tried to tell Sergeant Stoddard and me... what? It sounded like "antsy," but that was hardly a dying man's credible last word.

Tire tracks and "antsy." Hardly enough to keep me on the Sturdevant payroll. My next move would have to—

"Have you seen Max today?"

I turned from my window, banging the chair arm against the desk. Cliff Sturdevant. The Younger Brother looked like a college kid suddenly gone serious. I admired his practice of seeing employees in their offices instead of calling them to his, but his expression told me he'd brought trouble with him.

"Have I seen Max today? Not yet. Should I have? Some days, I never—"

"His car's in his space. You can see it down there."

"So he's got to be here somewhere. Maybe one of the other offices."

"Nope. Checked 'em all."

"Maybe down in the shopping level on a rental problem?"

Cliff shook his head. "I sent Pris down to take a look. No sign of Max."

"There's got to be some reason..." A disturbing thought hit me. "Let's check his car."

"God, you don't think he's had a—"

"I don't think anything yet, Cliff." Though I damned well did. "Let's get down there. First, though..." I picked up my phone, tapped in Max's office. "Is he in yet?" I asked Pris."

"No. He's never been this—"

"If...when he calls or comes in, call Cliff right away, okay?" Almost said "call me," but the historian taking the helm could be a blatant move. I stood and headed for the door. "Let's go, Cliff." I'd taken the helm after all.

In the pleasant morning sun, the parking area was filling with the shopping crowd. We strode toward Max's Lexus. I didn't like what I was thinking. Max slumped in the front seat. Heart attack? Stroke?

But both front seats were empty. Back seat, too. I tried the driver's door. "Unlocked, Cliff." I tried the left rear door. Locked, as were both right side doors.

"No briefcase," Cliff said. "He always comes to work with his briefcase. So he stepped out with his briefcase, forgot to lock the driver's door."

"Or couldn't."

"What's that mean?"

"Someone else shut the door. Just a possibility."

Cliff frowned. "And that leads us...?"

"Nowhere for the moment. But I've got a suggestion. Get the word around the office: did anybody see anything unusual here in the parking lot this morning?"

"Worth a try."

Back in my office, I felt like a hobbled race horse. As Max's non-appearance became a real concern, my "historian" cover seemed less and less useful.

Cliff walked in, pale and frowning. "I just called Elaine."

"Elaine?"

"Max's wife. After I got the word out asking if anybody up here had seen anything unusual down there, I wondered if Elaine might know about Max's schedule this morning. I thought maybe he'd planned a meet in the lot then drove off with whoever—and forgot to tell Pris about it in advance."

"Elaine shed any light?"

"Nothing. Said he left like he always did. Smack on the cheek, reminded her they had a dinner date, drove off. So we are nowhere."

"Well, not quite, Cliff. We know he got here—at least to the parking lot. Took his briefcase with him but forgot, or was unable to lock the Lexus driver's door."

"That's still nowhere. I did get the word around asking if any of our people had noticed something unusual down there. So far, nada. I feel like I'm—"

A discreet tapping on my open door cut him off in mid-sentence. She was slim and trim, in a sea-green pantsuit. "Millie Fleming," she said. "I'm a temp in the blueprint room. Your administrative assistant said I'd find you here, Mr. Sturdevant."

"What can I do for you, Millie?"

"The office email said you want to know if any of us saw anything unusual in the parking lot this morning. Maybe it's nothing, but when I pulled in, I did wonder why somebody had backed into the space next to the president's space and was just sitting there."

"What time was this?"

"About ten of nine. I always try to get here a little early."

"You notice what kind of a car it was?" I asked her.

She glanced at Cliff. He nodded.

"An SUV. Black," she said.

"Had Mr. Sturdevant's car arrived at that point?"

"No, his space was empty."

"You remember what the driver looked like?" I asked.

Again, she seemed hesitant to talk to this mere historian until Cliff gave her another little nod.

"All I remember, he was wearing a cap with something written on it." She frowned. "I wish I could tell you more but I..." She swallowed. "There's a rumor that Mr. Sturdevant has...hasn't..."

"He's unusually late to work, Millie," I told her, my cop-reflex taking the helm again. "Thank you for your help."

She gave me a little frown then walked out, peering back at me as she turned into the corridor.

"Well," Cliff said, "that's a step forward, but we're still in the woods."

We went over what we had, and even with Millie's input, we still didn't have much.

"Maybe this is all some weird coincidence," Cliff suggested. "Max forgets to tell anyone he has a morning appointment. He did take his briefcase with him."

"Assuming he had it at all this morning."

"He always has it. So off he goes on foot. And there's no connection between him and the guy in the black SUV. Just coincidence."

A good cop never puts any faith in coincidence, but I didn't say it. Cliff slapped my desk top, "God damn it! I gotta do something, but I don't know what the hell to do. Call in the police, maybe?"

"If we had anything solid to go on, yeah. But at this point, they'll just tell us to wait the standard twenty-four hours."

With a long, frustrated sigh, Cliff pushed out of the desk side chair. "'Fraid you're right. I'll be in my office trying to get my mind back on some piled-up work."

I knew how he felt because I felt the same way. Indecisive. So I pondered. I didn't like that either.

A few minutes after eleven, Cliff walked back in, plunked down. "I wonder if —"

"Mr. Sturdevant!"

Pris stood in my doorway, her face white. She gestured frantically at Cliff. He looked at me, eyebrows high. She motioned again, a subordinate's unseemly demand to have the acting boss come to her.

He gave me a puzzled shrug and joined her at the door. They stepped out of view. I couldn't make out what she was saying, but her tone sent a ripple across my shoulders.

Cliff reappeared, a shaken man. "You just lost your historian status," he said. "I'm calling a department heads meeting in ten minutes. Be there, Rod."

***

In the conference room, I could feel the tension, like static electricity before a menacing storm. Behind his wire-rimmed specs, CFO Ed Fletcher's sharp little eyes flicked around the table. Cranelike PR Director Mitch Newman seemed unable to stop drumming his fingers on the glass-topped table. Chief Planner Marty Elman fiddled with a curly black forelock. And between jittery fingers, Pris Killian turned her ballpoint pen over and over. Only Cliff, now at the head of the table — for the first time, I suspected — appeared collected and purposeful.

He didn't have to tap for silence. He already had it. "I know some kind of word has gotten around, but to make sure we're all on the same page, here's the situation: Max has been abducted, apparently from his car when he pulled into his parking space this morning. One of our people has reported seeing a black SUV with its driver aboard backed in beside Max's reserved slot. That, around eight-fifty. Max hadn't pulled in yet. Apparently when he did, the driver of the SUV forced him in and they drove off."

"You sure about all that?" Fletcher asked. "Sounds to me like a hell of a lot of speculation."

"It was speculation, Ed, until a phone call a few minutes ago. Pris?"

"I was out of the office, so the message was recorded." She held up her cell phone. "I re-recorded it on this." She clicked on the phone.

The voice was toneless and to the point. *Stop all work on Keystone or you will never see your boss alive again.*

Suspicions confirmed. I looked at Cliff, transformed from perpetual collegian to grim-and-purposeful man in charge.

"Jesus!" Mitch Newman burst into the shocked silence. "We gotta keep this quiet." Spoken like a true PR man. "It'll have our suppliers—"

Cliff shot him a hard look. "I'm not worried about our suppliers, Mitch. I'm worried about Max. To gain some time—for him and for us—we'll do what this son-of-a-bitch demands."

"Cave in?" Marty Elman looked physically pained. "That'll screw up the whole damned—"

"To gain us some time while we sort all this out, Marty, we stop construction on the Town Center building but keep clearing the forest behind it. As for the PR handling, we've got more than fifty employees who already know about our concern. The media are bound to get wind of Max's disappearance. In fact, an alert public could be an asset. We can play up our cooperation on stopping Town Center construction while we quietly go ahead with the clearing of the twenty-acre woods. Agreed?"

Somber nods all around. Chairs scraped on the hardwood floor.

"Hold on a minute." Cliff motioned everybody back down. "There is one positive aspect in all this. We have our own detective already on board. No need to make it public, but 'historian' Stevens is a private investigator Max hired to look into the series of 'accidents' we've had."

All eyes swung my way. Cliff had just put me back at the helm in what I felt was already a hurricane-whipped sea.

25

As the meeting broke up, I motioned to Cliff and he stayed with me in the empty room.

"I have an informal 'in' with a county sheriff's deputy. Name of Ben Stoddard. He was driving the third car in our chase after the groundbreaking balloon was shot down. The Maximall is in the county, so Max's kidnapping has taken place in county police jurisdiction. And at this point, we need all the help we can get."

"I can't argue with that." Cliff looked like he'd aged a full decade. "And I'm not the detective here. You are. One of Max's 'maxisms' was — God! is — 'Hire good people then stay the hell out of their way.' Just keep me up to date on progress."

Progress. At this point, "progress" sounded wildly optimistic. Back in my office, I used my cell to call Stoddard. Got him on the third ring.

"Rod Montgomery, Ben. We've got a situation here, a bad one."

"Can you hang on a sec, Rod?" As if I wouldn't. I heard traffic roll by, then — not quite muffled, he said, "Just write up the damned ticket, Harry, and give it to her with a smile." Then, "Sorry about that, Rod. New deputy too quick to go into lecture mode. What can I do for you?"

No reason to pull the punch. "Max Sturdevant has been abducted."

"Abducted or missing?"

"He didn't show up at his office this morning. Apparently he did make it to his parking spot. His car's still here."

"He could have—"

"We've gone through a list of benign possibilities, but that fell apart when a phone call came through just after eleven. The caller claimed he had Max, and work on Keystone must stop 'or else.'"

"Not good. Or maybe a crank call? Keystone isn't a unanimously popular project."

"Huh uh. At that point, only a few of us knew Max was missing. A random crank call on that? Hell of a coincidence."

"Yeah. I'm grasping. You said Sturdevant's car is still there at the mall?"

"Neatly parked in his reserved space."

"I'm on North Mountain Road, about fifteen minutes from you. Don't let anybody touch that car. I'm on my way."

***

At 11:40, when I saw Ben's blue-and-white roll into the lot, I headed for the elevator. I had one of the shopping level's security guards standing near the Lexus, but that didn't calm my conscience much. I had already violated a crime scene no-no when I opened the driver's door with my bare hand and tested the other doors. But at that point, we didn't know it was a crime scene... Oh, feeble, Rod. You already suspected it.

As Ben pulled up near us, I thanked the rent-a-cop. "You can go back to the mall. I'll call you if we need you again."

Ben stepped out, tall, heavy-set, the kind of cop you know you can't argue with.

"'Morning, Mr. 'Stevens.'" That with a half-smile.

"You can drop the 'Stevens,' Ben. The secret's out. I'm back to hired PI status."

He eyed the Lexus. "Anybody touched it?"

"Just one dodo that I know of. Me."

"You?"

"Yeah. Before I realized this was a crime scene. Thought Max might be collapsed in there. I tried all the doors, so my prints are on all four handles."

"So much for clever detective work, Detective."

"Try this." I'd been thinking while I'd waited for him. "Maybe the bad guy shut the driver's door. If he was holding a gun on Max, and in a nervous hurry, he could have slammed it shut with his free hand without using the handle. In fact, how many of us neatly use the handle to shut the door? We just give it a slap."

Ben chuckled. "Nice sidestep, Rod. But you have a point. Now I want to hear everything you've got."

"What I've got is the recorded threat call. Let's get upstairs."

As the elevator opened on Maximall's second floor, there stood Cliff. "Oh," he blurted, "I'm about to go down with a rent renewal for Soleful Shoes."

"Cliff Sturdevant, Deputy Ben Stoddard, County Sheriff's office," I introduced. "We're going to listen to the threat call recording."

"Good move," Cliff said, giving Ben a handshake. "I hope it tells you more than it told me. Rod, make sure you keep me up to date." He walked into the elevator, looking like a man shaken but hiding it, and a first class example of "…and stay out of their way."

"I think the original recording of the call might have more…uh, tonal quality than your re-recording," I told Pris. She agreed, though with a curiously impersonal attitude.

Couldn't be irritation at my bypassing her recording. What the hell was pre-occupying her? She led us into Max's office and poured us coffee from his personal machine. But she seemed detached from those simple tasks, as well.

"To activate message playback, press that button." She walked out, closing the door.

Ben surveyed the big, sumptuously appointed office. "Hell of a set-up, and with a great view." He eased into one of the chairs near the desk. I found myself unwilling to take Max's swivel. Took a side chair within reach of the answering machine and pushed the designated button.

The fourteen-word threat did sound less metallic on this machine. "Play it again," Ben said, "and this time, listen to the voice, not the words."

Not easy, but I understood Ben's suggestion. I pressed the button again.

"What do you think, Rod?" he asked when the chilling message ended.

"Teen-ager? Guy in his twenties? Older?"

"In his thirties, I'd guess."

"I agree. Accent?"

"New Yorkese? But not boroughese," I said. "That general area, though. Or maybe New Jersey?"

Ben nodded. "I'll buy that."

"I think he's a replacement for Vincent Parson. Both of them working for a person or persons unknown, obsessed with some damned reason to screw up the Keystone City project."

"Gotta tell you, Rod, I'm limited here. The County Sheriff's Department can determine if a crime has taken place. Max's non-appearance, then the phone call, sure as hell confirms that. So this is as far as I can go."

"Even though the crime has taken place in the county?"

"Yep. The Sheriff's Department is charged with traffic control, running the county jail—though that's actually in the city—and determining if a crime warrants further investigation. Which this one obviously does. So I'll go down, string some crime tape, and call in the State Police detectives. They'll take over. You make sure nobody fiddles with that answering machine. I'm sure they'll want to impound it."

After seeing Ben to the elevator with mutual assurances to "keep in touch," I walked back to my temp office to jot down a note about Ben's and my "finding" from the threat message recording. Now in overt detective mode, I'd replaced the prop three-ring notebook with a more convenient pocket pad from the stationery store downstairs.

I considered asking Pris to another of our recently neglected downstairs lunch get-togethers. I walked down the corridor to her cubby, stuck my head in. "You game for a quick lunch?"

Her expression oddly blank, she shook her head. So I BLT'd alone, wondering what was happening to such a normally super-controlled lady.

***

Back in my office around 2:15, I swiveled to my window to gaze down at the bright yellow crime scene tape Ben Stoddard had strung from a shrub edging the parking lot pavement, then around the Lexus's rear and back to a shrub on the other side.

"Mr. Montgomery?"

I swiveled back in place. "That's me."

"Detective Tremaine and —" A hard voice from a hard-looking guy in my doorway. As he stepped in, a short guy slipped in behind him. " — Detective Lawson. Pennsylvania State Police investigation department."

I stood, shook Tremaine's dry, bony hand, then Lawson's damp fleshy one, and motioned them to my two visitor chairs.

"Deputy Stoddard filled us in on what's known so far. We have a crime scene unit on the way."

They both wore gray suits, maybe an echo of their days in Pennsylvania trooper uniform gray. Both were somber-faced, Tremaine's lean with a piercing sea-green gaze, Lawson's chunky-cheeked, with brown eyes sweeping my barren office as if he expected lurking trouble. Though I had nothing to hide, both of these state gumshoes set my nerves ajangle.

"So," I said, "what can I do for you?"

"Why," said Tremaine, "did Mr. Sturdevant hire you, Detective Montgomery?"

"Because of the string of sabotage incidents." I reeled them off, ending up with a summary of Ben Stoddard's and my activities this morning. Then I threw them a question. "What about FBI involvement?"

"If a kidnapping involves crossing a state line," Tremaine said. "At this point, we have no indication of that. In the meantime, we will impound Mr. Sturdevant's answering machine. Make sure it's replaced in the event the suspect makes further calls. And we will assign a unit with recording and tracing equipment here and at his home."

Elaine's going to love that, I thought. Pris, too. Especially in her odd state-of-mind.

Tremaine stood. Lawson bounced up right behind him. I joined in.

"Thank you for your cooperation," Tremaine said. "Notify us the moment you have anything at all to report." He dropped a card on my desk like it was a printer's cast-off. I felt the same way, and let them find their own way back to Max's office to pick up the answering machine.

I sat down. Tented my fingers. Cogitated. With the case now crawling with detectives, what in hell could I—"

"Ro—"

Pris, in my doorway, cleared her throat. "Rod, I...have to talk to you."

"Fine. Come on in." On closer look, I deduced she wasn't fine at all. Pale, shaky. Her fingers working with nothing to work on, she walked in apprehensively, sank into the desk chair, and dropped fidgety fingers in her lap.

"I have to...to tell you something, Rod." Voice absolutely flat, eyes downward. "I don't know how to...how to put it. I never thought things would get anything like this. Mr. Sturdevant kidnapped!"

I tried for an offhand tone. "You sound like you think it's partly your fault, Pris."

She looked up at me. "Oh, God. I'm...I've..." Her hazel eyes brimmed with sudden tears. I hopped up, strode to the door and shut it. No need for passing traffic to see a co-worker coming apart. I pulled my fortunately clean handkerchief out of my pocket and offered it.

"Th...thanks." She dabbed her eyes, gulped a couple times, straightened up in her chair. "I feel so awful about this. But what's happened to Max is so terrible, I just can't keep on... can't keep on working for...for two—"

"Two companies?" Half of that was a guess.

"You knew?"

"I deduced. Beginning with your reaction the morning after our adventure at the hotel. Like it never happened. Cold, as if the whole thing was planned."

"It was. Timed with the helpful storm. My story about a fear of lonely hotel rooms... All that was a plan to find out what you really were doing for Sturdevant Developers. In the morning, I was ashamed of myself. For the...duplicity. I am still. Then this morning, with Max not showing up— then that awful phone message. Oh, God, I just can't go on being a...a..."

"A spy." I went into friendly cop mode. "Who for, Pris?"

"A company in New Jersey. Amerman and Cassina. They're big building suppliers based in Camden."

"Building suppliers? Why would a building supplier want to spy on a big development company? You'd think... Oh, of course. To get a leg-up on sales possibilities."

"That's what I thought, too. They seemed interested only in the construction schedule and they had me report on anything that slowed down progress."

"So you were working for a company to report on another company, and, I assume, you were—still are?—being paid by both?"

She gave me a parched, "Yes."

"Did it ever occur to you that the Jersey boys could be arranging the schedule-delaying incidents? The motor pool fire? The runaway D-8? The flare shooting at the Town Center groundbreaking—though I doubt they had such a dumbass effort in mind."

"They never mentioned any of that to me. I just reported it."

"There's no contact between you and Vincent Parson, or that guy who has apparently replaced him?"

"None. My job with Amerman was and still is—until I tell them to go to hell—simply to report development progress, or lack of it."

"So you're on two payrolls with apparently nothing criminal involved."

She looked at the floor again. "I'm not proud of it. I'm going to tell them I quit."

"Quit which?

"Both. Here and in Camden."

I took a long breath, let it out slowly. In the mind muddle she'd imposed on me, an idea was being hatched.

"Don't be too hasty," I said.

She looked up. "What does that mean?"

"If what you've told me is strictly accurate—"

"It is. I swear it is."

"Then you've done something corporately reprehensible but nothing that could put you in court. And I think there's a way to turn your—what's the word?—your corporate ambivalence into an asset."

"I'm not sure I follow what you're—"

"You continue reporting to Amerman and... What was the other—?"

"Cassina. A and C for short."

"—continue reporting to them, but we work with you on those reports before you send them to Camden."

"I won't be fired?"

"Not if Cliff okays such an arrangement." I looked straight into her misty eyes. "We'll be putting a lot of trust in you, Pris. Can you handle it?"

"I think I can."

"'Think' isn't enough. Can you handle it?"

"With what's happening to Max, yes, I can handle it."

I leaned back, feeling a lot better than I'd felt when she walked in here. I had just created Sturdevant Developers' double agent.

But our immediate concern remained. Who had abducted Max and where was he being held?

26

In the gloomy basement, Max sat on the blanket. Checked his luminous dial watch. He'd been locked down here five hours. Five hours of absolute silence. More than enough time to fight panic and concentrate on how he might get out of this damned dungeon.

The two windows — one apparently beneath the mansion's front porch; the other in the rear wall — were about nine feet above the cement floor. If he could get up there, he could bust out the glass with a shoe and maybe pull himself up to climb out. The only possible way to do that: put the bucket upside down, step up, smash out the glass, then Good-bye!

Great idea, until he picked up the bucket. Cheap plastic. The damned thing would crumple under his weight. Next bright idea? Somehow, at least break out the front window's glass? Then if anyone were nearby, he could yell for help. But who'd be wandering down that long, overgrown entrance drive? A hunter maybe? But this wasn't hunting season. He'd keep window breaking "under advisement," an office quip often used to table an obstructing idea.

Next thought. In this corner near the rear window — the west window, the sun's appearance now told him — as he shifted attention to the huge furnace across from him. And the peculiar "stall" between the furnace and the west wall. The corner walls and an L of five-foot-high wood partitions enclosed a six-by-six-foot space. In its face, a two-foot-wide slot was closed by stacked boards, apparently slipped in place through the slot's open top. What on earth...Oh, of course. The big furnace was a coal burner, and the odd little stall was the coal bin. Filled through a ground-level access slot high in the west wall for the delivery truck's coal chute. Then, as the supply was depleted, the boards in the slot successively were removed for continued shovel access.

So...any possibilities over there? Max let his imagination dance around with that. Squeeze out the coal chute slot? Too damn small, even if he could somehow climb up to it. Slip out the boards, step inside then replace the boards? Hell of a shock to that kidnapping bozo when he unlocks the kitchen access door and clumps down here to find... nobody! Assuming he does show up again. Or has he locked me in here to... But why would he have left the blanket, the PB and J makings, the damned bucket; all that? He's coming back.

Hiding in the coal bin, though, wasn't escape. Hard Eyes wouldn't stay flummoxed for long. And his reaction might be more than unpleasant.

A remote possibility: hide in the bin until the bozo walks to the cellar's east end, then make a rush out? No, he'd have me before I even got to the stairs... The stairs. A possibility there? A long shot, but worth thinking about.

What now? Think, dammit. Back to the start of all this. Why has somebody gone to the trouble, the huge risk, of kidnapping Sturdevant Developers' president? Logical conclusion: a series of efforts to delay the Keystone project has failed. So, kidnap the president and threaten his not returning unless work stops? Gotta be it.

The next move is up to Sturdevant's second-in-command. Cliff. And I have no idea how Cliff is reacting to this desperate hide-the-president outrage. My fault. I've treated him more like a kid brother than a responsible executive.

Uh. Just realized I haven't been such a great responsible executive, myself; specifically, not in the matter of parking lot surveillance cameras. Mall manager recommends full coverage. Company head says fine — for entrance coverage. But parking lot coverage? "I'll take it under advisement." Great decision, Max.

What in hell can be the root of all this? Attempts to delay. A dead D-8 driver. A Susquehanna Contractors' temp killed in a hit-and-run which turns out to be murder-by-car. And now, a kidnapping. What can be driving all this desperate *need* to delay or possibly kill the project altogether?

Never faced anything like this. But, damn it, sitting here brooding is self-destructive. I've got to do something *con*structive. What now? Something I can control: A god-damned peanut butter and jelly sandwich.

***

Cliff's eyebrows shot upward. He leaned forward in his chair and slapped both hands on his desktop.

"*Jesus, Rod!*" he exploded. "You're telling me *Pris* is working for someone else while she's working for us? She's been *reporting* to — who the hell did she tell you?"

"Amerman and Cassina in Camden, New Jersey."

"Why?"

"Her? For the money. Them? I have no idea. Yet. What I do know, or at least strongly suspect, is that Amerman and Cassina, also known as A and C, have been behind the whole string of unusual problems you've had. Vincent Parson tried to tell Ben Stoddard and me. We thought he was delirious, muttering what we assumed was 'antsy' over and over as he died. Now, thanks to Pris, I realize he was saying 'A and C,' as Amerman and Cassina are known in the building supply trade."

"A and C. Never heard of them." Cliff sat back and folded his arms. A gesture of defense. I could see he wasn't comfortable with any of this. "Damn. I like — liked — Pris.

Now she's headed for the door, of course. And my congrats for clever detective work." He reached for his phone.

I held up a cautionary forefinger. "Hold on a minute, Cliff. Hear me out. We can literally turn this around."

"I don't follow."

"Clever detective work had no part in this. She's been 'undercover' since she was hired here, a reporter for A and C, and I had no inkling—"

"So how did you—"

"I did nothing. Max's kidnapping this morning shocked the hell out of her. She walked into my office and confessed."

"She confessed to *you?* There's some empathy there?"

"Some, I guess."

Now just one of his eyebrows hopped up. "I'm not a detective, but I think I detect some personal reason you're against showing her the door."

"I do have a reason, but it's a corporate one. Pris and I had a discussion. I suggested she continue to serve both masters, but be loyal to only one—Sturdevant Developers. She agreed. I believe her."

"Just like that? You believe a woman who was part of all the damned incidents—"

"She says she's had no part in any of that. She's been a reporter only. She did suspect A and C could be orchestrating the sabotage, but she says she never had any contact with Vinny Parson. Never even heard of him until the press coverage of his hit-and-run demise."

"I gather you're thinking she could be useful to us as a... what's the term? Double agent?"

"Right. She keeps reporting to A and C, but we have a hand in her reports."

He gave me a long look. Kid-brother status no more. Forced to be in charge, he was growing in that role. Fast.

"Hell of an idea, Rod. And I like it." He reached for the phone again. This time he picked it up.

A minute later, taps on the closed office door.

"Come in, Pris," he called.

Fingers twitching in her apprehensive jitter, she walked in. As she sank into the chair Cliff pointed to, she threw me what I felt was a pleading glance.

He gave her a long, hard look. "I gotta say I'm disappointed as hell with your...duplicity, I think is the word for it. Taking paychecks from two companies and reporting on one of them to the other."

"I'm so s...sorry, Mr. Sturdevant. It's been a terrible mistake. I had no idea — "

"Yeah, sorry. Your damned spying certainly was." He folded his hands on the desktop, stared at them, looked up at her again. "But I do appreciate your setting the record straight. Our thanks for that." He took a deep breath. "Rod tells me you have agreed to continue that arrangement, but with a significant...uh, adjustment. We vet your reports before you send them to Camden. Agreed?"

"Yes, sir." Her subdued tone sounded remarkably non-Prisly, not at all the confident in-charge Pris I'd known when she was manipulating body and brain at the hotel.

"Have you reported to A and C since Max's disappearance?"

"No, Mr. Sturdevant."

"'Cliff' will do. We're all in this little game together now."

"What's happened with your brother has sickened me about what I was doing. I want to do whatever I — "

Cliff held up a silencing hand. "We're with you, Pris, as long as you're with us. Now, if A and C orchestrated Max's disappearance, which seems obvious to me, they're certainly waiting for your report. By phone, I assume."

"My own cell phone."

Cliff turned to me. "So, Rod, what's your input on that?"

My input? Cliff was slipping comfortably into exec mode. "My input," I said, "is Pris reports that Max has been kidnapped and the company is complying with a phoned-in threat to stop all Keystone construction. But no mention of the continuing forest clearance. As you pointed out in the meeting this morning, that lets the project go ahead to a degree." Lord, I sounded like I was slipping into exec mode myself. "And, Pris, I'm sure you will tell us of anything A and C sends your way."

"Absolutely."

"Done," Cliff said. "Both of you keep in touch with me minute-by-minute, if it comes to that. Specially you, Rod. I want to know spot-on of anything you hear from the county cops or the state cops."

"You got it," I assured him. Pris and I pushed out of our chairs, and I followed her out the door. In the corridor, she suddenly turned and grabbed my hands.

"God, Rod! Thank you. Oh, thank you. I owe you so much." Those compelling hazel eyes had recovered most of their sparkle. "Maybe..." she said. "Maybe...a more relaxed evening at the Anthracite?"

"You're suggesting...?"

"I'm hoping."

How 'bout that? Another surprise in this morning of disarray.

"Well, Pris—" I cleared my throat. "I will certainly...take it under advisement."

27

As Mateo Cassina walked in, Harvey Amerman swung his plush swivel from the view of the sunlit Delaware River. His chubby jowls framed a grin, a novel sight in this usually tense A and C head office.

"What the hell do you have to smile about?" Cassina growled.

"Just got a call from our Keystone contact. Krag's plan has worked out exactly as he proposed. Max Sturdevant is now... uh, sequestered in a remote secure location. His company has been given the ultimatum, and all work has stopped. Dead. Nothing's going on. So Krag has bought us some time."

"How long?"

"As long as the status stays quo."

"The what?"

"As long as the work stays stopped, Mateo."

"So now what?"

"Progress, my friend. I've found the place that'll solve our problem — or at least get us permanently out of reach."

Cassina looked more than unimpressed. His vulpine face — he wouldn't know what that means, Amerman thought — wore a barely concealed sneer. Their partnership, warm and mutually enjoyed since their days in Hardington years ago, had become a tense matter of forced cooperation—because, Amerman reflected, of the goddam Keystone City project.

"What I'm saying, Mateo, is we're going on holiday. 'Holiday the Samoan Way,' as the travel promo puts it."

"Samoan Way? Where the hell is that? South America?"

"No, partner. I've done a pretty damn exhaustive Internet search for a country that has no extradition agreement with the U.S. There's a slew of them, but almost every one is a place neither of us would want to live. Bunch of Communist or African or Muslim hellholes. Then I spotted Samoa."

"Tell me it's in South America."

"Nope. It's a lot more isolated than anything down there."

"C'mon, dammit. Tell me where the hell it is."

"Seven thousand five hundred miles west. I checked a map. Samoa is in the South Pacific near Australia."

"Jesus H. Christ!" Cassina shook his head in disbelief.

This, Amerman realized, is going to take some selling. Not that he couldn't roll right over any objections Cassina had. But the situation had both of them well aware of the potentially fatal outcome they faced. If they weren't out of the country before work resumed on that frigging project north of Hardington, their world would fall in on them.

Krag had assured them his risky but effective scheme would guarantee at least a couple weeks' delay, maybe more, depending on Max Sturdevant's endurance. Having the guy die on them—something Amerman sure didn't need on top of the problem they already had—seemed a minimum risk if Krag could keep it all together. Timing was already tight enough to give them the sweats. But for a change, things were breaking right.

In a side chair, Cassina twitched his bony shoulders. "Samoa," he muttered. "End of the world."

"Sure as hell the end of our world if we don't get out of here before development of that damned city goes much further."

"You got me working like hell to sell our company so we can make a quick exit to nowhere."

"To a friggin' *resort*, Mateo. Samoa's no jungle island. It's a country where they hold the Miss South Pacific Pageant, jazz concerts, art shows. There's even an annual Swim Festival."

"I don't swim."

"Most important of all, Mateo, there is *no extradition*."

"You got a point there."

"I got more than that. I got us room reservations on-demand at the Coconuts Beach Club. When we get confirmation of the Garden State Suppliers buyout, we will be on the plane the same day with twelve million in an offshore bank." He paused to peer at Cassina. "How's that coming?"

"That's what I came in to tell you. I'm supposed to hear from Taylor, Ketchem today. About time, damn lawyers."

"You let me know the minute they confirm."

Cassina gave him an impatient glare. "Jesus, Harve, keep your pants on. It's just a business deal."

"Not if it falls through. I'd have to tell Krag to keep Sturdevant wherever he's got him. And the risk for Krag— hell, for Sturdevant, too—gets worse than it already is. This whole thing is like a—"

"A house of cards?"

Leave it to Cassina to come up with banality. "Yeah, cards. Go see if any word has come through on the sale. We could be out of here in twenty-four hours. I hope you're ready to travel."

"Packed and ready for the first plane…west. Samoa. Jesus." Cassina pulled his lean frame out of the chair. "I'll let you know the minute our legal eagles tell us the sale is a go."

He walked out, leaving the door open. Amerman sighed, heaved himself up and shut it. *I'd rather not ponder in public,* he thought. *And I'd much rather be airborne.*

He passed up his usual noontime solitary walk down the block to the Garden of Eatin'. Turned back to his panorama of waterfront Camden. And...pondered.

At 2:15, Cassina burst in without a courtesy knock.

"Got the call," he announced.

Amerman felt a thrill zip from nose to tail. Samoa, here we come!

"And?" he prompted.

"Sombitch buyer is bargaining. Offers half of what we asked."

"Half?" Did you say *'half'?*"

"They said half."

"That's only six mil... What the hell are you laughing at, Mateo?"

"I'm wondering how 'only six mil' would have sounded 'way back when we slapped A and C together."

"Good point. Call Taylor, Ketchem. Tell 'em we'll consider nine."

"Nine million? I thought we were in a sweat to get out of here."

"A few more days' delay, Mateo, is not too much to risk for a three million bump."

"I'll give it a try. We could...ah, apply a little pressure. You know, like Garden State's gas pumps somehow get water in 'em. Stuff like that."

"None of that, Mateo. Not in this situation. Just do as I say, dammit."

"Yeah. But it could...Okay. I'll call our ambulance chasers."

With a sigh of exasperation, he watched Cassina hustle out, again—always—leaving the door open. So the sale is hangfire. But—and the thought of protracted bargaining began to pop sweat—no less urgent.

***

In the isolated mansion's gloomy cellar, Max Sturdevant decided the boredom was as distressing as the uncertainty. The hard floor beneath the blanket had become painful. Last night he'd folded the blanket lengthwise as an inadequate "mattress." Getting any sleep seemed improbable until he remembered the mental game he'd invented during his college days.

Start with a pair of words beginning with A that sound alike but have different meanings. Like...Ark and Arc. That was easy. Now work down the alphabet. Born and Borne. A little too easy? How about Blue and Blew...Clean...Clean. Uh uh. Creak and Creek? Okay, if you're not a country boy... Mind's wandering. What's next? D? Done and Dun. On we go... When he reached L...L...he slept. The only escape.

Now gray morning oozed in both windows. Before revising the blanket back into a cushion, he'd used the bucket. Worst part of this, so far. Hope to hell Hard Eyes shows up for latrine duty. Or have I been abandoned to die? No, don't think that way. If that was his plan, he wouldn't have left that little pile of supplies.

Breakfast? Another PB and J. How long can a guy live on that? Better than nothing at all. He struggled to his feet and stepped to the tumble of stuff in the northeast corner.

He slapped peanut butter on a bread slice. What could they be doing about this back at our Maximall offices? he wondered. What was our own private eye doing? Earn your fee, Rod. For God's sake—hell, for *my* sake, earn your fee.

28

Cⁿounty Police Sergeant Big Ben Stoddard took a long drag from his coffee mug then set it down with a clunk. "Thought it was time we got together, Rod. Compare notes."

We shared a corner booth in the Hardington Hunger Hutch, uncrowded this misty morning. Ben, in uniform, probably camped in this secluded corner to avoid alarming any law-leery customers.

"Appreciate it, Ben." I took a bite of Denver omelet. "Want to tell me about that gray, windowless van that pulled into the Maximall parking lot early this morning?"

"The out-of-state license on the kidnap car lets the FBI suspect the victim could have been taken across a state line, so their Hardington field office is on the case now. The van is theirs, monitoring Sturdevant Developers' incoming phone calls with tracking equipment." He took another snort of coffee. "Oh, about the fingerprints on Sturdevant's Lexus. The crime scene guys found Max's, of course. Plus yours, as you expected. And on the driver's door, a five-finger print, as you predicted. Trouble is, neither the state's nor the FBI's AFIS system shows a match."

"So now it's a county-state-federal party — not to mention my PI input."

"And that's my main interest this morning, Rod. What you've got to put in."

"Try this." I detailed the jolt of Pris's tearful confession.

"She's been a damned *spy* for a competitor?" Ben looked a trifle bemused.

"For a building supplier based in Camden. Sturdevant Developers didn't even know they existed."

Ben scowled. "Why in hell would a New Jersey supplier slip a snoop into Sturdevant's employment roster? What was she supposed to be doing?"

"Reporting on the effects of the goddam delays Sturdevant has been going through."

"Delays engineered by the Camden outfit?"

"Seems obvious. What threw Pris for a loop was their asking her about the impact of Max's kidnapping. How effective it's been in shutting down work completely."

"So this outfit over in Jersey is at the bottom of all the problems Sturdevant's been having? Who the hell are they? I assume she told you that."

"A and C is the corporate name. Stands for Amerman and Cassina, Building Suppliers. You realize Vinny Parson tried to educate us with his dying breath? We thought he was in wandering delirium, but he was trying to tell us who'd set him up."

"Jesus! 'Antsy' was 'A and C'!"

"Now you got it. The agent of Vinny's demise apparently came out of Camden."

"Why would a building supply company in Camden, New Jersey, be so concerned about a construction project in this neck of the woods that they'd kill off their own subversive implant?"

"You just hit on it, Ben."

"On what?"

"On the question all of us at Sturdevant are asking."

"For a starter then, what have you found out about—what in hell did you say it was? Amerman and Cassia?"

"Cassina. Amerman and Cassina. The Internet says they're both originally from Hardington."

"Aha!"

"Started small here, then moved to Camden, where they've built A and C into a multi-million-bucks building supply operation. The Internet has a whole lot on their Camden success. Damned little on their Hardington start-up. Nothing at all on any possible Keystone City tie-in."

Ben toyed with his coffee mug, a distant look on his broad face. Then he snapped back into focus. "I've checked you out."

"I'm sure you have."

"Marine Corps, then a cop's background with early retirement from the Philly department over some mix-up about bribery. What was that all about?"

I detailed it for him. "Not a proud moment," I wrapped it up, "but I did save a slightly bent cop who had taken a bullet to save this cop's life."

Ben gave me a long eye-to-eye check-out. Then he said, "Not an easy time for you."

"Or for the department. They approved my bailing out with a retirement parachute and a 'case closed.'"

"I can go along with that. So, let's progress." Ben took a bite of toast. "Hate doughnuts," he muttered. Chewed, swallowed. "With your background, I'll bet dollars to dough—I'll bet you've made some procedural hay up there in Sturdevant's offices. Tell me you've got yourself a double agent."

"Perceptive, Ben. Perceptive. At least Priscilla swears she will be."

"You trust her?"

"Ninety-nine percent...make that ninety-five percent."

"Why the five percent hold-out?"

"Because she was damned sharp at...uh, pumping me for info one dark and rainy evening. That was before Max's disappearance tilted her gyros into near collapse."

"Well, that's intriguing. What went on in the rainy dark?"

"Classified."

He gave me an oh-come-on-Rod look.

"Took place in my hotel room. 'Nuff said?"

"What was she after?"

"She saw through my 'historian' cover and suspected I'd been hired for more than company archiving. That was before Max's disappearance blew her into greater reality."

"Or so you hope."

"Ninety-five percent. Now Cliff and I are masterminding her reports to A and C, and she's relaying to us anything they tell her. So far, though, nothing she's gotten from them sheds any light on anything."

Without our asking, our wait person refilled our coffee mugs. Ben nodded thanks and took a long pull. Set the mug down, stared at the table then peered at me.

"Put your personal feelings for this woman aside for a minute. Can you *really* trust that remaining 'ninety-five percent'?"

"Fair—if persistent—question. Same one I keep asking myself. Point one: she gained nothing by telling us about her A and C spy status. In fact, she risked being fired by Sturdevant, which would have ended her value to A and C. Her coming clean could have cost her losing both jobs—and gaining nothing. Point two: she didn't come up with the double agent idea. Cliff and I did. Whatever that may lead to could be a lot more helpful to Sturdevant Developers than her former status. You with me?"

"No choice, I guess. But none of this gets us any closer to A and C's other much more dangerous rep—the guy who probably killed Vinny Parson. And now he's grabbed Max Sturdevant."

29

Barton Krag clicked off his room's TV, an out-of-date one with a picture tube. A last-century relic, not even close to the flat-screen one he had in his apartment back in Jersey. He pried the flip-top off his second beer of the morning and poured half a canful down his throat.

Another day to lie low. Snatching Max Sturdevant and locking him away had been one of the most—hell, *the* most exciting caper he'd ever pulled. But this sitting around for two nothing days was really getting to him.

Wonder how long old Max can hang in there eating PB and Js? Do I care? If he dies down in that cellar in a forgotten old house, nobody will ever...

Or might the FBI—TV says they're in it now—and that sure raises the stakes. Way up. Might they get the bright idea of a helicopter search? Could infra-red get through three stories of house to find a glow in that cellar?

Krag felt a grab in his gut. If I let him starve to death and he's found somehow, A and C will blow their tops. A murder rap for all three of us. Is Pennsylvania a death-sentence state? I could disappear, hole up in Canada or Mexico. But Amerman and Cassina—especially that hard-nosed Cassina—have a much bigger footprint than I got. The pair of them could bug out and leave me holding the bag.

He couldn't just sit here snorting beer, staring at the crappy little TV. Just sit here and stew. One thing for sure: he had to keep Sturdevant alive until he got some kind of word from A and C. Or until he figured a way out of this himself.

He tossed back the last few ounces and flipped the empty at the wastebasket. Missed. Let the maid pick it up. He jammed wallet and keys into his jeans' pockets and slammed out to his coal-black Ford.

First stop, a grocery store he hadn't been in before. Coupla oranges, coupla apples, package of sliced cheese, box of crackers. He checked out, carried the bag to the SUV and wondered why he'd cared at all about what he'd grabbed in his fast walk through the food aisles.

Now he found his search for a previously unvisited grocery store on this misty morning had gotten him lost. Took nearly twenty minutes to pick his way to Ash Street. At what was a memorable intersection with Maple — talk about returning to the scene of the crime — he turned into Maple and, a mile or so further, began the climb into the Poconos.

Now he was nervous about other traffic, specially a damned green Subaru that had hung on his tail for more than two miles. Krag slowed to thirty-five. The Subaru slowed with him. Was the guy unwilling to pass on this narrow road? Or was he actually following? Had all the damned city, county, state police and the FBI somehow figured *this* black SUV… Hell, the city was full of black SUVs. But Krag was shook. Couldn't deny it.

As he climbed the now-familiar long hill, he edged toward the roadside brushline. He slowed, lowered his window, and motioned for the guy behind him to pull on by. The Subaru slowed, then drifted past. The driver, a young blond woman wearing a bright red beret, waved her thanks and rammed in the gas. The car disappeared around a curve ahead.

As Krag steered back onto the pavement, he realized he'd passed the hidden access lane to the abandoned mansion. He squeezed around a U-turn, and it took him awhile to locate the lane from this direction.

Minutes later, he pulled up close to the front steps of the old house, grabbed his grocery bag and took a quick scan around. If anyone appeared, how would he explain showing up here with a bag of groceries?

"I was just passing by and this looks like a good place for a picnic."

Or, maybe, "I'm lost. Is this where the Smiths live?"

Hell, there'd be no good way to talk himself out of this. But the long-neglected surrounding woods were silent. No hunters or hikers. He climbed the marble steps, swung open the unlocked front door and strode down the hall. He fished the padlock key from his pocket, opened the lock, swung the hasp aside and pulled the door open.

Below, not a sound.

"Sturdevant!" he called.

No answer. Could the guy have starved to death already?

He took a step down. Another. Peered into the half-lit gloom of the two high-set windows. Didn't see Sturdevant anywhere. What the hell?

Four steps from the bottom, his right foot suddenly became entangled in something. He grabbed for the bannister. The grocery bag flew out of his grip. He pitched forward, tumbled down the last few steps and fell flat on his face.

As he struggled for breath, he heard shoes scrabble on the cellar's concrete floor. Somebody in a real hurry—Sturdevant! Raced from beneath the open-back stairs. Jumped over him. Grabbed for the railing. Son of a bitch had hid under the steps, Krag realized. Reached through, grabbed my foot as I came down. Now he was halfway up the steps, feet flying.

"No, you don't, dammit!" Krag bellowed. He shoved himself up, spun around and dived on the flailing shoes. He wrapped his arms around Sturdevant's legs. In his office-softened fifties, the guy was no match for Krag's 210 pounds of mostly muscle. Krag yanked him backwards down the steps.

He scrambled to his feet and pulled Sturdevant up. They faced each other, both of them gasping for breath. "What the hell do you think you're doing?" Krag snarled. He drew back his fist. He'd slam this guy flat. He'd pulverize him. He'd —

Sturdevant stood there, glared at him. Krag pumped his fist toward him. The guy didn't flinch. An out-of-shape desk jockey in his fifties, he didn't even blink. His eyes showed... determination.

Krag found himself doing something he'd never done before. He dropped his cocked arm to his side. Gave Sturdevant's shoulder a shove. "Pick up your friggin' groceries and get back in your damned corner."

"How about emptying the bucket?"

Only now did Krag sense the smell. "Get in the other corner. Stay there."

He picked up the bucket, climbed the steps, shut the door, hung the padlock in place without locking it and took the bucket outside.

He returned, repelled by having to do latrine duty, but aware he'd brought all this on himself.

After making sure Sturdevant still stood in the far corner — calmly chomping on an apple, for God's sake — Krag clumped back down and set the bucket in its corner with the other stuff. Still some water in one of the gallon containers. The second one was full. Couple of bread slices left of one loaf. The other not yet opened.

He climbed back up the steps, locked the door and walked to his SUV. He spun through a 180° turn-around then drove off, shaken. Not by his tumble down the steps. He found himself rattled to learn he had something that could screw up the rest of his life.

He had a conscience.

30

The *Hardington Times* building, a three-story granite fortress in the city's close-packed center, looked as if it had been designed to withstand World War II bombing attacks. But it had been built long before that big war, and before the previous one. *Established 1909* read an age-worn brass plate near the brass-and-glass entrance door. I grabbed the big handle, swung the door open and walked into a narrow lobby. Behind it, a wooden railing fenced off rows of desks, half of them occupied by, I assumed, reporters ranging from frantic to snoozing.

At the waist-high swinging gate access to this last-century bull pen sat a woman at least in her sixties. Her white hair fluffed around a not exactly welcoming gaze. A metal placard on the desk front offered INFORMATION. On the desktop, a nameplate ID'd the steely-eyed gazer: *Lucretia Dean.*

"'Morning, Ms. Dean. I'm Rod Montgomery, working with Sturdevant Developers."

Her lemon look told me I probably shouldn't have been so specific. Not everybody in town loved the new city project.

"And?" she prompted.

"I'd like to check on some possible stories twenty years ago — in the files in your morgue."

"Morgue? Good heavens, Mr. Montgomery. Newspapers haven't used that term in years." She nodded toward the lobby's left end. "Our *library* is that way. Downstairs. Miss Porter will give you some help."

My thanks got a look that seemed to say "Dumb furriner." I walked to the lobby's far end then trotted down the creaky steps.

Behind her *Ellen Porter* nameplate, a pretty but bleary-eyed redhead in her late teens looked up from the mound of newspapers on her worktable. In a dark green suit, she appeared dressed for something higher than basement filing.

"How can I help you, Mr. Montgomery?"

A basement psychic?

She chuckled at my expression. "Ms. Dean called me, said you were on the way. What dates are you looking for?"

"Roughly, about twelve, fifteen years ago."

"Uh oh."

"Uh oh?"

She waved an arm over the worktable. "I'm scanning all these old copies of the *Times* into our digital library. Hackers erased the digital files saved since the Internet age began, so this is my job." She gave me an eye-roll. "Don't ask me why they did it. Anyway, it puts money in my bank account. Working backwards from today, I've finished year twenty-ten. These piles on the table are twenty-oh-nine. You're talking about twenty-oh-two or so." She thumbed over her shoulder. "They're in those stacks back there."

Three-hundred-sixty-five papers a year, I thought. And she's only on—I craned forward—June 2009—heading backward.

In the room's ancient overhead incandescent she squinted at me. Poor kid. A mountain of papers still to process, and she looked exhausted already.

"How far back do those stacks go?"

"Only to nineteen-thirty-six. The big fire that year burned up everything before then."

"Still leaves you about seventy years' worth."

"Times three-hundred-sixty-five papers per year. I'd be a hunched-over old biddy. But this fall I'm escaping to Vassar."

"Good for you."

"Fifteen years ago, you said. If you want to go back to the early two-thousands, you'll find those papers in the second stack on the left."

I glanced at that formidable pile and figured I would still be leafing through newsprint by the time Keystone City was up and running. A hopeless hope, coming here at all.

"Specifically," Ellen said, "what are you looking for?"

"A company called A and C. Amerman and Cassina. Started here about twenty years ago, then moved to Camden, New Jersey."

"Amerman...Amerman. I remember my father talking about him."

"Your father knew him?"

"Dad was assistant manager at the airport. That's where they found Mary O'Brian's car. She was Amerman's secretary."

I felt a sense of... I wasn't quite sure what. "He knew Amerman?" I pressed.

"He knew *of* him."

"Could I possibly speak to your Dad?"

"Oh, I'm afraid he...passed last year."

"I'm sorry." In more ways than one. I let a moment go by. Then, "You remember anything he said about Mr. Amerman?"

"Not when it happened. I was only three that year. But I remember his talking about it years later—exactly ten years later. The *Times* did a ten-year anniversary feature on it. No doubt buried somewhere in that avalanche back there."

"Maybe you can save me from it. How much do you remember?"

"The company was involved in some kind of drywall thing. An overheard scandal to this thirteen-year-old lurking near the living room door. Mary O'Brian left the company and nobody had ever heard another word from her."

"Didn't Amerman try to find her?"

"The conversation I overheard was ten years after she ran off, so Dad was talking about a decade-old memory. They found her car in the airport parking lot. And that's where the trail stopped. Couldn't find a record of her flight out. Nobody knew which airline. And records weren't like they are now, with everybody suspected of carrying a bomb. 'So off she flew into the night,' I remember Dad saying. But nothing after that. She was from out of town. Had no family here."

She flipped me a really warm smile. "I think that's about what you would get from that pile back there, so I've just saved you weeks of paper paging."

Almost a come-on for lunch, but she was less than half my age.

"Tell you what," I said. "I'll put in a good word for you upstairs." I thanked her and left with a smile of my own.

Now for my next trick. I determined to try a little psychology...psychiatry? Well, something I'd read about somewhere. I drove back to the Maximall, elevated up to my temporary office and picked up the phone.

"Pris, I'd like to talk again with the woman who noticed Max and the driver of the black SUV in the parking lot the morning Max was grabbed. Millie, I think her name was."

"Millie Fleming, a temp in the blueprint room."

"That's the one. I'm wondering if she might have seen more than she realized."

"You're hopeful?"

"I'm desperate. She's the straw I'm grabbing at." I put down the phone and placed my two visitor chairs in front of the desk fairly close together, facing each other. Then I sat back behind the desk.

A few minutes later, Ms. Fleming appeared in my open doorway. Moderately tall, shoulder-length dark hair, white shirt, navy skirt—and apprehensive as hell.

"Mr. Montgomery?"

I stood and made a little show of walking from behind the desk. "Come on in, Millie." I indicated one of the chairs. With a puzzled frown, she perched on its edge and smoothed her skirt with nervous fingers—a temporary employee wondering why she was about to be chastened for she knew not what.

"Coffee? I can have Pris bring us—"

"No, thank you." She gave me an apprehensive why-am-I-here glance.

I eased into the other chair and offered a reassuring smile. "I want to thank you again, Millie, for your help on the morning Mr. Sturdevant disappeared." I was trying my good-cop best to put her at ease for my try at mind-probing. "Apparently, you were the only person out there who noticed what was happening."

"I'm glad I could help. I wish I could have done more."

"I think you might be able to, Millie. That's why I wanted to talk to you this morning."

Another puzzled frown. "I told you and Mr. Cliff Sturdevant everything I saw. I'm sorry it wasn't much."

"People often see more than they remember. And I'd like to try something—" Oops, wrong words. She gave me a startled look. I raised a dismissive hand. "Only a sort of memory review. All you do is close your eyes, concentrate on what you saw that morning. Try to put everything else out of your mind. Focus on the two men between their cars."

"That's why I'm here?"

"That's it. Eyes closed now, Millie. Visualize the two men...the cars...one parked nose-in—"

"The other one with its front pointing out," she murmured. "Mr. Sturdevant, standing by his car. The other man...big man. With a cap."

"Can you see what's printed on the cap?"

"Too far away." Eyes still closed, she rested an elbow on the chair arm and lowered her chin into cupped fingers.

"Black SUV," I prompted.

"Yes. He backed in, so all I see are his head and shoulders behind the open driver's door. Big man…big man…"

"Anything else you might remember? Anything at all?"

"I'm sorry. Only the two cars. One pointing in, the other pointing out. License plates…"

"License *plates*? One on the *front* of the black SUV?"

"Yes. Not a Pennsylvania one. Different color. Sort of tan, I think."

"Can you read the numbers?"

"Too far away."

"Anything more? Anything at all."

She opened her eyes and slowly shook her head. "I'm really sorry I haven't been of more help."

"You have added something to what you saw."

"Oh, the license plates. Sorry I couldn't read the one on the SUV."

"Helpful just the same, Millie, and I thank you." I didn't tell her how helpful because I didn't want that to become public knowledge.

"Please shut the door behind you, Millie," I said as she walked out. I reached for my cell phone.

31

I tapped in County Sheriff Sergeant Ben Stoddard's cell number. Got a "Call you back in a sec." A two-minute-long "sec" later: "Just handed a ticket to a teen driver exceeding seventy in a fifty-five zone. Not a whiff of responsibility. Got a future as a statistic. Oh, well...I was about to call you, but go ahead. Whatchu got?"

"Just talked again with our only known eye-witness to the parking lot grab. This time she remembered something more. The black SUV had a front license plate. Tan, she thought. Any help there? Not many states still issue front plates."

"Tan, she thought? Could be New York. Or could be New Jersey—theirs are a kind of subdued yellow. Could've looked light tan from a distance on a cloudy morning."

"Should be of some help. There can't be too many black SUVs in town with Jersey plates."

"Correct, Rod. I'll add that to the APB."

"Wonder why he didn't cover himself with a stolen Pennsylvania plate? Vinny Parson thought of that."

"Lot of good it did him. He ended up a victim of overconfidence. That's apparently why whoever sent him here had to send somebody else to get him out of the picture."

"So now we're looking for a guy who's got a case of overconfidence himself. Could be an asset for us. You said you were about to call me, Ben. What was that about?"

"Got word in a roundabout way that the FBI visited the A and C Company over in Camden. Talked with the owners — Amerman and Cassi-something — "

"Cassina."

"You already heard?"

"I know they're apparently involved."

"Yeah, but they told the FBI they aren't. Said Parson was a disgruntled former employee who held a grudge and apparently cooked up all the sabotage efforts to make A and C look bad. As for Priscilla Killian, your friendly executive assistant, Amerman said the same thing about her. If he's anywhere near the truth, A and C must be one bitch of a company to work for."

"You're not swallowing all that?"

"Hell, no. Neither is the FBI. A and C has to be in this thing up to their butts. Trouble is none of us — city, county, state, FBI, and you — can figure out why. But with all that involvement, someone's bound to come up with the answer."

"Let's hope," I said. "I'll stay in touch." I clicked off, stood, and walked to open my unusually closed door. There stood Cliff, fist raised. About to knock.

"Time for an update, Rod. The pressure is really getting to me." He walked in, took one of my hard-back visitor chairs.

Sitting upright in my desk swivel, I took a good look at him. His mustard blond buzz cut needed a trim. His usual brink-of-a joke expression had been wiped away by dark patches under tired eyes and clenched-teeth grimness.

"I gather I'm looking at a tired man," I said.

"Tired, desperate and disillusioned, Rod. I'd never say this to anybody else here, but I trust you to keep it to yourself. When Max was in the pilot's seat, I admit I envied him. Basking in accomplishment, I thought, in not-too-brotherly moments. But now that I've got his seat, I'm burning up with frustration." He slapped his empty shirt pocket. "Damn! You have a cigarette? Forgot mine."

"Sorry. I don't smoke. Didn't know you did."

"I didn't, until all this Keystone crap fell in on me. Just got a call from Marlin Majeski, president of Susquehanna Contractors. He's pissed at the delay. Says he's had a major commitment of men and equipment on the Town Center site, sitting there waiting for my go-ahead. Says it's getting close to the default clause in the contract. He's threatening to pull out and take on a major contract down in Allentown."

"Not good."

Cliff threw his hands up in frustration. "With Max locked up somewhere and everything on hold, I told him he could pull his men off the site but give us a few days before doing anything more. Problem is, none of this makes any damned sense. Why in hell does some building supply company in New Jersey get into sabotage and now *kidnapping* to stall a new city project here? So far, two guys have died in accidents—"

"We think Parson was murdered, Cliff."

"Jesus! That makes things even worse. And God knows where my brother is or how he is." His voice shook. "Or even *if* he is."

"He'd be no use to them if they—"

"But how do we know he hasn't already been...put out of the way? The kidnapper could keep on threatening. We wouldn't know Max was already...gone."

I shook my head and hoped I could sound convincing. "I can't see any advantage in...uh, what you're thinking, compared to just keeping Max holed up somewhere until A and C accomplish whatever they're taking all these risks for."

Hell, that didn't even convince me.

"I hope you're right." But his voice was flat.

"Some possibly good news," I said quickly. "Before you came in, my County Sheriff contact told me the FBI has paid a visit to Camden. A and C claimed ignorance of what's happened here, but now they know the cold eyes of the Feds are peering at them. That should sober them up plenty."

"Hope so." But his tone stayed flat.

"Another possibly good thing. This morning, I talked with Millie Fleming again."

"Who?"

"She's the temp in your blueprint room. Only eyewitness we've got who saw Max with the guy in the parking lot."

"Oh. Yeah, I remember."

"Well, she remembered something more. The SUV Max was piled into had a front license plate—probably New Jersey, according to my county cop contact. So, they're able to narrow the search."

***

Jesus! Barton Krag slumped on his unmade East End Economy Court bed. Same old mid-morning crap on the rotten little TV. Dumb-ass political jabberjaw. Women's stuff. Health scares. Fuzzy on-air broadcast! Hasn't this place heard of cable? At least cable could offer an old movie. He resisted his impulse to chuck something at the babbling political babe. Only interesting thing about her was an insistent strand of blond hair she kept brushing back from her left eye.

His irritation with the draggy programming wasn't Krag's most pressing problem. What truly bugged him this dull morning was...nothing. Nothing at all to do. He had taken care of the problem A and C had sent him here to handle: shut down, or at least seriously delay the Keystone City project. Done that. So now here he sprawled, doing what bugged him like nothing else: doing nothing.

Maybe check on Max again? Krag had to admit he was still...uh, kind of rattled from that trip to the old mansion two days ago. He'd come away with the unsettling feeling Max had "won." A feeling he damned sure couldn't shake lying here on the unmade bed, soaking up nothing-TV.

Gotta *do* something. He pushed to his feet and snapped the damned thing off.

Something like maybe an "inspection" trip? Make sure Sturdevant Developers were sticking to A and C's demand to stop all work. Yeah, that'd be something he could report on. Give him a boost with Camden. He grabbed wallet and keys, stepped out and boarded his Ford Escape. Yeah, an escape from boredom.

Fifteen minutes later, he climbed the road past the Maximall, picked up to forty-five when it leveled out. As he neared the Y-intersection, he slowed down to take a good look at the Town Center construction site a couple hundred yards north. Not a sign of activity. Near the half-built foundation wall, a crane's upraised clam-shell hung motionless against the forest greenery beyond. The site was abandoned. For how long? Krag wondered. Did A and C expect him to keep Sturdevant in that cellar indefinitely? Gotta be some kind of delaying thing? But how long? And what the hell for?

He shrugged. Might as well take the whole tour. Maybe some Sturdevant bright-eyes think nobody will check beyond here. They could be building a whole new town up ahead.

He gunned into the left fork. Sailed past the Lake Linden access road. Not another car anywhere. Rolled north then around the eastward curve. Passed Susquehanna Contractors' motor pool sheds. Not a sign of life there, either. All closed up, except for a car in front of the office shack. Some workaholic doing shutdown paperwork?

A couple miles beyond the last curve, he raced past that big, isolated house where the stubborn won't-move-out guy still hung on. His car was parked out front. Gotta be lonely as hell out here.

Headed back south with only a few more miles to the Y-intersection, he still saw no sign of any construction work. He began to shape up his report to Camden. *Made a check ride around the whole project area. Not a sign of activity anywhere. How long should I —*

He craned forward. What the hell? A quarter mile ahead, a truck loaded with tree limbs had rolled onto the road.

Trees? As he neared the truck's exit point, he slowed, pulled to the shoulder and peered toward the woods. Two more trucks back in there. And a crane. Looked like a dozen guys working hard. Already had a couple acres open. Hell, they're clearing out the woods! Bastards! They'd stopped work on the Town Center building, but they were clearing away the woods behind it. Getting ready to build the whole Town Center area's shops and offices?

Amerman and Cassina will go ape over this. Krag rushed back to the Snooze Inn, parked, trotted to his room and yanked out his cell phone.

"They're cheating on you," he blurted to Amerman. "They quit work on the first Town Center building, but they're clearing the woods for the whole damned thing."

"You heard that?"

"I drove up there. I *saw* that."

Amerman exploded. "GOD DAMN IT! You better find a way to stop ALL work. You hear me! ALL work. Or you'll be looking over your shoulder from now on. You got that?"

Krag got that, all right. But he was already ahead of Amerman.

Max had a brother.

32

Harvey Amerman slammed down the receiver of his office phone. First call of the morning and it had been a chiller.

"Just took a tour around the Keystone set-up," Krag's aggressive voice boomed.

Set up. Amerman winced. "And?" he prompted.

"Nothing going on...there."

Did that little hesitation mean something? Amerman held his breath.

"So I drove on around. 'Cept for a car parked in front of the office, the motor pool looked shut down. Nothing else going on 'til I got back to the east side of the woods."

"The woods?"

"Yeah, the woods where the rest of the Town Center is gonna go, according to the newspapers here."

"What about the woods?"

"Looked like they're clearing it out."

Amerman felt a hot wave of panic then cold fury. *"Goddamit, Krag!* I told you to find a way to stop work on Keystone. That means *all* work. You find a way to stop that damned woods clearing, too. And quick. You got that?" Jesus God! All this was getting way out of hand.

"Got it," Krag rapped. "I'm already working on it."

Amerman took two long breaths. "I'm still counting on you, Barton. All work's gotta stop." Long enough to get us outta here, Amerman hoped. "Find a way."

He had hung up, banged his chunky fist on the desktop and fired up his third cigarette of the morning. Krag tells 'em to quit all work, and they're clearing the damn woods. That's done it. He grabbed the phone again and stabbed in Cassina's extension.

"Yeah?" Damned partner's typical tone of bored annoyance.

"We gotta leave, Mateo."

"I know that. What're you—"

"I mean we gotta leave ASAP."

"Wait a minute, Harve. You know damn well we're still in negotiation with Garden State Suppliers. Hangin' tight at eight mil now, with them still offering only six."

"I want you to call Ketchem right now. Tell him to notify Garden State that we'll take their offer of six."

"What the hell, Harve? What's happened?"

"Krag just called. Says they've stopped work on the Town Center Building, but now they're clearing the area behind it."

"The woods?"

"Yeah, the woods. I told Krag to delay 'em for another week. But we gotta be long gone before that. Call Ezra Ketchem right now. Tell our plodding legal eagle to contact Garden State and tell them we'll take the six mil, and make sure they transfer it to our Cayman account today."

"Jesus! We need that kind of a rush?"

"If we're going to have any kind of safety factor, we have to move fast. Call Ketchem *now!*"

"Will do."

"And call me back as soon as you do it."

Amerman took a long drag on his barely-smoked cigarette, stubbed it out, fired up another. Tapped his chair arms with nervous fingers. Christ! Just when you think you've got the lid on and the heat turned down, the damned pot begins to boil over.

He pulled out yet another cigarette then realized he already had one clamped between cold lips. Shoved the pack back in his shirt pocket. Started to swivel toward his view of the river —

His phone jangled. Cassina back already? "Yeah, Mateo. Tell me Garden State's already transferring the six mil — "

"Wish I could."

Ice rippled down Amerman's spine. "What are you telling me?"

"I'm telling you what our ambulance chaser just told me." Mateo Cassini's voice sounded tight with apprehension. Not reassuring at all.

"What's — " Amerman's voice faltered. He took a quick breath. "What's going on, Mateo?" A near whisper.

"I better come up there."

They'd agreed to Garden State's low bid. What could possibly go wrong at this point? Amerman yanked out a rumpled handkerchief and dabbed his forehead. He heard a pattering behind him. Swung around. His grand view of the Delaware River had faded in the gloom of a rain squall. He felt his stomach tighten. Screw that. He didn't believe in omens. That was for —

His door banged open. Cassina barged in, strode straight to the desk. Slapped down his bony hands and leaned his squint-eyed, pointed-chin face too damned close.

"What the hell?" Amerman blurted. "If Ezra Ketchem has blown this, we can hire another law firm in two minutes. You tell him that?"

"I told him nothing. He told me."

"Told you what?"

"Told me about Spencer Coates."

"The president of Garden State Suppliers? What about him?"

"He's had a heart attack. He's in the hospital up in Trenton. Happened during a conference up there."

"Good God! A freakin' *heart attack?*" Amerman felt his own heart thud. He pressed his palm against his chest. "I might be joining him." He nodded toward a pitcher on the cabinet near the door. "Glass of water, Mateo." He forced his breathing to slow down.

Cassina handed him the water. He took a couple of quick swallows. Sat back and blew out a long breath.

"Any idea how long it'll be before we can tell Coates we'll take the six million? We gotta get the hell out of here, Mateo!"

"I asked that. They have no idea."

"How about somebody else at Garden State? Vice-president? Treasurer, maybe?"

"Asked that, too." Cassina shrugged. "They told me it's gotta be Spencer Coates. Maybe it's not as bad as you think. If Krag can come up with another delay—"

"Look, dammit. When Keystone was a general threat, a general delay made sense. Now they're down to specifics— the whole Town Center including clearance of the woods. Krag got work on the building stopped. But they're still at it in the woods."

"I know, I know. You keep telling me. And you said you ordered Krag to find a way to stop that, too."

"Long enough for us to get outta here the minute Garden State confirms our taking their six mil offer and wires the damned money to Cayman."

"And they won't do that without Coates's say so? Jesus!"

Amerman slumped in his chair, scowled at his partner. "You packed? Ready to get out of here in a rush?"

"Yes, Harve. Carry-on in my office closet. Cripes, calm down."

"Calm down? *Listen* to me. If we don't get out of here pretty damned quick, we'll never get out. But if we leave without that six mil available, we'll end up as Samoan beach bums begging for handouts. We gotta get outta here pronto. Unless we're lucky as hell, our sky's gonna fall right on top of us."

33

In a remote corner of the East End Economy Court's parking lot, Krag sat rock rigid in his black SUV. He stared at the cell phone in his hand. Amerman had actually *threatened* him! Nobody had ever done that to Barton Krag.

He shoved the cell back in the pocket of his plaid shirt and scowled into the fading afternoon sunlight. What the hell had lit Amerman's fuse now? he wondered. A and C sent him here to get increasingly careless Vinny Parson "out of the picture." Which he had done with slick, if brutal, efficiency. Parson's assignment had been to slow down progress. Then, with the first building actually under construction, A and C demanded "all construction" halted. Krag's Max-in-the-cellar inspiration had done that. But now Amerman had gone bonkers over the clearing of the woods. What in hell could the woods have to do with anything?

His was not to reason why, so Krag pondered on prospective MOs. Force Max to use my cell phone? Tell them that unless they get out of the woods... But would that sound like a real threat or a sort of feeble P.S? "By the way, quit work in the woods, too." Nowhere near enough punch.

So, it's gotta be Cliff Sturdevant, the brother he'd read about in the *Hardington Times*. Grab him in the parking lot? Could be risky as hell now. They gotta be a lot more alert after he'd grabbed Max there. Take Cliff on his way home from work? Take him up to the old mansion...Both of them in that cellar?

Krag thumped the steering wheel with a chunky fist. Flexed his arm muscles. Forced himself to think, dammit. Think! Two brothers up there. Two desperate guys and him with only a knife. Could be tricky to handle. Maybe too tricky. So where in hell could he stash Cliff?

Or was this idea too full of holes to work? Cliff's picture never appeared in the paper, so Krag didn't even know what Cliff Sturdevant looked like.

Did he have a reserved space in the Maximall's parking area? A space with his name on it?

Krag checked his watch. Ten after six. The Sturdevant people had to be out of there by now, the parking lot occupied only with evening shoppers. He fired up the Ford, shifted into drive, and eased out of the lot into sparse northbound traffic.

Fifteen minutes later, he turned left off the Keystone-bound road to roll into the Maximall's largely empty parking expanse. As he'd hoped, the row of spaces marked for Sturdevant brass was empty. Hard to read the names in the lowering sun's glare.

He turned into the front row access lane, rolled along slowly, reading the names stenciled on the concrete headers. There it was, the third space to the left of the mall's main entrance: C. STURDEVANT.

At the far end of the front row, Krag 180'd left into the next access lane and headed back to the road into town. Next move: Be there tomorrow before nine to get a look at Cliff Sturdevant as he pulled into his space. Beyond that, Krag knew, with his palms slippery on the wheel: I gotta have a real plan on where to stash the guy.

***

The next morning Krag suddenly realized the ominous demand from Amerman had blown responsibility for Max right out of his mind. For three days Krag hadn't driven into the Poconos foothills to check on his prisoner. Surely the guy needed more water, and the cans from the last trip, the baked beans, corn, peas, and the package of sliced salami had to be empty by now. He'd felt a little twinge when he handed over the plastic spoon he'd kept from the previous night's supper at McDonald's, and the can opener he'd bought at Broadbent's Hardware. Could a really desperate guy kill you with a can opener? He'd have to keep a closer eye on seemingly compliant Max. Then, of course, there was the friggin' bucket. This job of jailer had turned into a real drag. He'd pictured himself as a stern warden, but now he felt trapped by the responsibilities of a goddam nanny.

No way around it. He had to find another obscure ma-and-pa grocery, buy up Max's resupply. Second thing tomorrow. First thing: before nine tomorrow morning, the beginning of the Sturdevant workday, he'd show up at the mall to get a look at Cliff.

***

At 8:40 a.m., Krag pulled into the third row from the mall entrance and parked nose-in, facing C. Sturdevant's reserved slot. No car there yet. Krag settled low in his seat. No cap on this time. He'd quit shaving his scalp and already wore a quarter-inch dark fuzz; yet another "look," though he hoped to be unnoticed sitting here while cars pulled in and Sturdevant employees strolled toward the mall entrance.

By 8:50, brother Cliff had not yet arrived. He was not the early-bird Max had been. Or was Cliff keeping an appointment somewhere in town? Out of town? Sick at home?

Am I wasting my time with this ID part, Krag wondered? He'd considered using the same knife-threat procedure that had so neatly nabbed Max in less than a minute. But now they must have tightened parking lot security. No patrols in sight, but there could be a guy up at a second-floor window with binocs. Possibly a car or a couple of cars with their drivers sitting and watchful, like him, but for a different purpose.

At 9:05, a silver-gray Corvette had turned into the front row access lane, slowed then pulled into Cliff's reserved space. The driver stepped out, pressed something in his hand. Krag heard the door lock beep. He watched Cliff Sturdevant stroll toward the mall entrance. Medium-size guy with a sandy brush cut, rust-colored slacks, short-sleeved tan shirt. Not exactly top executive garb, like his brother's dark coat-and-tie. Cliff wore the rig of a guy protesting office conformity—a guy who could be much more of a problem to snatch.

Okay. So now Krag knew what Cliff Sturdevant looked like. Next problem: how to grab him. And the problem after that: where to put him. First, though, he had to get some stuff up to Max before the guy starved to death. A body in that cellar would send Krag out of here fast. West. A thousand miles from any connection with A and C. And off their generous but dangerous payroll. He started his Ford, backed out of the space and headed down into Hardington.

At The Korner Grocer, a seedy looking little store at Vine and Oak, Krag grabbed two cans each of baked beans, peas and—give the guy a little variety—a couple cans of stewed tomatoes. Throw in a package of sliced ham. Loaf of bread. Add two gallon jugs of water. He checked out and drove on across town.

At the all-too-familiar Ash and Maple intersection, he turned south. Then up the hill into the Poconos. Almost a mile of scattered houses, then the empty stretch to the old abandoned driveway. Harder to find since he'd gotten rid of that battered long-forgotten sign. He checked ahead and behind. No car in sight. He spotted the hemlocks, slowed, turned into them, and bounced into the rutted lane. A few minutes later, he pulled up in front of the deteriorating old mansion.

He lugged the grocery bag and the two gallons of water— Jesus, they're heavy—up the steps then down the musty hall to the kitchen. The lock on the cellar door was still in place. As if he'd expected otherwise. He set down the bag and bottles, fished out the padlock key. Swung the door open.

"Sturdevant?"

No answer.

He picked up bag and jugs, took four steps down and stopped. "Don't try your little trick again, Max." He peered into the gloomy light from the two small windows. Made out Sturdevant slumped on the blanket in the corner under the west window. Was the guy still alive? Then Max raised his head and glared at him.

Krag stepped on down and set the food and water in the east corner beside the growing pile of discarded cans, water jugs and food wrappings — and the damned bucket.

Latrine duty again. He lugged the bucket upstairs, swung the hasp in place and hung in the padlock. Leaving it unlocked, he emptied the bucket in the weeds out front, clumped back in and down.

"How long—" Max rasped then cleared his throat. "How long do you plan to keep me in this dungeon?"

Surprised at Max's strong voice, Krag muttered, "Not up to me." He set down the bucket.

"What the hell does that mean?"

"Just shut up, will you?" Talking to his captive made Krag uneasy. He always felt this way talking to people he figured were a lot smarter than he was. But with corporate president Max hunched on the concrete floor and Krag standing over him...

"Your company's cheating, Sturdevant."

"What's that mean?"

"That means you're here until they quit clearing the woods."

Max scowled. "The woods? What the hell difference can the woods make?"

"That's what I wonder, too." Bad move, Krag realized. He'd just said something in common with his prisoner.

"So?" Max prompted.

"So shut up!" Krag jabbed his thumb toward the other corner. "Have a drink, damn it. I'm getting tired of playing water boy." Telling Max how he felt? Another slip.

The prisoner struggled to his feet. "And if they don't quit work on the woods?"

"Just shut up, will you? I only do what I'm told."

"By whom?"

"Go eat your lunch, Sturdevant." With that, Krag pounded back up the steps, locked the door and walked back to his car.

How long? He hated this as much as Max did. He stuck the ignition key in place. Then he sat back. God Almighty. This was really getting to *him*. And it was his idea. All this work, the risk. And now whatever he did with Cliff would make it worse. Much worse.

Maybe...

He slipped his cell out of his shirt pocket. Maybe a really hard-nosed reminder of Max's situation could be as effective as adding Cliff to his high-risk collection of captive dependents. One is a real pain in the ass to handle. Two would really —

He thumbed the phone. Waited...

"Sturdevant Developers." A female voice. "How may I help you?"

"*You tell them if they don't quit work in the woods —* " His voice cracked. What in hell was he doing? That had sounded last-ditch-feeble, even to him. He clicked off. Stick to the plan, he told himself. Good advice, he thought. If he had a plan. He was back to square one: snatch Cliff Sturdevant.

34

Another day of wondering what the hell I was doing to justify my "detecting" fee. The high point, and that happened days ago, had to be the car chase from the chaotic Town Center groundbreaking ceremony. Not its near miss of grabbing saboteur Vinny Parson. The big benefit of that ineffective pursuit turned out to be my helpful and continuing access to the County Sheriff's Sergeant Ben Stoddard. Without Ben's —

The phone in my borrowed office derailed my nearly stalled train of thought.

"Cliff, Rod. Need you in Max's office." He hung up. Not at all like the light-hearted Cliff I'd known before Max's kidnapping. Cliff had taken over the Sturdevant reins, but he was a distracted driver. Max had been out of the picture for almost a week, and the strain had changed Cliff's attitude from near-collegiate enthusiasm to glum worry.

I trotted up to Max's office and my guilty feeling of frustration came with me. I wondered if this might be the moment I would be told my currently ineffective services were "no longer needed."

As I stepped into Pris's little anteroom, she and Cliff broke off their conversation.

Cliff nodded a non-committal greeting. "I want you to listen to this," he said. "Just came in. It was recorded, like all calls to Max's office."

He turned to Pris, seated behind her desk with her hand on the call recorder. "Play it."

She pressed replay. "You tell them if they don't quit work in the woods—"

"That's it?"

Cliff shrugged. "That's it, Rod."

"Either he got cut off somehow," I guessed, "or he changed his mind. Sounds like the same guy who phoned in the threat after Max disappeared."

"Why could he possibly be concerned about the woods?" Cliff wondered.

"He could have been concerned about something else," I suggested, "by the sudden thought that cell phone calls to this number might be traced. And they can be traced, I'm told, by that FBI van down in the parking lot."

Cliff took a deep breath then let it out in a rush. "Let's hope so. I'm just about done in by all this."

"I'll call my County Sheriff contact. Let you know as soon as I know."

"Good."

That single word was the only positive note I'd heard from Cliff since Max had been abducted. Back in my office, I called Stoddard on my cell.

"I know what you're about to ask me," Ben said before I could say anything. "And yes, the FBI picked up that cell phone blurt and determined it came off the relay tower south of the city. So it could have come from almost half of Hardington and a lot of the northern Poconos."

"Well, that sure narrows it down."

"Yeah, only a few hundred square miles. But the FBI guys are as frustrated as we all are. They're sending a couple cars into that area for what it's worth. Between us, I don't think it's worth much. But keep in touch."

"You'll have to fight me off, Ben."

I clicked out, switched to the office phone, and called Cliff.

"They've traced the call down to half of Hardington," I told him, "and the adjacent Pocono area. They'll cruise around looking for likely locations, but don't get your hopes up too high. It might be only the first step on a long staircase. I'll keep in close touch with Sergeant Stoddard and you."

I hung up and swung around to stare out my window... Jeez! No, not that again. I pushed out of the chair and walked back to Pris's little cubby.

"Some semi-good news," I told her. "The FBI has traced the tower that relayed the call. It's in the north part of the Poconos. In fact, on a clear day and with the help of binoculars, you can probably see it from here."

"So, they know—"

"I think they assume what we've already assumed. Max's kidnapper is somewhere in or near the city, despite the out-of-state plates on his car."

"Or in the Poconos," she said.

"True. But that cut-off call has told us something else we didn't know. Sturdevant's clearing the woods up there has really lit someone's fuse—at least, Max's kidnapper's fuse. And he's obviously working for A and C. So the question is: What the hell is it about the woods that's got them in an uproar now?"

"And you, too, Rod."

"My problem... Yeah, my basic problem is a guilty conscience over how little I've been able to do that's of real value."

"Coffee."

"No, th—"

"That's not a question, Rod. It's an order." She stood and stepped around her desk. "We're going into Max's office.

I've got his coffee machine going, and you need to get less emotional and more analytical."

"Oh, come on, Pris. I think you're—"

In the doorway to Max's inner sanctum, she turned back. Even with showing the strain we all felt, she was a striking woman. Tall, slender, with her hazel eyes crinkled in a little smile that offset the stick-to-business effect of her gray pants suit.

"You think I'm...what, Rod?"

"Reading too much into my little outburst."

"No, I think you are underrating yourself."

"Hard not to. I'm hired to find out who is sabotaging the Keystone project—and why. Now we do know who, but—"

"Something about the woods might tell us why. I'd say you're more than halfway to the answer." She stepped behind Max's impressive desk, poured and handed me a steaming mug. "Drink up," she said. "And calm down."

"Good advice, but I can comply with only half of it."

***

Krag pulled his black SUV into the parking area flanking a strip mall on Hardington's north side. He shut off the engine and sat staring at the yellow front of the Savings Mart without seeing it.

Then he pounded the steering wheel with both fists. He'd never felt so frustrated. The problem he wrestled with now was not grabbing Cliff. He'd worked out a couple of low-risk ways to get that done. The big challenge was where to put him. Krag had come up with nothing even close to the advantages of the old mansion.

...The old mansion. Perfect for holding Max. But two desperate captives down in the cellar could be more than he wanted to handle. Yet the old abandoned house was a perfect location.

Another room there for Cliff? He and Max would be separated, but in the same location. Easy to handle, convenient, and well-concealed. Then his elation faded as fast as it had bloomed. All the rooms on both the first and second floors had big, bright windows. Too easy to see into or break out of. There had to be some —

Krag slapped his forehead. Got it! The walk-in closet in the master bedroom. Big enough to park a limo in. Perfect.

Step one: same as when he'd made the cellar ready. Put a padlock on the closet door.

He scanned the strip's storefronts. No help here, of course. That would be too easy. He backed out of the parking slot, drove into Larch Street and spent twenty minutes searching for a hardware store. Found one conveniently on the south side of town.

Fifteen minutes later, with padlock, hasp assembly and screws in a bag, and his screwdriver in the dash compartment, he turned into Maple Street and headed for the climb into the Poconos.

The mid-afternoon sky was darkening. At 3:30 p.m.? He peered upward. Clouds moving in. Dark as charcoal. Gonna rain.

The road ascended past the several set-back houses. He'd never seen activity at any of them, but today cars were parked in the well-kept drives of two.

As he neared the hidden lane, he checked ahead and behind. Then he pulled off the road and bumped down the slight grade to the mansion. Every time he'd arrived here, he'd held his breath. The presence of another car would be an alarm as shocking as a siren. But the parking area in front of the mansion was reassuringly empty.

He parked, grabbed his hardware bag, climbed the front steps, pushed through the unlocked front door. Halfway down the hall, he wondered what Max might make of footsteps overhead but not to the cellar door. Hell, let him wonder. Break the monotony.

He mounted the broad staircase to the second floor. Up here, he turned left and walked down the dark hallway to the master bedroom. He remembered it as an unusually large room with big windows, bright with sunlight when he'd first checked out this upper floor. But with the overcast outside darkening, the room was cheerless now. As he set down his hardware bag, the silence gave way to a pattering sound. Rain had begun to spatter the north side picture window.

He opened the closet door, peered in. Lots of empty shelves. A built-in light overhead, but electric service had long ago been discontinued.

He lifted out the hasp and screws, pulled the screwdriver from his belt, and got to work. Fifteen minutes later, he had converted what had once been a luxury closet into what was about to be a dismal and totally lightless prison cell.

Krag left the padlock hanging open on the hasp. He added the key to his key chain, carried the screwdriver and empty bag downstairs, then plodded through the long, echoing hallway to the front door. The light rain shower had stopped. The afternoon air felt comfortably cool and damp. Lots of clouds, but that had been only a flurry.

He stepped into the SUV, swung it around then drove slowly up the long, overgrown lane toward the mountain road. A sudden flare of sunlight brightened the soggy dirt driveway. An omen? He didn't believe in omens—unless they were good ones.

As usual, he stopped a hundred feet from the county road. Still hidden in the lane's overgrowth, he cut the engine and listened. Not a sound of traffic out there.

He started the Ford again and pulled onto the two-lane macadam road. Time for details now. Time to stop *all* work on Keystone City. He grinned in satisfaction at having come up with a plan that would have stumped anyone else A and C might have sent here.

He was unaware he had just made a potentially disastrous mistake.

35

"They interviewed everybody on that road into the Poconos, Rod. And they learned nothing."

That had been Ben Stoddard's "courtesy call" this morning, and maybe his way of venting some of the frustration we all felt. The FBI's tracing the south tower as the relay point of that blurted cell phone call had seemed a sure giveaway. But that "giveaway" took in a whole lot of territory.

I scanned the map of Hardington and environs I'd spread over my desk, a more constructive non-activity than gazing into the parking lot. If I were the guy who'd snatched Max, where would I have put him? The congested City of Hardington spread across the whole valley. Heavily-traveled Interstate 81 crossed the valley north-south. North of Hardington, two county roads accessed open country—farmland, with property owners acutely aware of what went on in their properties. What were the chances of finding a secure place out there to imprison a kidnap victim? Not so good, I thought. And presumably the FBI thought likewise.

So they looked at the other side of the valley, along the lone county road winding south into the Poconos. Logical. But according to Ben, they found nothing.

I knew I was looking for a reason to get off my butt and do something my conscience would let me call "positive effort." Ben had said the FBI concentrated on interviewing residents along that road. How far into the Poconos' rolling hills had they driven?

I folded the map, stuck it in my pocket and headed for my Jeep. The morning's bright sun had given way to early afternoon's increasing cloud cover. By the time I reached the Ash and Maple intersection and turned south on Maple, the murky overcast threatened rain. I gunned my rented Jeep up the long slope past the scatter of houses the FBI had no doubt already checked, topped the long climb a couple miles farther on, and wound into the rolling, densely forested hills of the northern Poconos.

I checked both sides of the road, looking for anything that could hide a kidnap victim. A few miles later, a framework tower loomed over the treetops ahead. Had to be the tower that relayed that fragmented cell phone call.

Rain began to spatter the windshield. I flipped on the wipers and drove deeper into the Pennsylvania wilds.

And found—nothing. Not a house nor a building of any sort. Only trees...trees...trees. All I'd gotten from this check drive into the forest was a stiff neck. I was getting nowhere in the middle of nowhere. A few miles past the relay tower, I turned around in the empty road and headed back toward Hardington. The brief rain had stopped, but my frustration persisted.

From all the scanning back and forth, my neck ached. Now I kept my eyes on the road. As I coasted down the hill leading back into Hardington, the sun managed to flare briefly between the overcast's breaking clouds. That was the only bright moment of this day, another day of—

I rammed down the brake pedal. The Jeep juddered to a stop. Had I seen what I thought I saw?

I levered into reverse, opened my side window. Steering with my right hand, I stuck my head out and kept my eyes on the damp pavement.

Yeah! There they were: brief arcs of faintly muddy tire tracks. Too intent on peering for buildings, had I missed these tracks on the way up? More likely, they were made following that rain flurry after I'd passed.

The brief tire marks emerged from the left, the overgrown west side of the road, curved downhill and faded out. I studied the roadside tangle where the tracks emerged. Yep, I spotted a barely noticeable break in the brush line, weed-choked and obscured by low-hanging hemlock branches.

I spun the wheel left, then eased forward through the hidden break. Past the obscuring hemlocks, I bumped along a gently descending dirt lane, somewhat softened by the recent rainfall, and marked with the tracks made by the exiting vehicle. I eased down a long-neglected stretch of packed earth with occasional flat stones. Four or five hundred yards in, the lane veered left around a stand of towering maples, then right, to continue downslope.

I realized this had been a driveway. At its end loomed a huge two-story frame-and-stone house. A mansion. Down in a hollow? No wonder it had been passed by.

After the oddly-inspired original owner passed on, I figured, the place became a Realtor's nightmare. Location, location. A house like this one should be on a hilltop.

But the big question kept my foot on the brakes. Was Max down there—and was he alone? Plus another big question: could his kidnapper be down there with him, watching my SUV ease down the driveway? If he has a gun... Should I call for back-up, then wait who-knew-how-long for a platoon of cops to appear, then storm into a maybe embarrassingly empty house?

Or was Max only a few hundred feet away, tied up or locked up, surely hoping to hell *somebody* might somehow...

I didn't see any vehicle down there, and those tracks back on the macadam were exit tracks.

I quit debating with myself and swung my foot from brakes to accelerator. My heart thundered in my ears. I revved the Jeep down the last few hundred feet of driveway, pulled up in the weed-strewn parking area in front of the decrepit mansion. Cut the engine. And listened.

All I heard were ticks of the cooling engine.

I surveyed the stone steps to the front entrance, steps flanked by the lattice work of a crawlspace beneath the narrow front porch. Then I shoved the Jeep's door open, slid out and climbed the entrance steps. Tried the age-dulled brass latch. The door was unlocked. I pushed it open, peered through a small foyer into a long, gloomy hall. Great place for a Halloween party. I stepped in, listened. Not a murmur. Walked down the hall's creaky hardwood floor. Big rooms along both sides. Halfway down on the right, a broad staircase led to the upper floor. I walked on, almost on tiptoe; this was that kind of place, a hulking relic of decades' past, long left to molder in the remote woods.

There wasn't one stick of furniture in any of the barren rooms I glanced into as I walked past. No curtains nor shades on the big windows.

I walked to the end of the hall and into the kitchen. Except for the dusty sink, it, too, had been stripped bare. I stepped to the back door and peered through its window. Nothing out there but a weedy, brush-strewn area that must have been a back lawn—bordered by dense woods beyond.

Nothing down there or in here. I decided to take a look upstairs. More emptiness up there? As I turned back toward the hall, my hopeful hunch was fading fast.

But halfway across the kitchen I stopped. I'd noticed another doorway, this one obscured between flanking shelves. No doubt the cellar access. And I felt the hairs on the back of my neck ripple.

The door's flaking paint was gray with age, but its padlock and hasp above the doorknob on the right side were silvery new. Why a brand new lock assembly in this deserted old relic of a forgotten past?

A hot wave of elation swept through me. I banged on the door with both fists. "Max!" I shouted. "Are you down there, Max?"

Silence. God, don't let that mean —

I banged the door again. "It's me, Rod Montgomery! Are you down there, Max?"

Again, silence.

Then I heard a muffled voice. Couldn't make out what he said, but that sound alone sent my adrenaline level straight up to red-line.

I yanked open every drawer in that kitchen, every cupboard, desperate to find an overlooked knife or spoon or anything I could use to pry off that hasp and padlock.

All drawers and cupboards were empty.

I blew out a frustrated gust. Probably no cooking utensil would have been of much use anyway. I stood in the middle of the naked kitchen and forced myself to think...*think!*

Of course! My rented Jeep. I raced up the hall, jumped down the steps, yanked open the Jeep's back door, found the spare tire — but no jack or tire iron. In this age of ubiquitous cell phones, apparently this car's rental agency wanted you to call for help rather than risk actionable injury changing a flat yourself. I slammed the door shut and leaned against it to catch my breath.

I sure as hell wasn't going to leave Max in that cellar... Cellar...

Inspiration struck. Cellar doors had to open outwards, not over the steps. That put the hinges of this one on the kitchen side.

I rushed back into the house, tore down the hall to the kitchen and checked the three hinges on the door's left edge.

Possible? I needed something pointed and something with an edge and something to hammer with. Where would I find all that in this stripped-bare house?

Hopeless. But I'm not a big fan of hopeless. There had to be... Got it!

I raced back to the front entrance, jumped down the steps then crouched by the left side lattice panel. I grabbed one of the crisscross slats, gave it a desperate yank. It broke off, a foot-long, half-inch by two-inch hunk of hardwood, square at one end, the other end shattered by the break. The nail in its square end had a rusted head, but its protruding inch looked iron-solid.

I scanned the ground. Found a baseball-sized rock. With stick and rock in hand, I ran up the steps and down the hall. Fifth trip of this hundred-foot dash. In the kitchen, my heartbeat shifted from high-exertion hammer to hopeful-expectation thud. I stuck the nail's point into the open bottom of the middle hinge. Gave it a tap with the rock. Another tap, and the hinge pin cracked loose and moved up a half-inch — enough space to place an edge of the lath strip's square end under the hinge pin's head. Then I tapped the broken end of the lath with the rock until the pin popped loose. One cleared, two to go.

A few minutes later, all three hinges were free of their retaining pins. I set down the rock and lath piece. I grasped the top and middle hinges, tried to keep my fingers on the hinge segments attached to the door itself, and pulled. I felt the door's edge move out — a little. Only a little.

Tried again. This time, the door slid a fraction of an inch leftward, taking up the loose fit age had given it — or as much of it as the slot in the hasp would allow. But that was enough to let me slide my fingertips around the door's left outer edge. I took two deep breaths. Then with all the strength I had left, I gave the damned door a desperate pull.

It grated open a couple inches…a foot, a couple feet. Then it pivoted on the obstinate hasp and creaked sideways until it jammed at an awkward angle. With the door hanging on the bent hasp, I had space enough to squeeze between the jamb and the left edge of the tilted door.

I hunkered down and edged through.

36

In the dim light of two small, ceiling-high windows, I made out Max standing at the foot of the steps.

"My God!" he gasped. "Am I glad to see *you!*"

As I stepped down to the cellar's gritty cement floor, he threw his arms around me, a gesture most out-of-character for the Max I'd known.

"Really —" His voice cracked "Really glad," he managed.

"You okay, Max? You sound okay."

"Yeah, but I look like hell. Let's get out of this stinking dungeon."

I glanced at the little pile of stuff in one of the corners. "Anything you want to take with you?"

"You kidding me? Let's get the hell out of here."

"Can you make it up the steps?"

"To get out of this hellhole, I could make it up a rope. Just clear the way." He started strong, but halfway up, he stumbled. Close behind, I caught him as he lurched backward.

"Slow and easy, Max."

I helped him squeeze under the angled door at the top of the staircase. In the glare of the kitchen windows, he leaned against the left side shelves, his chest heaving. The president of Sturdevant Developers looked like a street vagrant in salvaged clothes. Tangled black hair, more than a week's worth of beard, his dark suit rumpled and stained. And he'd noticeably lost weight.

"Soon as you feel fit to travel," I prompted, "we'd better get you some medical attention." I took him by the elbow and urged him into the hall.

He shook me off. "Hold on a minute, Rod. Just before you showed up, I heard somebody walking around in here. Sounded like he went up the stairs to the second floor. Wondered what he was doing up there. Thought maybe I wasn't the only prisoner in this damned jail."

I wanted to get Max out of here as fast as I could. The tire tracks had told me somebody had just left, but how did I know he wouldn't be right back for some reason or other? If he had a gun, then both of us could be locked in the cellar — after he forced us to replace the hinge pins I'd left on one of the kitchen shelves.

But if the footsteps Max had heard —

"I'm going to check upstairs," I told him. "Wait right here. But if anyone drives in, duck into one of the rooms and do your best to stay out of sight. I'll be right back."

I left him leaning against the hallway's dark-paneled wall, and I ran up the broad staircase. Took quick scans of the two eastside bedrooms. Nothing but bare walls. I rushed to the master bedroom at the other end. Nothing here, either.

Except... Was that a glint of something shiny? I looked in again. A new lock had been installed on what looked like a closet door. A hasp and padlock identical to those on the cellar access door. On this one, though, the padlock hung open. I crossed the big, barren master bedroom, lifted out the padlock and opened the door. The walk-in closet was empty, its shelves bare. I shut the door and stuck the lock in my pocket. This set-up had to be a cell in preparation for a second abductee. The missing lock might at least disrupt sinister scheduling.

Taking Max had stopped work on Town Center construction, but that aborted phone call—the call the FBI traced to the south relay tower—had said A and C was concerned about clearing the woods. Could Cliff be the next target?

I raced down the stairway two steps at a time. Max still leaned against the hallway wall. I took him by the elbow again. This time he didn't shake me off.

"Looks like your warden is setting up another cell upstairs, Max. Taking you got the Town Center construction work stopped, but they kept clearing the woods. Now A and C wants that dropped as well."

"Cliff!" Max's voice sounded parched.

"My thought, too. Let's get out of here." I reached out to steady him.

"I'm okay, Rod. Getting my sea legs back. Let's move."

He did need help to climb into the Jeep and buckle up. Then I drove up the long, rutted lane, hoping not to see another car heading toward us. I didn't need any delays; I needed to get Max a medical check-up. The old driveway was clear all the way. I swung onto the county road, pulled out my cell phone and keyed in Ben Stoddard's cell phone number.

"I've got Max. He says he's okay but I think—"

"Where are you? I'll send an ambulance."

"Don't need an ambulance. We're already headed into town."

"Hospital, then. Nearest one is—where the hell are you, Rod?"

"I don't need a hospital, either!" Max barked, overhearing Ben's insistent commands.

"He's got to be checked over," Ben persisted. "You're no doctor. There could be any number of—"

"Take me home," Max ordered.

"My boss says to take him home, Ben. How about a compromise? I take him home, you send EMTs there to check him out." I glanced at Max. He nodded.

"Okay, agreed," Ben said.

I gave him Max's address, then I said, "Better arrange for some security for Cliff Sturdevant. He could be the next target."

"Way ahead of you, Rod. After that fragmented phone call they traced, the Feds ginned up their presence in the Maximall parking area and the city cops have been keeping an eye on Cliff's house and his travel."

"Any suspicious activity?"

"None so far. Except where A and C is concerned. Their claim that all this is a matter of vengeful ex-employees is pretty well out the window."

"Why don't they go ahead and pick up Amerman and Cassina? You and I know they're guilty as hell of abetting a whole casebook's worth."

"You know the Feds, Rod. They want to make sure the paperwork is right."

"Roger that. One more thing. I'm sure the guy holding Max won't show up again, once the news gets out, but there's got to be fingerprints, maybe other evidence—"

"Location?"

"South on Maple, then up a long hill. About two thirds up, look for an entrance on the right. Hidden by hemlock branches. Might be some exit tracks, if through traffic hasn't scuffed them out. Big house is about two tenths of a mile down. Max was holed up in the cellar."

"Up a long hill, look for hemlocks on right. Got it, Rod."

"Glad to help. Keep me posted."

As we rolled into south Hardington, I handed the phone to Max. He tapped in a number.

"I'm on my way home, Sweetheart! Rod found me, got me out of there... What?... I'm fine. Don't be upset by an EMT ambulance showing there. It's routine. They're just going to check me out... No, I really am okay. See you in a few minutes, Hon. Love you."

He keyed in another call. "Pris? It's Max!...Yeah, I'm with Rod, our corporate hero of the day. He got me out. I'm on my way home...Yep. I'll be at work tomorrow...What? The shutdown? Hell with the shutdown. Full speed ahead on Town Center...Yes, on clearing the woods, too, 'long as they've already started. Tell Cliff. And ask him to come to my house right now. I'll be there in a few minutes. See you tomorrow, Pris. Full report then."

He handed me the phone. "What's with the clearing of the woods, Rod? That wasn't scheduled for another month."

"After you were grabbed, A and C's guy who did it told your people to stop all construction, or else. Cliff shut down construction on the Town Center building and switched to clearing the woods behind it. Figured that would — "

I hit the brakes for a red light.

" — Cliff figured they were concerned only about the building, for some reason or other, not the woods. But your kidnapper went into orbit over that, too. It's obvious he works on A and C's orders. Nobody seems to have any idea why they're so intent on delaying your Keystone City project. Amerman and Cassina left this area a couple decades ago."

"What in hell could they be concerned with at this late date?"

"I don't know, Max. But I am beginning to get an inkling of a theory."

The light turned green and I drove on.

"Care to let me in on it?"

"Not yet. For the moment, it's more hunch than punch."

***

Max's street looked like a major disaster had hit the neighborhood. EMT ambulance, city and county police units, an unmarked sedan I assumed had brought in a squad of FBI agents, two TV units... And, of course, a still-growing crowd of the curious. I had to sit on my horn to get Max to the foot of his jammed driveway.

Elaine Sturdevant, tall and determined, hair flying, elbowed her way through the crowd, threw herself into Max's arms and held him tight. As I struggled out on the passenger side, she turned to me, eyes streaming. "Thank you, thank you, thank you!" she shouted over the tumult. And I got a solid kiss on the cheek.

The media loved it. "Again!" one of the TV reporters yelped. "Wanna make sure we got it." My frown backed them off, but only a little.

Max was hustled into the EMT rig, and I found myself surrounded by the press of the press, a moment of glory I could happily pass up. I'm no publicity hound. I fobbed them off with a comment about dumb luck—which, in part, it was.

After a going-over in the ambulance, Max stepped out, plowed tight-lipped through the media madness, and stepped close.

Voice husky and near my ear in the milling mob, he said, "The EMTers say I'm a tad undernourished—no surprise there, and a pleasure to remedy. He grabbed my arm. "Rod, I don't know how I can ever repay you for this."

"You've been paying me every week, Max. Call it part of the job." I maneuvered us away from the pestiferous media minions. "Trouble is, it's not over."

Big Ben Stoddard wormed his way out of the crush. "Damned good to see you, Mr. Sturdevant. Hell of a piece of work, Rod."

"Wish it was the end piece," I told him. "The big question still hangs over us. Why are Amerman and Cassina so damned concerned about Keystone City?"

***

As he drove from the old mansion back into Hardington, Krag faced his next decision: grab Cliff Sturdevant and lock him in that upstairs closet, then get the water, bread and whatever. Or get that stuff now and snatch brother Cliff after the closet was already supplied?

Krag mentally kicked himself. If he'd picked up the supplies at the same time as he'd bought the lock and hasp, everything back in the old house would have been ready now. He was a doer, not a planner. This whole thing was ballooning into—he had to admit it—into more than he wanted to handle. Hell, he was coming unglued. If he hadn't been so eager to get that lock in place... Dumb, dumb, dumb.

So, okay. Get the damn stuff now and lug it up there. Then he could concentrate on exactly how to grab brother Cliff.

A half-hour later, Krag headed back up the long hill toward the mansion. Two loaves of bread, jar of peanut butter, jar of grape jelly, plastic knife—this one pilfered during a quick coffee stop at IHOP—two gallons of water, a plastic bucket. Same set-up Max was surviving on. Get it in place, and finally concentrate on the riskiest part of this thing. Grab and lock up Cliff. Then make the call to Sturdevant Developers. As Krag neared the hidden driveway, he was already framing the threat: *You didn't listen to me the first time. You'd better listen now. Stop ALL work, or you'll never see...* Or maybe, *Listen to me! This is your last chance to save...* Or something more like: *You'll never see them again if you don't shut down everything right now!* This was the part he liked most. The threat. All the damned planning, all these details—that's for the birds.

He spotted the hemlock-hidden entrance. And scowled at the faint tire tracks until he realized they had to be his, made just after the rain had stopped earlier this afternoon. Through-traffic would soon scrub them away. He checked the road ahead and behind. Not a car in sight. He swung the Ford into the old driveway.

In front of the ancient mansion—his mansion, he thought of it now—he unloaded the bags of supplies, lugged them up the entrance steps, down the hall, up the stairway to the second floor, then strode down the upstairs hall to the master bedroom and its big closet.

He set down the bags and— Where was the padlock? Had he absently stuck it in his pocket while installing the hasp? Hell, no. He distinctly remembered hanging it in place, unlocked.

Jesus H. Christ! Somebody had—

He stumbled over the bags, rushed down the hall, tore down the steps, ran into the kitchen. And stopped dead. The cellar door hung at a crazy angle on its hasp. He scrambled around it, banged down the steps.

Gone! Who in hell could have—

A wave of hot sweat broke across his shoulders. To hell with A and C. His problem now was himself. He had figured he'd be long gone after eventually freeing Max and Cliff. His fingerprints were all over the place, but he'd never been fingerprinted.

They'd describe him, of course, but descriptions could be deceptive.

All that was by the boards now. This place could be crawling with cops any minute.

He stood at the foot of the cellar steps, shivering in growing panic. He grabbed the stair railing to steady himself. Think. THINK!

37

Halfway down the long hill into south Hardington, Krag slowed his racing Ford Escape, but his heart thudded on. No other traffic. Then a car emerged from Maple Street's distant tree-lined blocks below and headed up the long climb toward him. Just another Pocono traveler?

As the dark blue sedan approached then rolled past, Krag was relieved. Its driver and front seat passenger took no notice of him. Both heads were turned away, apparently interested in the roadside more than the road. Looking for... Jesus! Krag glued his eyes to the rearview mirror. Dark blue with a white license plate. Feds?

Three-quarters of the way to the top, the sedan's brake lights flared. Full stop. Then Krag's chest constricted. The car turned to its right and disappeared into the roadside brush. *They've found the place.*

Krag felt hot sweat soak his sports shirt collar. That was *close!* If he'd delayed leaving the mansion by only a few minutes, he would be trapped now by that incoming car.

He tramped the accelerator. And ran. He hated running. He was supposed to be in charge, the guy to derail the Keystone project until blustering Amerman and sneaky Cassina got done what they needed to do. That part was not his concern.

And now he knew this damn assignment was no longer his concern, either. His number one—and only—project had just become a one-worder: RUN. Get out of here fast. Before those prowling Feds tumbled to the fact they had passed him on their way up the hill. To hell with A and C and their Keystone paranoia. He had to disappear and damned quick, before the Feds or the local cops or the swarming staties put everything together. A and C owed him, but forget that. He could find other clients for his kind of specialized work. When A and C's cash ran out, he'd get the word around that he was available. Do all somewhere out west. Way out west.

First a quick stop at the motel to pick up his— No. Too risky. Might be possible his black SUV with Jersey plates had been spotted—reported?—when he'd grabbed Max in the Maximall's parking lot. Shoulda replaced the plates with a new set of stolen ones, but his couldn't be the only dark-colored Jersey SUV in Hardington. And so far...

Kidnapping's a federal offense, he'd heard or read somewhere, if the victim isn't released within hours. Max had been locked away for a lot more than that. And the car climbing past him on the hill sure looked like Feds. They could be checking motels, too. The hell with going back there. He'd leave his meager belongings at the East End Economy Court, stiff the place for the room bill...

His brain whirling, he almost rushed straight through the Maple-Ash intersection. Sure didn't want to go back into the city. Had to get out of Hardington, out of this damn valley. Barely in time, he swerved leftward into Ash Street. Minutes later, he raced past the abandoned warehouses he'd once thought as possibilities to hide Max. Then he tore out of Hardington's western outskirts—not on a speedy, four-lane interstate, but on a winding two-lane down-valley macadam county road.

Hunched over the wheel, he gunned up to sixty-five, braked only for occasional curves, then stomped the gas hard again. Only when Hardington was far behind, and with a long, straight stretch ahead, did he settle back. And grin. Free at last!

Then he heard a distant siren wail. Glanced at the rearview mirror. A quarter-mile back, a motorcycle with blinking red light. Where in hell had *he* come from? Could a Ford Escape outrun a cop on a bike? He floored the gas pedal. The SUV lunged up to 75.

Trees flanking the narrow road zipped by in a blur. He howled past a gas station. The golden arches of a McDonald's. A sign: NORTOWN 25 MPH. Four parked cars, but the street seemed clear. He ripped through, broke into open country again.

Checked the rearview. The cop had slowed through town. More than a quarter mile back now, but closing.

The road paralleled a creek on the right. A sign flashed by so fast Krag could barely read it: BRIDGE 20 MPH.

Christ! It was dead ahead, at a rightward angle over a leftward twist in the creek. Racing toward him. He floored the brake pedal. Tires screaming, the SUV swerved. He fought it straight. Overcorrected. The bridge loomed dead ahead. Leaving a wake of blue smoke, The Ford plowed through the left side of the bridge's steel railing.

He was airborne—until the Ford slammed into the far-side bank.

***

The motorcycle cop raced across the bridge. Skidded to a halt. Jumped off. Scrambled toward the crumpled SUV—

No need to hurry. The guy hadn't been wearing his seat belt. His head had rammed through the bloody windshield. He stared wide-eyed but unseeing.

***

When I walked into my temporary Maximall office at nine the next morning, my cell phone jingled before I sat down.

"Yo, Rod!" Sgt. Ben Stoddard's voice. "You heard?"

"About the New Jersey SUV guy killing himself in a losing race with a motorcycle cop? Yeah, on the radio this morning. Any ID?"

"What you haven't heard is that in his wallet, a Jersey driver's license for a 'Leonard Lewis' turned out to be phony. Plus, a Discover card in the same name. A quick check told us the charges on it went to 'Book Buys,' apparently a dummy company in New Jersey, with the charges paid by postal coupon."

"No connection with A and C?"

"Not in the wallet, but his cell phone had only one number in its memory. The FBI traced it to A and C. And he was carrying food, water, and a bucket, same as you'd told me about Max's cellar supplies. Is he okay today?"

"Surprisingly, for a guy in his fifties who was cooped up in a cellar until yesterday. Saw his car in the lot when I came in, so he's showed up for work earlier than I have, and I'm on time."

"Four stars for him—and for you."

The desk phone buzzed. "Front office call waiting, Ben. Thanks for the briefing. Get back to you later." I signed off and picked up the other phone.

"Good morning, Rod." Pris's voice, lilting. "Talk about a smart detective! How did you ever figure out where—"

"Luck and tire tracks, m'dear. If the weather had stayed clear, Max would still be in that grubby basement."

"Well, he's flying now. Wants you up here."

"I'm on my way."

In his customary office attire—shirt sleeves and tie—Max looked and acted like a man back in charge. "Coffee, please," he barked at Pris then turned back to me. "Have a seat."

I took one of the two chairs in front of his desk. In her dark green, knee-length dress with a saucy lime-green sash, Pris poured two mugs from Max's personal coffee maker on the sideboard near the big picture window, set them on the desk, gave me a quick smile and left, shutting the door behind her.

Apparently, Max's clipped style had been an effort to convince her he was back in the chief's chair at full steam. Now with a grin on his still pale but now far less haggard face, he reached into his center drawer then slid a check across the big desktop. My weekly fee...plus a startling $1,000.

"For remarkable service expertly rendered, Rod. Thank God. And thank you again."

"And thank you, Max."

As I pocketed the check, he sat back, took a long drag of coffee. Set the mug down. "We're back on schedule. Work is already — "

"Got something to tell you, Max."

"About what?"

"About the bastard who locked you up. Dead in a car crash yesterday. Just got the word from Stoddard. Black Ford Escape, Jersey plates, fake creds. No help there. But he was carrying a load of food, water, and a bucket. Same as you had. Apparently, he got spooked and ran."

"I'll be damned! Thank God for that." Max lifted his coffee mug in salute. Then he looked...pensive. "You know something? He was a son of a bitch, all right. Locked me up and could have just walked away. But he came back a couple times. Brought more food, emptied the goddamn bucket. Hell, I sound like I got a touch of — what do they call it?"

"Stockholm Syndrome, when the prisoner begins to feel a relationship with his captor."

"That's it. I used to think that was a lot of bull, but now... Cripes! When word of his dying in a car crash gets around, my damned phone will light up like a Christmas tree. After yesterday's stampede, I've had enough of the merciless media."

"Until you need them for Keystone publicity," I said with a wry smile.

He nodded. "You got me there." He waved that aside. "Hell of a project. Three people dead, a spy unveiled—"

"True, but now Pris is on our side."

"Yeah, she is. But we still don't know why that damned company in Camden is so intent on slowing up progress. Didn't you tell me yesterday you had some idea about—"

"Only an inkling, Max. That's a couple degrees less reliable than a hunch."

"Can I pry it out of you?"

"I don't think you should. It could unnecessarily corduroy our smooth relationship if I turned out to be a touch wild-eyed."

He gave me an eyebrows-raised chuckle. "You got any thoughts on where we go from here? I've given project management a 'full speed ahead,' but I'm still holding my breath."

"With luck, the FBI's presumably exhaustive investigation will at least keep A and C off-balance, if not pre-occupied." I took a coffee sip. "I wonder if we might…"

"Might?"

"Might be able to push them closer to whatever they're trying so hard to avoid."

"Not sure I follow."

"Let's consult with our counterspy."

"Worth a try." Max picked up his phone. "Pris, we need you."

She stepped in, eyebrows raised in expectation. Max nodded at the other desk-side chair.

"All right, Rod," he said. "Let's hear your idea on where we should go from here, concerning A and C."

"As their 'spy-in-residence,' Pris has to update them on what's happening." I turned to her. "To maintain credibility with them, you have to report Max has been freed and returned to work, and the guy who kidnapped him has been killed in a car accident—"

"He was? I hadn't heard that!"

"Just heard it myself, Pris. Turns out he was working for A and C, but you're not supposed to know that. So you tell them about Max's being found, the car crash, and that work on Keystone is going ahead full blast. We'll see how they react."

Max gave me a dubious look. "You're hoping they'll try something that will get them nailed by the city, county, state police, or the FBI, all of them swarming the project now?"

"Right. We came close, until their guy died in the car crash. Could be a long shot, but Pris has to report something or A and C surely would cut her out when reports on the fatal car crash are picked up by national media."

"Good point," Max agreed. "I'll arrange for police protection at the Town Center building and the woods behind it. Clearing the woods wasn't to be on schedule for six weeks, but since they're already at it, I told them to keep going."

"And I'll work through Stoddard for beefed-up police surveillance here and for your key people."

Max scrawled a note then looked at Pris. "Make the call."

She stood. "I'll get my cell phone. All my calls to A and C have been on my cell so they wouldn't appear in Sturdevant phone records."

She stepped out to her reception alcove, came back with the phone. She tapped in a number. "Amerman's personal cell." Then she set the phone on the desk, and we clustered around it.

"Yes?" a male voice grated.

"Max Sturdevant has been rescued and he's back in the office. The man who took him has been killed in a car crash."

Silence. A long one. I looked at Max. He frowned. And shrugged.

Then the phone's metallic voice asked, "And the work on Keystone?"

"Already going ahead. The building and the woods behind it."

I heard a gust of expelled breath. Then the phone went dead.

"Mr. Amerman has hung up," Pris said.

Max straightened up from his crouch over the now-silent cell phone. "You think we've planted a time bomb?" he asked me.

I felt a surge of anticipation. "I do indeed, Max. I can almost hear it ticking."

38

Harvey Amerman shoved his cell toward his shirt pocket. Missed. The phone tumbled into his lap. He snatched it up, hit the pocket this time. Then he grabbed his desk phone. Call Ezra Ketchem again and get another lawyerly plug for patience on Garden State's heel-dragging? *Patiently* wait for their response to A and C's acceptance of their offer of six million? Hell, no. Not with Keystone back on schedule.

Amerman stabbed in a number. While he waited, he felt a goose flesh chill creep down his spine.

Goddammit! Even with their president in the hospital, Garden State Suppliers had to make a move. Buy A and C or get off the pot. *Now*—before work in Hardington went fatally further.

Three rings, then: "Garden State Suppliers."

"This is Harvey Amerman, A and C. With Coates laid up, who's in charge out there?"

"Mr. Narlek, sir, our senior vice-president."

"Is he there now?"

"I'll connect you."

"Just tell him to stay put. I'm coming out there." Amerman hung up and heaved out of his chair. He'd been telling himself to lose weight, eat less. But Garden City's delay had him nervously stuffing down more.

Take Mateo with him? Not this time. His fist-shaking attitude was helpful with reluctant delay-payers, but this confrontation called for a cool face-to-face. Right now.

***

Hands tight on the wheel of his dark green Buick, he drove north to Federal and 3rd, turned east and rushed four miles into the Camden boondocks. Garden State Suppliers' big yard, sprawling warehouses and flat-topped, white-stucco office building lay along meandering Pennsauken Creek. He pulled into the gravel parking area in front of the offices, slammed the Buick's door and marched in.

From her PC at the desk near the entrance, a fluffy-haired woman in a rust-colored blouse glanced at him. "Help you?"

"Harvey Amerman, A and C, looking for Mr. Nar..." What the hell was the guy's name? "Your acting CEO with Mr. Coates in the hospital."

"Mr. Narlek." She pointed down the hallway to her right. "Last door at the end." She reached for her phone.

Puffing from his overweight rush, Amerman trotted down the hall. The door at the end was open. He walked in. "Amerman, head of A and C. With Coates out of commission, you're the one I'm told to see."

The balding guy behind the blond oak desk stood. Looked to be in his late forties.

He thrust out a hand. "Hugo Narlek, vice president."

Amerman shook hands and squinted. "Yeah, now I remember you. Well, your name. From our lawyer's report on one of his early discussions with Garden City. Look, this should be a simple matter. We've already agreed to accept your counteroffer of six million. I'm sorry Coates is indisposed, but we need that amount transferred fast, or I'll have to go to another offer."

There was no other offer, but Narlek didn't have to know that.

"You put me on the spot. I'm not eager to make such a large transfer Spencer Coates should personally authorize. And he's in no shape at the moment to even think about it. You can be certain payment will be made as soon as he returns to work."

Jesus! Amerman felt anger boiling. Choked it back. "Well, Hugo, as acting CEO you will have to confirm the offer yourself and transfer the money to the account number I will give you. Or we will cancel the whole damned thing and go with the competing offer. You understand that?"

He watched Narlek's face pale a bit. Got him?

"I'm afraid—"

"And I'm afraid I have no alternative. The other party is waiting for my call this afternoon." He turned to leave, then turned back. "Hope Spenser Coates recovers soon. But by then, someone else will own A and C."

Hoping Narlek hadn't noticed the sweat breaking out on his forehead, Amerman headed for the door.

"You make a good point," Narlek said, his tone suddenly conciliatory. "Phone me your account number."

Amerman stopped. "Got it with me." He reached into his hip pocket and stepped back to the desk to hand an envelope to Narlek. "I'll appreciate your burning this after the transfer."

"Agreed. Confirmation to you at your office."

"No. I'll check via the Internet precisely at three this afternoon. Then Ezra Ketchem, our rep, will contact you concerning the A and C transfer documents."

***

Back in his office, Amerman needed a few moments to pull himself together—from the press of downtown traffic, but more from the stress of putting all that pressure on Hugo Narlek. Pressure was Cassina's game, but today Amerman had resorted to exactly that.

Now that the deal was made, he did have to bring Cassina back into the picture. He had considered a Samoan future without Mateo's often overbearing pressure, but leaving him here could be disastrous. Mateo giving state's evidence in return for...

He picked up his phone. "Need you right now, Mateo."

Four minutes later, Cassina strode in, sprawled into a chair. "Yeah?"

"Bad news first, Mateo. Krag is dead."

Cassina lurched forward. "Jesus! How?"

"Car accident. That's not the worst of it. They found Max Sturdevant, and work on the Town Center building—"

"And the woods?"

"And the woods. They're back at it, which means—"

"Which means we've gotta get the hell out of here quick."

"Precisely, Mateo. That's why I drove to Garden State Suppliers—"

"Today?"

"Just got back. Turns out Coates is in the hospital. Heart attack. So I told their acting CEO, a veep named Narlek, that we needed the six mil deposited by three this afternoon. He agreed. As soon as I confirm the money transfer, I'll notify Ketchem to bring over the property transfer paperwork. Then we'll be outta here. Get ready to move. Tomorrow. I'll activate the standby tickets. Delta to Atlanta to L. A., overnight there, then Papeete the next day."

"Pa-what?"

"Papeete, Mateo. Had to look it up myself. It's in French Polynesia. From there we take Air New Zealand to Apia."

"I thought we were going to Samoa."

"Apia is part of Samoa, Mateo. One of its three islands, the one with the airport on it. We're going to need a bundle of cash. As soon as I confirm Garden City's transfer to our Cayman account, I'll pay all outstanding bills here and cash out our Camden account."

"While you're doing all that, what do you want me to do?"

"Just be ready to get out of here in a hurry, Mateo. I'll do the rest."

Cassina walked out. Amerman tried to concentrate on routine paperwork. Couldn't. Kept staring at the PC on his desk. He wasn't much of a computer op, but he knew how to access the Cayman account he'd set up with a few Gs a couple months back. Patience...He watched the wall clock's minute hand creep...creep...

Oughta pat myself on the back, he thought. This was shaping up as one smooth escape from calamity. If only that damn Sturdevant outfit had picked another spot to build their city, none of this would be necessary. He and Cassina could have kept building A and C into a major Mid-Atlantic builders' supply center. A dream shot to hell now.

He dragged his gaze away from the clock. Spun around. Through his office window, he stared at the sluggish Delaware River. Time dragged, too. He stood, strode to the coffee room. Neither he nor Mateo had an "administrative assistant" to cope with such trivia as coffee chasing. Poured himself a Styrofoam cupful. Checked his watch. Walked back to his office. Sat down.

Finished the coffee. Fiddled with a ballpoint. Checked the wall clock. 2:54.

He fired up his computer.

Checked the time again. It was 3:00 on the nose. Give Hugo Latex... What the hell was his name? Narlek. That was it. Let him have a couple more minutes to make the transfer.

Now it was 12 past. That ought to do it. He tapped in the Cayman bank's code. Took a while to flash on. Then he keyed in the confidential account number. Scanned the data...

Had he missed it? Read it again, Harvey. Carefully. Last deposit: *a month ago?*

What the hell?

Had he screwed up somehow? Gotten a backdated report? He hit *delete current tab*. Entered the number again. Same thing came up. The account showed no recent deposit.

He grabbed his desk phone, banged in Garden State's number.

"Mr. Narlek!" he barked to the answering female. "Tell him Harvey Amerman's calling, and tell him to get the hell on the phone!"

"I'm sorry, sir. Mr. Narlek is out of the office."

"Out of the office? He was supposed to—where the hell is he?"

Long silence.

"You still there? Where is Narlek?"

"In Trenton, sir." Her voice sounded oddly subdued.

"In Trenton?"

"At Mercer County Hospital, sir. Mr. Coates has had a serious setback. He's in the ICU. On life support."

"My God! Narlek was supposed to...Didn't he leave any message for me?"

"He suspended all company activity until Monday. Then I'm sure he will return your call. I'm very sorry—"

Amerman slammed down the phone. Monday. Today was Wednesday. Five more days. He picked up the phone again. Jabbed in a two-digit number.

"Change in plan, Mateo. Better come up."

Change in plan? Some change. Every hour of delay could drag them an hour closer to disaster.

39

If anyone had told me the unravelling of the Keystone project's sabotage effort would begin in the Yellow Pages, I would have had my week's only chuckle. But on Friday, I had an actual idea. I picked up my desk phone.

"Morning, Pris. Wonder if you have a phone book up there with the Yellow Pages."

Three minutes later, she plunked a thick Hardington phone book on my desk and gave me a pixie smile. "Looking for another job?"

"Following up on a brain flash, m'dear. Amerman and Cassina left town two decades ago and set up A and C in Camden. Other building suppliers here in Hardington must have been aware of the disappearance of…what was her name?"

"O'Brian, according to office gossip that popped up when word got around that A and C wasn't happy about Keystone."

I picked up the fat phone book. "I think it might be worthwhile to do a little chit-chatting with someone who was in the building supply business here when that happened."

"In other words, Rod, you're as mystified as the rest of us."

"In one word, not quite."

"That's two words." She tapped the phone book. "Good luck." At the door she paused. "Lunch sometime?"

"You asking for a date?"

"You playing hard to get?" She gave me a flip grin and walked out, a playful Pris I hadn't seen enough of before.

I leafed through the phone book to Building Suppliers. My theory: those in the same business back then could have had more interest, maybe more insight about an employee's disappearance—maybe more...hell, gossip. Yeah, Pris was right, this was a wild shot, but it beat sitting here nursing a wild guess.

Six companies were listed. I was about to go through a company-by-company search for those in business two decades when a display ad on the listings page caught my eye. Established 1950. Picked up the phone.

"Hardington Suppliers," a chirpy voice announced.

"Rod Montgomery." My Rodney Stevens persona had long since been superseded by reality. "I'm with Sturdevant Developers. Like to come out there and talk with your boss soon as possible." I have a lot more faith in face-to-face discussion than phone-to-phone.

"Hang on a minute," she said. More than a minute later, she announced rather grandly, "Mr. McClave can fit you in at three-thirty this afternoon."

***

The cinder block office, big fenced-in yard and warehouses of Hardington Suppliers sprawled across several acres on the sparse south edge of the city. I parked between a pair of dusty pick-ups then walked into shivery air-conditioning. A pony-tailed blond in a fuzzy pink sweater peered up from her paper-strewn desk.

"Help you?"

"Rod Montgomery to see Mr. McClave."

She picked up her phone, announced me in her chirpy tones then nodded over her shoulder. "First door on the right."

I walked down a barren, chilly hallway, found the door marked "Jacob McClave," and walked in.

He was a big guy, like a football tackle crammed into a blue work shirt, sleeves rolled up, and denim jeans. He stood, shoved out a huge hand. We shook.

"Sit, Mr....uh..." Looked at a note on his chaotic desk. "Montgomery."

I sat. Another hard office side chair.

McClave reassembled his bulging muscles behind his desk. "I've been hoping to hear from Sturdevant, now that you're into building construction out there. We've got a whole range of what you're gonna need. All top quality stuff—"

I held up a hand. "Not my department, Mr. McClave. I'm—"

"Jake. Call me Jake."

"Fine, Jake. I'm a...consultant with Sturdevant. Looking into problems the company has had with—"

"I've heard. Motor pool fire, guy killed in the runaway dozer, Max kidnapped. Wait a minute. Hmm. Montgomery... Aren't you the guy who found him? Read it in the Times. Hell of a thing."

"I got lucky."

"Yeah, sure. If you aren't here to order a couple tons of cinder block, what can I do for you?"

"You familiar with A and C, some kind of building consultant in Camden?"

"Yeah. They offered to put us on their 'list'—for a cut of the proceeds. We don't do business that way. They got started here in Hardington. Amerman and Cass-something."

"Cassina. You have any dealings with them back then?"

"That was—what? Twelve, fifteen years ago when they left? I was still in my teens. Thinking about a pro-football career, not how many board feet of two-by-tens I could sell."

"But you did end up selling lumber."

"Busted a leg first year at Penn State. Didn't heal the way it should. So yeah, I'm selling lumber. And anything that goes with it. Dad started this company a couple years after World War Two. I took it over when he died five years ago. So I don't know anything about A and C when they were here — before they moved to Jersey. Sorry you wasted the trip out here."

He stood. My cue to leave. I thanked him, apologized for taking up his time and headed for the door. I grabbed the knob —

"Hold on a sec, Montgomery. Just realized I've got somebody here who might be of help. My chief bookkeeper, Eddy Connell. A Hardington old-timer. Last door down the hall."

I thanked him and walked down the rest of the echoing hallway. Heard someone typing. Typing? I thought the nation's last typewriter must be in the Smithsonian by now. But no, in the last office down, a cramped cubby oozing cigarette smoke into the hallway, a woman with her back to me hunched on a revolving stool and whanged away at what looked like an old Smith Corona like my father'd had.

"Excuse me," I said over the machine-gun typing. "I'm looking for Eddy Connell."

The clatter quit. She swung around, a woman surely on the far side of sixty, with a dandelion fluff of white hair and gunmetal blue eyes that seemed to look right through me. She stubbed her cigarette butt in an ashtray on her adjacent desk, and flicked an ash from the sleeve of her rumpled tan cardigan.

"You found her," she said. "What can I do for you?"

"You're Eddy? Mr. McClave said I should — "

"Eddy as in Edwina. Mr. McClave said what?"

"I'm Rod Montgomery, consultant working with Max Sturdevant on the problems he's had with the Keystone — "

"So he's hired a P.I.? About time. The local cops have been going in circles." She squinted at me. "'Montgomery,' you said? You're the guy who pulled Max Sturdevant out of that cellar?"

"I'm the guy." I nodded at her typewriter. "I see a computer over there in repose."

"I use the typewriter to address envelopes and fill out forms. My breath of air while drowning in electronics." Still perched on her stool, she pointed at her desk chair. "Have a seat, Montgomery. You're the first visitor I've had in a month of Sundays who hasn't had some damned problem with paycheck deductions or withholding taxes. But how can I possibly be of help to you? I spend my days in fiscal purgatory and my nights watching reruns on TCM."

"Mr. McClave told me you were in Hardington when another building supplier got caught up in the beginning of the Chinese drywall thing some fifteen years ago. You remember that?"

"Hell, honey, I almost remember the Maine. Harvey Amerman, his name was. Him and his pal, Cassino."

"Cassina."

"Right. Mateo — that's Eye-tie for Matthew — Cassina with an a. They both slipped out of town just in time."

"And set up some kind of builders supply thing in Camden."

"Way I heard it, they buy up surplus materials at completed jobsites and sell them cut rate. Got three or four warehouses somewhere, with an office in the city. Called themselves 'A ampersand C' back in the day, A and C now. So what about them?"

"It's probable they have something to do with the Keystone project problems. They deny that, and claim it's disgruntled ex-employees plotting against them."

"Huh! But why would A and C give a damn about Keystone City?"

"That's what I wondered. So I went to the *Hardington Times* library. But they're a couple decades behind in scanning to disc, and the papers of the Chinese drywall era are buried in a heap coupla feet deep."

"You're looking for something A & C did, or were involved in, that connects them with Keystone City? I can't imagine anything that far back could have a thing to do with sabotaging Sturdevant's project. Heck, they were so concerned with bad publicity back then, I think they'd steer clear of anything at all to do with Hardington now. Mary Louise even told me—"

"Mary Louise?"

"Mary Louise O'Brian. Their girl-Friday."

"You knew her?"

"I was with a CPA service back then, and she needed some help with her tax return. We had lunch together a couple times. She was a peppery redhead, bright, full of fire and do-goodism. She was all fired up over the Chinese drywall thing. Especially how it could affect A & C. I gathered she was worried more about the future of the firm than any personal future with Harvey Amerman—there were rumors... God, listen to me—a real prattle-tale!"

"That's why I'm here, Eddy. Hoping to get inside insight. Woman disappears and nobody seems to have looked any deeper than a surface scratch. You seem to have known her pretty well. What do you think happened?"

"I think what everybody else thinks—as far as her disappearing. The airlines lost track of her. But I've thought beyond that. Last time I saw her was a couple days before she evaporated. She was totally wound up over the drywall thing. Told me she'd even written a report on it, and wanted Harvey to present it at a builders' supply conference coming up. They'd had a hell of an argument over that, and he turned the idea down flat, of course."

"But you think she decided to present her study to the conference in person."

"Yes, I do. And she knew that would finish her with A & C. And I'm sure she assumed that weasel, Cassina, would see that she never worked anywhere else. So I think she decided Mary Louise O'Brian would disappear, and she would become...Well, who knows? When she flew off into limbo, I was stunned but not overwhelmed."

"Bought a ticket, gave a false name."

"Exactly, Rod. Remember, this was years before nine/eleven. You just gave your name, bought a ticket, got a boarding pass and flew away. So I think she parked as Mary Louise O'Brian—her car license plate told the world that—then walked to the ticket counter as Jane Don't-Even-Remember-Me. She's somewhere way west where they never heard of Hardington and the looming A & C drywall monster."

Eddy cupped a knee with her hands and leaned back on her typewriter stool. "So that's what I think. What do you think?"

"You've reasoned it a lot further than her car at the airport. Everybody else seems to have shrugged it off as 'the airline lost her, and she didn't want to come back.'"

"And Harvey Amerman went along with that. In fact, he probably found it helpful in a way. The mystery of her disappearance pushed the Chinese drywall story to the back burner."

"Surely not to A & C's disappointment."

"But they didn't exactly sit back and enjoy it, Rod. A couple weeks later, they moved their little company out of town."

"Out of state."

"And now they're throwing an interstate hissy fit over something they apparently have no connection with at all." She shrugged and shook her head. "I'm afraid I haven't been any help at all."

"But you have, Eddy." I stood and stepped to the door. "I know a lot more now than when I barged in here. And you've turned a wild thought I've had into a full-blown hunch."

40

Saturday brunch in the Anthracite Hotel's archaic dining room was a Hardington custom I eagerly supported. This early summer mid-morning, Pris grinned at me. When she'd accepted my suggestion yesterday afternoon, she had gleefully twitted, "Aha, an actual date!" She had appeared in the lobby this morning precisely at ten-thirty, frisky in electric blue with a sassy white sash, mahogany hair smoothly lustrous.

From our foray to the steaming breakfast buffet, we walked back to our table. Western omelets for both, grilled tomatoes for Pris, hash browns for me. Toast, marmalade, coffees constantly refilled by a super-attentive roving waiter.

Then I said, "Tell me again how Amerman reacted when you called him yesterday."

"When I told him what you and Max wanted me to tell him—"

"That work had gone into overtime on the Town Center building and the woods."

"Yes. When I told him that, all I got was silence. Then I heard...well, a sort of whisper to himself. Very softly, he said, 'Jesus!' Then he said, and I don't understand this at all, 'No need for you to call anymore.'"

"You're sure those were his exact words?"

"Positive. From that, I gather I'm fired."

"By A and C. You think he's caught onto our double-agent act?"

She took a nibble of omelet. "Sounded like that. When his monthly check doesn't arrive, I'll know."

"Money from two employers. Does that tweak your conscience?"

"Not when one of them apparently has had three men killed."

"No actual proof, Pris."

"But doesn't actual logic confirm speculation?"

"That it does." I gave her a smile and raised my coffee cup in a toast. "Here's to my favorite spy." First really enjoyable morning I'd had in this burg, I realized. A brunch with an ever more compelling companion. The disturbing hunch reinforced by Eddy Connell's memories receded into the restaurant's cozy aura. I found myself speculating on where Pris and I might go from this pleasant point...

***

Every time Mike Melhado settled his ample butt into the seat of his Cat Track Loader and started it up, he found himself wondering: Will this be a normal controlled start-up? Or will this big Cat howl out of control like Gary Samuels' sabotaged D-8 earlier this year? Kill him like the racing D-8 had killed Samuels in Lake Linden? In all his start-ups since, Melhado had experienced nothing of that sort. The only fear he had, he thought every time, was fear itself. Read that somewhere.

Behind him and on schedule, the debris hauler truck pulled off the Keystone project's east road, rumbled to the edge of the nearby woods and stopped. Melhado took a final puff on his Marlboro—only time he could sneak a cigarette without his wife's or even a fellow employee's icy stare—and tossed it aside. He pulled his safety helmet low over his eyes, held his breath and fired up the loader. Chug...chug... Then a no-problem rumble. He raised the big, toothed scoop clear of the ground out front and headed for the brush line. This Saturday work was for the birds, Melhado thought, but Sturdevant has ordered it, and Susquehanna is paying time-and-a-half, so I'm doing it.

His target: the clump of staghorn sumac at the woods' edge. Weed trees that looked like a northern effort to imitate southern palms. The little grove, five or six feet high, stood at the edge of longer-established towering maples and beech. Tree-felling crews with power saws for those. Melhado's game was brush, sapling stands and sumac groves, like this one. The palm-like stuff looked dense and heavy, but that was deceptive. Their velvety trunks were nothing but soft pith, their roots shallow.

He lined up, rumbled into position. At the edge of the stand he lowered the scoop, rolled forward to dig its toothed bottom edge into the ground. When he had a full load of sumac roots and brush, he raised it a couple feet and turned toward the nearby truck. Then he squinted and leaned forward. What was that hanging from one of the scoop's big teeth?

The truck driver saw it, too. He stepped out of his cab and sauntered over, a lanky guy in faded tan shirt and pants. He pulled the cloth loose, walked back to the Track Loader's cab. "Just a rag." He handed it to Melhado. A greenish rag, filthy with clinging dirt.

Melhado held it at arms' length, shook off most of the loose soil. "Not a rag, Harry. Looks like, I dunno. Maybe a scarf somebody dropped years ago."

The truck driver sauntered to the hole the Track Loader had scooped out. Melhado watched him peer in, then rear back mouthing something Melhado couldn't hear over the idling engine. The trucker gave him an urgent "get-your-butt-over-here" wave. Melhado left the Track Loader in idle and stepped down from its little cab. He strode to the gouge he'd made in the edge of the sumac grove, the rectangular hole the toothed bucket had scooped out, about a foot and a half deep. Broken sumac roots and — what the hell was *that?* Looked like —

"Kee-rist!" Melhado cried. "You gotta cell phone on you? Call 911!"

***

Fifteen minutes after he got the call from the Sheriff's Department dispatcher, Sgt. Ben Stoddard raced up the road past the Maximall, veered to the right at the Y-intersection. He gunned his patrol unit around the road's northward curve. Pressed on another half mile. Then he spotted the truck and dozer on the wood's edge and scruffed to a halt on the macadam's left shoulder.

From the front of the dozer, a stubby guy in jeans and a blue work shirt trotted toward him. "Damn glad you're here, officer. Soon's we saw it, we stopped everything and called 911."

He stuck out a callused hand. "Mike Melhado. I drive the Track Loader."

"Ben Stoddard, Sheriff's Department. What've we got here?"

"That's what I wonder, too."

"Working on a Saturday?" Ben asked as they headed for whatever the hell it was that had summoned him out here.

"Boss says we're making up for time lost when Sturdevant was locked away. I don't know what's behind it all. I just do what they tell me to do. Clear the brush. No problem. Until this morning. Never had anything like this before. Not in all the years I've worked for Susquehanna. Nothin' like this."

The man was rambling, Stoddard realized. Trying to cover his consternation over whatever had happened here this cloudy, warm Saturday mid-morning.

They rounded the front of the silent dozer. Another guy back here, pacing back and forth until he saw them appear. Thin guy in what looked like surplus Army suntans.

"Harry Duncan," Melhado said. "Drives that truck over there."

Stoddard nodded, glanced at the clump of sumac in the Loader's partially upraised scoop. Then he peered into the shallow excavation at the forest's edge.

A pair of bones a little over a foot long poked from the disordered dirt. Radius and ulna—Stoddard was a crossword addict. His assumption was confirmed by the easily recognized skeletal remains of a human hand resting on the distorted soil.

"Awful thing," Melhado muttered. "I couldn't get myself to dig any further."

"Good thing you didn't." Stoddard crouched, scanned the disturbed soil. "That's a job for the forensic guys."

"There's something else," Melhado stepped around them, walked back to the cab and reached in. "This came up hooked on a bucket prong. He handed Stoddard the dirty cloth. "Shoulda left it hanging?"

"I don't think you have to worry about smudging fingerprints on this. I'll give it to the forensics crew."

He headed toward the road then turned back. "Sorry, but you both'll have to stay put until they have a crack at you."

In his car, he made a call to request the State Police crime-scene unit. Crowd control? Shouldn't be much need for that way out here. He called for backup anyway. Then he shut off the radio and pulled out his cell. Bending some rules on this one, but so far, cooperation had paid off.

Stoddard tapped in Rod Montgomery's number.

41

Our Saturday morning brunch dishes cleared away, Pris and I sat back with coffee refills. The Anthracite Hotel's dining room attendance dwindled, but we lingered. A "date" Pris had insisted this to be. "Now," she said, "what would you like to do?"

For a teenaged dater, that could have been something of a come-on. For this 40-something P.I., it turned out to be a question unanswered. In my shirt pocket my cell phone vibrated and chimed.

Ben Stoddard. "Got something you'll want to see, Rod. Edge of the woods up the east fork of the Keystone ring road."

"Where they've been clearing?"

"Yep. A body."

A chill zipped through me. "I'm on my way."

I stuck the cell back in my pocket. "Gotta go, Pris."

"I thought we—" She peered at me. "What's happened?"

"That was Ben Stoddard, County Sheriff's Department. He's at the work site where they're clearing the woods. They've found a body."

"A body!"

"Yeah. He wants me up there."

"I want to go with you."

"To see a dead body? That's no way to top off what's been a really nice breakfast."

"Neither is leaving me here wondering what's going on."

I shrugged. "Your choice, Pris. Let's go. We'll come back for your car later."

***

We wound through downtown's sparse Saturday traffic then rushed uphill past the Maximall. At the Y intersection, I turned right. We raced around the road's northward swing. A mile or so further, I spotted what had to be the scene of Ben's call. Not hard to spot, with its cluster of blue-and-white county police cruisers and a gray State Police crime-scene van along the road's left side. I slowed, pulled off the road, stopped on the shoulder.

At the edge of the woods, a couple hundred feet beyond the parked wheels of the law, a cluster of cops and the forensic team milled around a truck and some kind of dozer.

"I don't think you need to see what's causing all this excitement," I told Pris. "I'm not too eager to see it, myself. Why don't you stay here, and I'll fill you in."

To my surprise, she murmured, "Gladly." Not the insistent lemme-see-it reaction I'd expected. That's why I'd lied a bit about my not being so eager myself, hoping to keep her in the car. Now I realized she hadn't come along to see the apparently grisly find over there. She'd come along to be with... Get a grip, Montgomery.

I stepped out and walked across the road. Not all the cops were at the woods' edge. Two of them stepped from behind the parked units.

"Hold it, sir," the taller one ordered. "No spectators."

Actually, that's what I was. A Philadelphia P.I. had no jurisdiction here at all. But before I launched into a song-and-dance to charm my way past them, I spotted Ben Stoddard trotting toward us.

"Glad you're here, Detective," he called. "Let him by, Jake."

The tall cop backed off. I joined Ben and we walked toward the woods.

"The Track Loader dug up an arm — well, bones of an arm. The crime-scene crew has cleared away enough dirt so we can see the arm belongs to a whole body."

"And I'm sure you've figured out that's what A and C has been so damned agitated about."

"Gotta be. Which means they had something to do with whoever it turns out to be."

"Hell, Ben, it's a woman. Right?"

"Wearing woman's clothes, as best we can make out. How'd you know that?"

"I know more than that. I know who she is."

"How in hell...?"

We rounded the front of the loader and stood at the edge of the hole it had scooped out. I stared down at a skeleton dressed in a filthy, deteriorating skirt and jacket.

Once bright green, I thought. Now dirt-crusted remnants with only traces of green visible amidst the soil. Her high-heeled shoes were dull black, but intact.

I peered at the skull's wispy hair strands. "Red-haired," I said. "And O'Brian was a flaming redhead."

"Not significant," piped a skinny little guy standing beside me with a pocket notebook. Steel-rimmed glasses and a prissy blond mustache made him look like my idea of a college lecturer. "Hair color is made up of two pigments," he said. "One of them is black, brown or yellow. The second one is red, and it is more stable. So, over time after death, the other pigment fades faster than the red pigment. Thus, all long-term corpses have reddish hair."

Jeez, he *was* a lecturer.

"Arthur Mortensen," Ben said. "State Medical Examiner." He turned to Mortensen. "This is Detective Montgomery, Arthur. Working with us on the Sturdevant case."

Mortensen nodded, scrawled something in his notebook and walked away.

"Before I told you anything about it," Ben said, "you knew this was a woman. And you said you know who she is. How so, Rod?"

"Deduction. She's Amerman's and Cassina's upstart assistant, Mary Louise O'Brian. She was about to attend a conference out west and apparently tell all about A & C's questionable dealing in troublesome Chinese drywall. That could have ruined them. They killed her, faked her departure at the airport then buried her up here way before anyone had any thought of developing this area."

"That's theory," Ben said as we walked back toward the road. "Not fact. Could be anybody in that hole."

"Any red-headed woman?"

"Mortensen pretty well blew that for you."

"The hair color aspect. But the clothing backs me up. Green is the favorite color of every redheaded gal I've ever met."

"Flimsy, Rod."

"Yeah, you're right. No good in a courtroom. DNA maybe?"

"Don't know how long she's been up here. I'll start with your claim, but O'Brian disappeared twenty years ago. And I don't think she was from this area. Hard to track down a relative. But I'll have to give it a shot." He stopped. "I'd better get back there. I'll keep you posted."

I stepped into my rented Jeep and sat there pondering.

"Rod?" Pris prompted.

"It's got to be Mary Louise O'Brian. Everything fits. Especially A and C's delaying tactics." I started the SUV and we drove on north. A tour for thought.

"Delaying tactics?" she said.

"Has to be. They knew she'd be found eventually, so they've been delaying progress to give them time to —"

"To run! That's the only way delaying things makes sense."

We rolled past Ivan Sikorski's impressive—and still standing—old homestead. Unfinished business, but I'd had an idea, not yet presented to Max and Cliff.

"You're right, Pris. They've been delaying the project to give them time to dispose of A and C and get out of Camden. When clearing the woods began, no wonder they got desperate. Desperate enough to plan a second kidnapping—Cliff. Makes no sense otherwise. And while the police follow procedure to positively identify the body I just identified for them, you can bet Mary O'Brian's two murderers will be racing to fade away into the blue."

42

I'd made my case, so to speak. Now I waited for the creaky wheels of official justice to confirm exactly who had been buried years ago in what had been remote, undeveloped countryside. If my assumption panned out, I knew we should keep a lid on the thing long enough to "detain" Messrs. Amerman and Cassina. Otherwise, two of Camden's citizens would promptly disappear. Ben Stoddard agreed, though somewhat hesitantly. All this was obvious to me, but until science prevailed, to Ben, the body in the woods remained an unhelpful "Jane Doe."

So here I sat, peering down vacantly into the parking lot, restless fingers tapping on office-chair arms. With Sturdevant's need for further P.I. work in limbo, the time had come to head back to Philadelphia. But before I signed out, I decided to yield to temptation and insert myself into the development business.

I shoved my chair around to face the desk, pushed out of it and walked over to Cliff's office. I tapped on his typically open door. "You got a minute for a wild idea?"

He looked up from his littered desktop and ran fingers of frustration through his blond brush cut. "What this country needs is less regulation strangulation. Wild ideas always welcome. Specially one that might get me out of this office for a while. Whatchu got?"

I walked in and laid it out for him, my intrusion into the development game.

" — The three of us," I suggested, as I finished. "You, Max and me."

Cliff gave me an eyebrows-raised grin. "Wild idea, indeed. I'll check it out with Max." He stood. "Wait here. I'll be right back."

Five minutes later, he reappeared. "Max is dubious."

"Well, I just thought — "

"He's dubious, but he says nothing else has worked, so it's worth a try. Without him, though."

"He doesn't want to be part of this?"

"He said he's already been too much of a part. Thinks you and I could make a better go of it without him."

"He's got a point, Cliff. You game for a try?"

He swept his paper strew into a neat pile. "Gladly. A great excuse to let all this procedural nit-pickery wait. Think we should call ahead?"

"Nope. Let's be an off-balancing surprise."

***

With Cliff at the wheel of his silver-gray Corvette, we climbed the ridge to the Keystone site's Y intersection, swung to the right and rode east, then around the curve to the north. "That's where the body was found," I said, as we passed the site of recent excitement. No vehicles or police presence at all now. At the edge of the woods, only a multi-stake-supported ring of yellow crime-scene tape marked the event.

"You heard anything from your county contact?" Cliff wondered.

"Not yet. They're still trying for a positive ID. Can't find any relatives for a DNA match. But it's gotta be A and C's former secretary. Fits the picture exactly."

A few miles later, Cliff slowed down. We coasted into Ivan Sikorski's driveway and pulled up beside his hulking midnight-blue Hummer. Cliff switched off. "Looks like he's here."

"He's been here every time I've passed this place. Must slip out early in the morning when he needs groceries — or has them delivered. Not exactly an outgoing sort of guy."

As we stepped out of the Corvette, the mansion's impressive front door swung open. There stood six-feet-plus, 200-for-sure-pounds of irritation: Ivan Sikorski. In black Levis and blue sweatshirt. Hands on hips, jaw jutting.

"So now what?" Not exactly a friendly, "Howdy."

"We've got a proposition for you, Ivan."

Cliff's friendly tone didn't warm up Ivan's glare, but the hands slipped off the hips. He wrapped his fingers around the porch's railing and leaned over us.

"Proposition or ultimatum?" he demanded. Then he looked at me. "You the writer came to see me weeks back. Dunno what the hell you wrote. You here for a sequel?"

"Rod Montgomery, Ivan. I'm here with an idea. Something that could clear the air and let everybody breathe again."

"No matter how you say it, Montgomery —" He scowled. "Thought you said you were 'Stevens' before."

"That was for cover, Ivan. The cover's off. This time, I'm here on my own."

"So why's brother Cliff standing there with you? And where's Max?"

"This idea's not mine or Max's," Cliff said. "It's Rod's. I'm just along for the ride."

Well, not quite. With his past meetings here "unproductive," as Max had put it, he had delegated Cliff to be Sturdevant's official rep on this one.

"Along for the ride," Ivan muttered. Then he pushed back from the railing." What the hell. I got nothing better to do. Might as well have coffee while we reach a disagreement."

"Don't prejudge, Ivan," I said as Cliff and I climbed the five broad marble steps to the entrance. We followed Ivan through the huge front room to the hall beyond, then past the spiral staircase, the dining room and into his last-century-style kitchen. He motioned at the chairs around the kitchen table, grabbed mugs from a cupboard, clunked them down. Then he brought a nearly full coffee pot from his up-to-date and apparently always-hot coffee machine.

"I'm sure not going to pour for you two," he rapped. "Help yourselves." He banged down milk and sugar then plopped onto one of the hard-on-the-butt kitchen chairs.

"Okay," he said. "Get it over with, finish your coffee, then goodbye. I'm not leaving this place, and the court case is pending."

"Tell him," Cliff prompted.

"I'm no developer," I began.

"Apparently you're no writer, either, Montgomery... or Stevens, like you said the other time, or whatever your name really is."

"It's Montgomery. A private eye from Philadelphia. I — "

"Jesus! You've dug up some sort of — what the hell is this? Some kind of phony baloney blackmail plot?"

"Steady, Ivan. Nothing like that. In fact, I'm way out of my depth in this, but ever since I was here before, I've been thinking over your situation — "

"Situation, hell. It's a legal fight now."

"Yeah, it is. And you could lose, Ivan. In fact, you're already losing. Remember what I told you about the litigants pulling on the cow while the lawyers get the milk."

"I'm not losing this house without a fight!"

"Rod's idea has you keeping the house," Cliff put in.

That left Ivan momentarily speechless. Then he managed, "Huh?"

"The house stays," I said. "That huge front room makes an ideal community meeting place."

"In fact," Cliff joined in, "knock out the partition between it and that other front room — "

"The sitting room."

"Take out the partition, Ivan, and you have one really impressive meeting room across the whole front of the mansion."

"Wait a minute. Wait a minute!" Ivan yipped. "What happens to my, uh, privacy?"

"Simple. We put a doorway in the front of the hall," Cliff proposed. "That gives you complete privacy from the big room. And access when you want it."

"And where would I get the money for all this?"

"Sturdevant handles the work—gratis." Cliff said. "And for the community use of the meeting area, we will pay you a monthly stipend until the Village of Stag Run is fully developed. After that, we'll encourage the village association to continue to share your household expenses."

Ivan shot Cliff a hard look. "That's it?"

"That's it." Cliff took a drag of coffee, set down the mug and leaned forward. "Save your money, Ivan. Drop the lawsuit, and we'll get going on the front room remodeling."

A long silence was broken by my refilling my coffee supply. Ivan sat back in his creaky chair. Glared at Cliff then at me. Studied his folded hands. Looked back up. Cleared his throat.

Then: "It's a goddamn bribe!" Studied his nails again. Gave each of us a scowl. Cleared his throat. "But it sure beats the hell out of lawyer fees. Put all that in writing and I'll sign it."

As we walked back across the huge living room, I glanced at the M-14 over the front door. That assault rifle and the ominous dark Hummer had made Ivan my first suspect in the sabotage effort.

"When you're ready to welcome your new neighbors into their town's meeting hall, you—"

"I know, Montgomery, I know. I'll move it to my bedroom upstairs."

***

In the warm glow of victory, we headed back toward Sturdevant's Maximall offices. As we turned south at the Y intersection, my cell phone chimed.

"Ben Stoddard, Rod. Got a positive ID on the body in the woods."

"Not DNA. Not fingerprints. Let me guess. Dental record."

"You got it. Hardington has six dental offices. One on the west side took a look at the crime lab photos of the jaws. Bingo. No question about the oddly-angled incisor on the left side. You aced it, Rod. Mary Louise O'Brian."

"The problem now," I said, "is keeping that under wraps until the FBI or Jersey State Police can nail Amerman and Cassina."

"FBI's on it. Figured Max's kidnapping plot crossed state lines. But they've gotta hustle. Though we cautioned him to play mum, our helpful dentist couldn't keep his mouth shut. Hardington TV's got the story."

43

As he clunked down his coffee mug, Harvey Amerman's fingers trembled. Another miserable day waiting for the call from Ketchem's office – the confirmation that Garden State's buyout was signed at last. How many more days could he and Mateo afford the risk of waiting here in Camden until that confirmation freed them to flee west, way west? Out of reach in balmy Samoa.

In their office closets, they both kept hand luggage packed with minimal essentials, one bag each. They had arranged month-to-month leases at Maple Grove, convincing management they were seeking lodging arrangements "closer to our offices." Their cars were rentals. No problem if they simply walked away. Everything was in place for an abrupt fade-out, with Garden State Suppliers efficiently moving in. All they needed was that damned confirmation call from lawyer Ezra Ketchem.

Harvey let out a long, shaky breath and picked up the *Camden Courier-Post*. Damn fingers still jittering. Friggin' tension, even with all the bug-out planning in A-1 order.

He paged through the paper. Thirty car pile-up in Boston's early morning fog...Another senator questioned about his blending personal push with political pull...

A body found near Hardington, Pennsylvania…

The hair on the back of his neck bristled. Discovered by workmen clearing woods for new city project…ID'd through dental records as Mary O'Brian, who disappeared fifteen years ago — *Great God Almighty!*

He grabbed his phone. *"They've found her. Get the hell up here!"*

Forty seconds later, Mateo burst in, slapped both hands flat on Harvey's desk and leaned over him.

"Found her? How in hell — "

Harvey shoved the paper at him. "Page four," he said through gritted teeth. "We're getting the hell out of here *now.* Get your travel bag, and get yourself down front. I'll meet you there soon's I make a call."

"What about — " Mateo struggled for breath. "What about the sale?"

"I'll handle that. Get your damned bag."

Mateo gave him a wide-eyed look. Like a fox who'd just heard the too-close baying of onrushing hounds. "Shoulda done this weeks ago, when Sturdevant began working on the Town Center. We damned sure shoulda got our asses in gear when they began clearing the woods."

"I didn't think we should leave everything in Ketchem's hands until the buy-out money was transferred."

"So now we got no choice."

"Get your damn bag, Mateo!"

Cassina glared at him. Then he whirled around and raced out the door.

With twitching fingers, Harvey fumbled the phone number. Tried again. "C'mon, c'mon…" Then: "Ezra? Harvey here. Plan A. Got that? Plan A. Send me Internet confirmation of the sale and money transfer soon's it happens. Details all yours now."

He banged down the receiver. Had to trust the guy. If he gooses his fee, so be it. There'll still be a bunch of money for our Samoan sunset.

He yanked open the tiny closet's door, grabbed his carry-on bag and rushed for the elevator. The small staff would be in disarray until Ezra could get them in line—until Garden State moved in. But on a sun-drenched beach seven thousand miles away, he and Mateo wouldn't give a damn.

First step, literally, in what Harvey planned as a series of trail-breaks, he and Mateo walked three buildings east and around the corner from their own. Then Harvey hailed the first taxi to appear. Were the driver to be questioned later, he would identify their pick-up point as the Benbow Building on North 5th Street.

"The Marriott up in Cherry Hill," Harvey told the dark-skinned driver. Looked to be a Mex. Sounded like one, too, when he repeated, "Cherry Hill Marriott, si."

Through the agonizingly long minutes of the four-mile ride north, Harvey resisted the temptation to glance behind. Whatever he might see back there wouldn't prove anything anyway. He was struggling with...with bug-out fidgets, you could call it. Fought them all the way to the Marriott's entrance.

He gave their driver a medium-size tip, big enough to be appreciated, small enough to be unmemorable. The cab pulled away into Cherry Hill's traffic swirl, and with it, per plan, went any direct connection to Camden. He and Mateo hurried into the lobby to join the modest crowd awaiting the next Philadelphia International shuttle bus in the day's frequent runs.

Twenty anxious minutes later, they shuffled aboard—two business travelers in slacks, tieless shirts, and sports jackets. Increasingly comfortable, Harvey felt, as casual nonentities in a bus load of nonentities.

They stepped off at the international terminal, sweated through a ticket counter tango of activating the standby tickets of "Herbert Hargrove" and "Martin Hazlet" — the names on the phony driver licenses and passports Mateo had secured through a reliably secret source of any forgery enough money could buy. Boarding passes in hand, they endured pat-downs and shoe inspections as their pocket contents and carry-ons crept through the scanner. Then up the ramp and aboard.

"Hargrove" and "Hazlet" sank into seats halfway down the tourist class section.

Harvey found himself irritated by Mateo's smug confidence — an emotion he, himself, didn't enjoy until the cabin door slammed shut, and the big Boeing was eased backwards to the taxi strip. The engines wound into jet wails, and their grand escape — step 3 of Plan A — rolled toward the runway.

In the window seat, Harvey watched a jetliner ahead of them turn onto the runway, accelerate with a roar, and roll away. Now he saw the taxiway's bordering turf apparently pivot as their turn came, and the jetliner swung ponderously onto the runway.

Harvey glanced at Mateo. His partner's fox-faced grin matched his own chubby-cheeked smirk. They had done it! The engines howled. The plane began its take-off roll.

Abruptly, the engines' howl subsided. The jet slowed to walking speed. What the hell —

"Captain speaking," the overhead intercom announced. "We have been ordered back to the terminal."

A protesting murmur swept the cabin. Harvey glanced at Mateo then upward in irritation.

"All passengers are to stay aboard," the overhead speakers grated. "We are assured the delay will be brief."

I'll be damned, Harvey thought. We're right on the edge of escape, and some ass has left a gas cap off or screwed up some paperwork. He gave Mateo another disgusted glance and shrugged.

The ponderous jetliner rolled slowly to a turn-off, swung left toward the terminal, and stopped on the taxiway at the International Terminal. Behind them, a woman's voice muttered, "Damned short round trip." He watched a portable stairway roll up to the cabin's exit forward. A flight attendant pulled the door open then stepped aside as two men in dark business suits stepped aboard.

They huddled over a paper one of them held out to her. She nodded aft, and the two stern-faced guys walked slowly, purposefully, down the left-side aisle, referring to the paper.

Christ! Harvey's guts curdled. The damned paper was a photograph.

He turned away, stared out the window. The pair of "businessmen" walked closer. Stopped. "That's them," Harvey heard one say.

"Harvey Amerman, Mateo Cassina," the other announced, "FBI. You are under arrest."

Handcuffs appeared.

"Stand up, hands behind your backs."

And they were escorted off the plane.

***

"They had their getaway neatly planned." Ben Stoddard downed a bite of his Denver omelet then looked up at me. At his suggestion, we'd met in Maximall's Ye Olde Pub for a breakfast briefing on exactly what had taken place yesterday in Camden and Philadelphia. "Camden cab to Cherry Hill shuttle to Philadelphia airport," he said, "but the FBI was on 'em the minute they stepped into the cab. The driver was FBI, watching A and C's building since O'Brian's body was found. You can take some credit, Rod. Your tying it all together put them on watch in Camden."

"Already told you, Ben, I'm not looking for 'credit.' Just satisfaction in closing a case for my client. So...the taxi left them at the Marriott in Cherry Hill. Then?"

"Then the FBI almost lost them. Their taxi driver had trouble finding a spot near enough to watch the hotel.

Figured they might be meeting someone there. Maybe had a car there. He missed them getting on the shuttle but figured it was a likely reason for them to be at the Marriott. The shuttle has a frequent schedule there for transportation to Philadelphia International. The FBI raced agents to all the airport's terminals — it's a damned big airport — including the international terminal. Got there just as a westbound flight was loading passengers. A check at the ticket counter ID'd their photo of Amerman and Cassina. By then, the plane was lined up on the runway, but they got it stopped. And there sat our two persons of a lot more than mere interest. Shot down before take-off."

"Circumstantial evidence seems strong enough, and I can make a pretty solid assumption at what happened fifteen years ago. Mary O'Brian, a budding whistle-blower, sees big problems looming with Chinese drywall. Not only could the stuff finish off their budding company, it could open them to litigation for knowingly distributing a health hazard — as that drywall was found to be a few years later."

"So Amerman and Cassina tell her to shut up about it."

"Right. But she gathers her notes and is about to head for a tell-all at a national builders' conference — which could potentially sink their Chinese drywall-centered business. They strangle her in the office. One of them drives her car to the Hardington airport, his partner trailing behind. Leaves her car in long-term parking, and rides back to work with the partner, probably with O'Brian's body in the trunk. After dark, they drive into the then-neglected open country north of Hardington. And they bury her."

"Then fifteen years later comes Keystone City."

I nodded. "Out of the blue, that project is more than likely to expose — literally — the murder they'd perpetrated long before. They decide to get out of Camden. Out of the country. But they need time to close down or sell out, and their delay strategy — the sabotage — begins. The motor pool fire, some vehicle altercations, then three deaths. All that, plus the O'Brian killing would lead both of them straight to a Pennsylvania life-term lock-up. Or a shorter term fatal fade-out. Only solution: disappear."

"Tickets to Samoa, it turns out."

"Samoa?"

"Yeah, Rod. I wondered, too. Turns out there's no extradition from there."

"Smart choice, for two dumb-bunny murderers." I finished my coffee. "Check's on me."

"Can't accept gifts." Ben grinned. "I'm on duty."

"Okay, check's on you. Plus, any credit for solving the case. Publicity can get in a PI's way.

"So now it's back to Philly."

"Good closing line."

But I wasn't quite ready to close. I'd had another wild idea.

44

The day after Amerman and Cassina were tagged before take-off, Max called me to his office.

"Shut the door, Rod. This has to stay confidential."

No coffee offer. He thumbed me to the chair nearest his super-sized desk. I sat and decided to make this easy for him. "I think my services here are wrapped up, Max. Figure I'll pull out tomorrow."

"I'm paying you weekly, Rod. You're on the payroll through Friday. No need to rush."

He paused, tapped the mammoth desktop with his pen then looked me straight in the eyes. "Tell me what you think of Pris."

That shook me a little. "What *I* think?"

"She came here as a damned spy and worked for A and C until we caught up with her."

"We didn't 'catch up with her,' Max. Her conscience did. She turned herself in."

"True, true. What I'm really saying is I just can't get myself to trust her in the long run. Is she a loyal Sturdevant employee now, or an opportunist who took a smoother road? I can't get over the feeling she can't be trusted one-hundred percent. I know that's a hell of a hang-up over my own administrative assistant, but I can't get around it. Any thoughts?"

The boss with an employee hang-up is asking his hired PI for an opinion? "I don't quite know if I..." I left that hanging while I brain-raced for a halfway intelligent response. Put her where no company secrets are accessible? Fire her for cause, though she'd ultimately been an asset?

Then lightning struck.

"I'll see what I can do, Max." I stood, thrust out my hand. "It's been a...an experience working with you."

"And personally saving my butt, Rod. That I'll never forget." He stood and gave my extended hand an enthusiastic shake. "I'm going to keep you in my Rolodex—on paper. I don't trust the damned cell phone."

I walked out and paused in Pris's little station. "Come to my office," I said quietly, then strode on down the corridor.

In three minutes, she appeared. Tall and trim in honey-colored slacks and jacket, her mahogany hair agleam. But her expression didn't match her sartorial elegance.

"What did Max tell you?"

"Thanked me for my work here."

"I mean, what did he say about me?" A terse expression of perception if ever there was one.

"Sit down, Pris." She sank into one of my two hard chairs, hands in her lap, eyes on mine. I pulled the other chair over to join her in front of the desk. Psychology 101.

"How do you feel about working here?"

She frowned. "You sound like a company morale counselor."

I chuckled. "I don't care what I sound like. I'm asking about you."

"So, that's what Max was—he doesn't trust me, does he?"

I said nothing. But silence was the answer.

"Oh, hell, Rod. I'm forty-plus. Sold my soul—or rented it—to those two sleazes in Camden, then shoved them under the bus when you and Max offered... You know how all that will get around—maybe already has. Every day I can sense Max is... well, dubious about me. That's not a good cloud to work under." She sighed. "I know I can't go on working here."

Wow! I'd won my case before summation.

"Think about this," I said. "It's not a proposition, but I have two empty rooms in my house down near Philadelphia. You're welcome while you establish a new life down there."

"In a strange city."

"It's in the suburbs."

"In a strange city's suburbs. With a man I barely know."

"Oh, c'mon. I've slept with you."

"Once. What you're offering *is* a proposition."

"I don't look at it that way. It's—"

"I like it."

***

On a sunny Thursday, this PI-for-hire and his now-unhired former double agent drove out of Hardington into the Poconos, headed downstate. Destination: my Orchard Glade digs in Philly's southwest suburbs. Was I driving us into a promising future, perhaps with us working together? Or was I no more than Pris's convenient transport out of town?

She had returned her rented car and checked out of the bed-and-breakfast where she'd talked the owner into longer-term boarding. Both transactions hinted at her expectation of less-than-permanent employment with Sturdevant.

As the Pennsylvania Turnpike's southbound extension raced us through Hickory Run State Park, I glanced at her. She gave me a smile. Contentment or contrivance?

That, as they say, remains to be seen.

-END-

If you have not had the chance to read Bill Hallstead's first Rod Montgomery novel, *Hard Days in Paradise*, please be sure to check it out at www.bluewaterpress.com/paradise. Also investigate his other books by surfing through Bill's titles at www.bluewaterpress.com, or on Amazon. We are sure you will enjoy his other yarns as well as this one.

www.ingramcontent.com/pod-product-compliance
Lightning Source LLC
Chambersburg PA
CBHW060349030726
47497CB00003B/656